FLESH & BLOOD

A NOVEL

ALLISON HOBBS

STREBOR BOOKS
NEW YORK LONDON TORONTO SYDNEY

SBI

Strebor Books
P.O. Box 55471
Atlanta, GA 30308
www.simonandschuster.com

This book is a work of fiction. Names, characters, places and incidents are products of the author's imagination or are used fictitiously. Any resemblance to actual events or locales or persons, living or dead, is entirely coincidental.

© 2018 by Allison Hobbs

ISBN 978-1-59309-693-9
ISBN 978-1-50117-254-0 (ebook)
LCCN 2018955224

First Strebor Books trade paperback edition October 2018

Cover design: www.mariondesigns.com
Cover photograph: © Keith Saunders/Keith Saunders Photos

10 9 8 7 6 5 4 3 2 1

Manufactured in the United States of America

For information regarding special discounts for bulk purchases, please contact Simon & Schuster Special Sales at 1-866-506-1949

The Simon & Schuster Speakers Bureau can bring authors to your live event. For more information or to book an event, contact the Simon & Schuster Speakers Bureau at 1-866-248-3049 or visit our website at www.simonspeakers.com.

Dear Reader:

Allison Hobbs, who has thirty-plus titles published with Strebor, has spun tales of erotica, paranormal and child sex trafficking. With *Flesh and Blood*, the prolific author delves into the meaning of family ties and male bonding.

Former drug addict Malik Copeland loses his fiancée, Elle, and then his infant son, Phoenix, after he is adopted by her new husband, Everett. Malik also starts a new family life when he relocates, marries Sasha and becomes a stepfather to her young daughter, Zoe.

At age thirteen, Phoenix becomes a permanent part of the Copeland household, and soon, their world starts to spiral out of control, especially with recent criminal activities in the neighborhood. As the newest community resident, Phoenix is viewed as the likeliest of suspects.

The novel is a testament to the challenges of father-son relationships and the adjustment of blended families. Readers will be surprised at the plot twists as Phoenix's secrets are revealed to Malik who must decide how far he'll go to stand by his own flesh and blood.

As always, thanks for supporting myself and the Strebor Books family. We strive to bring you the most cutting-edge, out-of-the-box material on the market. You can find me on Facebook @AuthorZane.

Blessings,

Zane

Publisher
Strebor Books
www.simonandschuster.com

CHAPTER 1

Passion mounted and perspiration fused our bodies together.

Elle wrapped her legs around my back and then locked her ankles, pulling me deeper into her warm abyss. Our hearts beat like drums, setting a fast tempo for our harmonized moans.

Embedded deeply inside her, I found my way to uncharted territory. For a brief moment, I ceased thrusting and marveled at the cushiness of a well-hidden patch of flesh. I pressed into that sacred place known as the G-Spot and Elle cried out in prayerful appreciation.

After she finished thanking Jesus, a litany of profanity spilled from her lips as she alternately praised me and cursed me for possessing such good dick.

I'd never been much of a talker during sex, and therefore, my response to her outpouring of lustful gratitude was to resume my forceful stroke, pounding the pussy the way she liked it—the way we both liked it. I hammered inside her in a manner that was so brutal, she was prompted to claw at my back, encouraging me to continue pulverizing the delicate flesh of her nether regions.

Intent on pleasing this woman whom I loved with every fiber of my being, I growled through clenched teeth as I fought against the overwhelming desire that was building inside me. I refused to focus on the tiny clutching muscles that tugged determinedly on my rigid length. Her scent wafted up to my nostrils, and although I found the pungent aroma of sex to be an intoxicating fragrance, I refused to allow it to get to me.

I blocked out everything and concentrated on my stroke game, keeping it strong while making sure I didn't prematurely flood my baby with a torrent of hot passion.

As a man…as *her* man, I felt obligated to hold back until she released that familiar, high-pitched wail, which told me she'd been satisfied. And when she finally screamed out my name, I was reassured that I'd put in good work and could finally indulge my own urgent need for release.

The moment I let go, it seemed like time stood still. Nothing existed except the electric orgasm that charged throughout my body. As a windstorm began to roar inside my ears, I felt as if I'd become one with multiple universes and other galaxies. It wasn't until I had deposited the last drop of ejaculate that I returned from the cosmos and back to Earth—once again, a mortal man.

"That was fantastic, baby," she whispered.

"Mmm," I agreed in a low moan.

"I love you so much, Malik." Her voice cracked with emotion, reminding me that no matter how good I gave it to her, she would never quite trust that my love was as strong and as true as hers.

After all the hell that I'd put her through, I couldn't blame her.

Feeling remorseful for the sins of my past, I wrapped both arms around her. "I love you, too, baby. More than life itself," I assured her. My lips found hers and I kissed her, trying my best to reassure her that the dark days were far, far behind us.

I'm a changed man, I told myself.

I bit down on my lip to stave off the troubling feeling that began to stir inside me, and I held on to Elle, tightening my grasp around her as if she were an anchor that could keep me from being swept out to a stormy sea.

She disengaged my tight hold on her and curled into a more comfortable position.

"I love you more than life itself," I whispered in her ear.

"I love you, too," she murmured.

Moments later, she was blissfully asleep.

But sleep eluded me.

Many things triggered my substance abuse problem, but sex had never been one of them. Yet, for some unknown reason, the amazing sex I'd just shared with Elle had aroused my demons. Now I lay awake, tossing and turning, and struggling with the overwhelming urge to get high.

Refusing to cave in to my self-destructive desires, I repeated the Serenity Prayer in my mind, hoping the words would bring me solace. Desperate for peace instead of turmoil, I directed my thoughts to the wedding that Elle was planning. I imagined the beautiful future that lay ahead of us.

She wanted children one day—we both did—and so I tried to imagine a big house filled with the sound of children's laughter. But my head was in such a messed-up place, I couldn't conjure up the sound of happy laughter. All I could hear was a tormenting cacophony of demonic shrieks and hellish cries.

Times like this, I should have called my sponsor. It wasn't wise to try to deal with my issues alone, but I stubbornly told myself that I'd be all right. I simply needed to enforce my willpower in order to subdue my urge to use.

Minutes ticked by...maybe hours. Despite my best efforts, my thoughts continually focused on the eighty dollars that I'd tossed on top of the dresser. Unable to resist my urges for another moment, I eased out of bed, crept to the closet and quietly got dressed. Like a thief in the night, I scooped up my money and pocketed the bills.

Before exiting the bedroom, I crept over to Elle's purse that she'd set on a chair. With an eye on her, I reached inside and found her wallet. I extracted the special bank card that she used for wedding expenses. That particular card had a balance of well over ten thousand dollars, and I needed the square piece of plastic for backup. Eighty dollars wasn't nearly enough. However, I planned to use the card sparingly, withdrawing only a few hundred dollars.

On payday, I'd put the money back. Elle would never notice that any of the money was missing.

This won't be a major relapse, I reassured myself. I've been clean for fourteen months, and I only need a little something to take the edge off. I'll be home before Elle wakes up. I'll get to work on time, and no one will be the wiser.

I skulked toward the bedroom door, looked over my shoulder to make sure that Elle was fast asleep, and I swore to God this would be the last time that I'd ever give in to my cravings.

With my hands stuffed inside the pockets of my jacket, I slipped out of our apartment and blended into the dark night.

A week and a half later, I woke up in the hospital.

The doctor said I'd suffered a seizure from an accidental overdose of the synthetic opioid, fentanyl.

"Fentanyl?" I furrowed my brows together. "I don't mess with fentanyl," I explained to the doctor.

"It was in your system. Lots of it," he said in a judgmental tone of voice.

I glanced around my hospital room and saw a blackboard with the date written on it. My mouth gaped open when I realized that more than a week had passed. How had I lost an entire week?

"My fiancée…she's probably out of her mind with worry. I have to call her." I glanced around the room, wondering where my cell phone and other belongings were.

"Your fiancée was here yesterday and the day before. She's been here every day," the doctor said as he perused my chart. "The nurse will give her a call and let her know you're awake." He peered at me over his glasses, and I could tell by his expression that he viewed me as a scumbag that didn't deserve a decent woman like Elle.

He was right, of course, but I still didn't appreciate his self-righteous attitude.

The doctor told me that the nurse would be in shortly to give me my meds, and then he turned to leave.

"Hey, wait! When can I get out of here?"

"I want to run a few more tests before you're discharged," he responded.

"All right, but I can't stay overnight again; I have to return to my job."

This time he gave me a pitying look, and I slumped against my pillow with the realization that I'd screwed up royally. After missing so much time from work without an explanation, it would be a miracle if I still had a job.

I had a degree in African American Studies, but due to my heroin addiction, I'd lost my career in education. Now, I worked with my hands. Thanks to Elle's dad, who looked out for me, I had a new career as a power plant mechanic at the same company he worked for. It was damn good pay. More than I'd made teaching. But I still hadn't gotten used to being a blue collar worker and wearing a uniform with my name stitched on the front.

No doubt, Elle's dad was professionally embarrassed over my disappearing act and personally infuriated that I'd disgraced his daughter. Hopefully, I'd be able to smooth things over with both of them and be able to hang on to my job and resume my personal life.

But who was I kidding. Elle had to be at her wits' end with me. And no company was going to put up with a no-call, no-show from any employee.

Undoubtedly, I'd ruined my life again.

Some addicts could function within society and somehow maintain their jobs and family obligations. Unfortunately, I wasn't that kind of substance abuser. Each time I slipped up, I tended to swiftly spiral out of control, always ending up right back in the gutter.

I didn't know how I was going to face Elle. What could I tell her? I didn't have any right to ask her for another chance, but I truly loved her and didn't want to lose her.

I tried to retrace the past week as best I could. Scanning through my hazy memory bank, I vaguely remembered hooking up with a skinny white chick who was also buying heroin from the dude I copped from. I agreed to go back to her place where we could get high together, and she took me to a roach-infested apartment. She cooked and shot up her drugs while I opted to snort mine. I'd always told myself that snorting was less harmful than injecting, and there was the extra bonus of no track marks for anyone to detect.

As I tried to remember what had happened, I came up with a dim memory of another chick joining us. A black girl with a sexy body and an alluring smile. I fucked both of them—raw dog—and gave them both oral sex.

Goddamn, I'm immoral and nasty as hell when I get high!

I shook my head in self-disgust. My freak-level went through the roof when drugs were in my system, and there was no telling what kind of STDs I'd picked up during my week-long binge.

I worriedly dragged my fingers down my face as sharper memories surfaced. I recalled a full-on orgy that lasted for days and included a number of nameless and faceless women and men. I pondered the horror of going home and possibly passing a communicable disease on to Elle. I decided that it would be a good idea for the doctor to run a battery of tests on me before I was discharged.

I racked my brain trying to remember everything that happened during those lost days before I was hospitalized, but I didn't have any clear memories. In my confused mind, I only saw blurry images of a stream of junkies and drug dealers coming in and out of the apartment. Through the fog of my mind, I could recall clusters of drug paraphernalia, pills, heroin, cocaine, and empty liquor bottles everywhere.

I recalled naked bodies entwined. Apparently, I had participated in a Caligula-style orgy.

Then, it dawned on me that each time we ran out of drugs, I had allowed the two chicks to use my car to go get more. I also remembered handing over the bank card along with the PIN.

Oh, my God! I had funded a drug marathon. I'd allowed a pack of bum-ass strangers to fuck up the money Elle had put aside for our upcoming wedding.

In a sudden panic, I looked around my hospital room. Where was my shit—my wallet, key fob, and my fucking cell phone? Frantic, I buzzed for the nurse, and the moment she stepped inside the room, I demanded my personal belongings.

She opened a drawer and took out a small plastic bag. "You didn't arrive here with much. Only this," she said, pointing to my wallet that was encased inside the plastic bag.

Panicked, I seized the bag and tore through my wallet, searching for Elle's bank card. My heart plummeted when I realized it wasn't there. In fact, my wallet was empty except for a few old business cards and my work identification. Those motherfuckers had stolen my driver's license, registration and insurance cards…everything of value.

"What about my phone and my car keys? Were they in my pockets?" I inquired in a shaky voice.

"You only had a wallet on you when you got here," she reiterated solemnly.

Anguished, I covered my face with my hands.

Hopefully, Elle had put a freeze on the card before those bastards had managed to deplete all of the money.

Where was my car? Did I stupidly exchange it for heroin? Was some unscrupulous drug dealer wheeling around in my silver Dodge Charger right now?

Elle had co-signed for the car, and she was going to be stunned and outraged by my recklessness and sheer stupidity.

The nurse handed me two miniature cups that contained pills. I didn't bother to ask what I was taking. It really didn't matter. Nothing mattered except making amends with Elle.

After the nurse left my room, I held my head in my hands and let out a long, anguished groan. Once again my life was ruined, and there was no one to blame except myself. In the midst of my pity party, I was taken off guard when Elle suddenly strolled through the door.

"Why?" she demanded as she pulled a chair close to my bed. "Do you realize you almost died?"

I nodded grimly. "I fucked up, baby, and I'm sorry."

"You're sorry?" She shook her head incredulously. "The police located the car…"

"Thank God," I said with audible relief.

"A pair of twenty-year-olds were driving it…and apparently

living out of it after they wrecked it. The driver's side is smashed in and so is the rear. The trunk and backseat was filled with all kinds of trash, empty beer bottles, and all sorts of clothes, blankets, and pillows."

"Baby, I'm sorry. I'll get the car fixed."

She sucked her teeth. "Don't concern yourself with car repairs. It's in the shop, and after it's fixed, I'm selling it."

I bit down on my lip and then nodded.

"And there's more bad news. You were fired. My father tried, but he couldn't save your job."

I flinched. "I'll start looking for something else immediately."

"I don't understand, Malik. You were in recovery—doing fantastic. What happened?"

Not having a plausible explanation, all I could do was shrug.

"I don't understand how you could go inside my purse and steal from our wedding fund? You spent thirty-six hundred dollars on drugs and probably would have completely wiped out the account if I hadn't put a freeze on the card in the nick of time."

Feeling like scum, I dropped my head into both of my hands, and sat there like that.

"In most instances, the bank would cover theft, but not when the culprit is your fiancé who has access to the card," she said with disgust.

I raised my head and looked her in the eyes. I wanted her to see the full scope of my remorse. "I was dead wrong, Elle. But I only meant to take a couple hundred, and I planned to put it back before you realized it was gone."

"That doesn't make it right, Malik."

"I know, baby. I know."

"I truly believed that your drug use was behind us. I believed in you," she said with her voice rising and tears beginning to flood her eyes. "I realize now that I don't know what you're capable of. After you made love to me that night, you told me you loved me more than life itself. But apparently that was a lie. You love drugs much more than you'll ever love me."

"That's not true. Elle. Please—"

"Please what? Give you another chance?" She made a scoffing sound. "I've called off the wedding, Malik. I can't do this anymore— it's humiliating. You've done rehab, you attend recovery meetings, and I don't know what else can be done for you. You made a decision to throw your life away, and I refuse to allow you to take me down with you."

"I wish I could make you understand what it's like when that need overpowers me."

"I don't care what it's like. Not anymore. You blew through money that I worked hard to save, and you almost killed yourself with that fake fentanyl that you took. I don't want to ever go through this kind of ordeal again."

I scowled, once again trying to remember taking fentanyl, and I finally concluded that the heroin I snorted must have been laced with it.

"I can't spend my life not knowing whether you're really happy or whether you're merely pretending to be," Elle continued. "Am I supposed to lock up all the valuables every night before I go to bed?" She pulled her diamond ring off her finger and set it on the bedside table.

"Elle, please...you're all I've got. I can't live without you," I said pleadingly.

"I'll send your things to your parents' house." She stiffened her chin, trying to be strong.

But through her hard exterior, I could see the raw pain in her eyes, and I felt like a piece of shit. All I'd ever done was bring her heartache, and it was time for me to man-up and let her go.

"I don't blame you, baby. You're a good woman. Smart. Beautiful. And you definitely deserve a better man than me," I admitted.

"Oh, Malik, what happened to us?" She sat on the bed and started weeping. I held her in my arms and fought to hold back tears of my own.

After a few moments, she pulled away, gathered herself, and wiped her eyes. "Goodbye, Malik. I honestly hope and pray that you find the strength to get your life together."

"I'm going to try my best," I said, swallowing down a big lump of pain and remorse.

CHAPTER 2

My parents allowed me to move back home. Being back in my old bedroom was humbling, and seeing the hurt in my mother's eyes was like taking a knife to the gut. She'd been so proud of the progress I'd made, and I knew it was hard for her to see me at such a low point...once again.

My dad was enraged over my relapse. He could barely look at me without mumbling under his breath or banging a fist on a table or countertop. My parents, Ruth Ann and Winston Copeland, had worked hard and had sacrificed to put me through college. They felt a huge source of pride in that their sacrifices had spared me from the burden of student debt.

But here I was...a full-grown, educated man, back under my parents' roof. My life was so depressing that I quickly started getting high again. In order to pay for my drugs, I resorted to stealing items that my parents wouldn't miss. Items such as jewelry my mom only wore on special occasions, emerald cuff links that my grandfather had passed down to my dad, and other family heirlooms that my parents valued. I rationalized that the trinkets would one day be passed down to me, anyway, so who was I hurting?

After a month, I noticed that the tension between my mother and father was growing increasingly worse. I could hear their muffled arguments on the other side of their closed bedroom door.

From what I could discern, they were arguing about me. My dad wanted to use tough love to get through to me. He said that kicking me out of the house would teach me that there were consequences for my actions, but my mother felt that I needed family support more than ever.

My dad was right. At thirty-one years old, I had no business being the cause of the strife within their marriage, and there was no telling when I would graduate from stealing small items to stealing TVs and computers. To spare them from the pain of my addiction, I packed a few things while they were at work. I left my mom a note, telling her I'd be in touch after I got situated.

With nowhere to go and no money to my name, my only recourse was to pawn Elle's engagement ring. Believing that Elle and I would one day get back together, I'd been using every ounce of my willpower to hold on to her ring. But I needed money badly—not only for drugs, but I also needed somewhere to live.

I went to a pawn shop and I could see the delight in the clerk's eyes when I handed over the two-and-a-half-carat ring. He didn't expect me to retrieve the expensive ring in thirty days, but I vowed to myself that come hell or high water, I'd get Elle's ring back.

The moment I tucked the money and the receipt inside my pocket, I literally bumped into a tall, willowy chick with wind-blown hair. She whizzed into the pawn shop like a tornado, carrying a dusty-looking table lamp in her arms as she dashed toward the counter.

Feeling shitty about pawning Elle's ring, I was in a hurry to get out of there, and the chick with the lamp was in a hurry to pawn her lamp. Due to our haste and our combined frenetic energy, we collided into each other. The lamp tumbled from her arms, and when it crashed to the floor, the glass shade shattered.

"Goddamit, motherfucker! Look what you did," she shrieked. "This is a handmade vintage lamp that's been in my family for generations. It's worth a fortune. A fucking fortune!"

I bent down, trying to salvage the remnants of the broken lamp, picking up the colorful shards of glass. I noticed the woman was teary-eyed and shaking, and I felt bad for her. Even though the accident wasn't totally my fault, I couldn't help feeling a degree of responsibility for the mishap.

When the clerk came from behind the counter to inspect the damaged lamp, he smirked. "There's nothing vintage about this lamp. It's dusty from sitting around, but it's not an antique, nor is it handmade. It looks like it came from Target or Walmart, circa nineteen ninety-four," he quipped.

"Screw you, smartass," she fumed at the clerk. Then she kicked the lamp in anger before storming toward the door.

It didn't require much scrutiny for me to realize she was a junkie. It takes one to know one.

One look at her and it was clear that she was nothing but trouble. I should have lingered inside the pawnshop for a bit longer to avoid further contact with her. But instead of listening to my better judgment, I exited the store right behind her.

She turned around and stared at me. Despite my polished appearance, she quickly sized me up as drug abuser, also. She was also aware that I'd made a transaction and my pocket was full of cash.

Judging by her jerky movements and the look of desperation in her eyes, it was apparent that she was going through withdrawals and was too dope sick to bother with girly flirtatiousness. She viewed me as a means to feed her addiction, and she got right to the point.

"What are you about to get into? Wanna party with me?" She

delivered her inquiry with a serious expression and didn't offer a flicker of a smile.

My plan had been to rent a room, get settled in, and then get high. I also intended to start making the rounds to various job fairs around the city as soon as I took the time to put together a new resume. I was sure I could do drugs and maintain a job as long as I kept to myself and didn't get involved with other addicts—especially female addicts. I tended to spiral down to the gutter whenever I combined drugs and sex.

But I was lonely, disillusioned, and feeling hopeless—a combination of emotions that I didn't want to feel. Suddenly, I yearned for the company of a woman along with the numbing effect of heroin.

I took a moment to appraise the young woman. She was around five-four and had a delicate build that made her seem fragile. She had smooth, cocoa-colored skin, dark moody eyes, and plump lips that added to her quiet sex appeal. Even though her hair was messy and her mascara was smeared, she was still pretty. Drugs hadn't robbed her of her beauty, yet. But it would only be a matter of time.

Hanging out with homegirl was risky and no doubt she'd entice me to spend more money than I wanted to, but throwing caution to the wind, I agreed to party with her.

She told me her name was Kaloni. Aside from asking if I'd buy her a gram of heroin, she didn't say much else. She drove a beat-up Volkswagen Jetta that was cluttered with everything from clothes to bags of dog food.

Apparently the car was home to her and a little brown Chihuahua that sat in the front seat, yapping away. The dog did not look well cared for. It wore a raggedy rhinestone collar with several missing stones. With mangy fur and cloudy, bulging eyes, it was clear that the little dog was no young pup. It was old and mean, and probably pissed off at having to depend on an irresponsible addict for its care and well-being.

Upset by my presence, the dog continued to bark even after Kaloni put it on her lap.

"Don't be jealous, Paris Hilton," Kaloni cooed as she petted her dog.

I hope I don't pick up any of Paris Hilton's fleas, I thought as I strapped on the seatbelt.

We copped from a dealer she knew who lived near Kensington and Allegheny Avenues. With money to burn, I bought a gram for Kaloni and a gram for myself. Then, we drove to a motel. I would have preferred if she'd left noisy Paris Hilton in the car, but I didn't bother to protest when she brought her into the room with us.

There were two twin beds and I took my bag of powder and camped out on the bed closest to the door. I immediately went to work, using the screen of my phone as a base and then breaking up the rock and making lines with the plastic keycard that the motel clerk had given me.

I kept an eye on Kaloni as she sat on the other bed. Her works consisted of a syringe, a lighter, a spoon, and a cord to tighten around her arm. She gave herself a shot, and I didn't snort one line until I was sure she was okay and hadn't overdosed.

Her head tipped forward as she began nodding, and when she didn't pass out or go into convulsions, I felt she was in the clear and it was okay for me to get high.

"This is some good dope," I muttered as I was hit with a rush of euphoria. In a matter of moments, I was free of all problems and was drifting on cloud nine.

Paris Hilton jumped on my bed and started growling at me. High as a kite and feeling complete bliss and utter contentment, I didn't feel the least bit annoyed. With my eyes half closed, I reached out and stroked her mangy coat. She calmed down and stopped barking, and I continued petting her as if she were my very own beloved pet.

After we both came down a little from our high, we took the dog for a walk in a wooded area near the motel. With drugs still in our systems, it wasn't a brisk walk. Kaloni and I ambled along slowly.

I took a seat on the ground, resting my back against a tree trunk. Kaloni sat next to me.

"Your pooch seems happy being in an open area," I commented as the dog scampered.

"Yeah, she's having a good time." A smile blossomed on Kaloni's face for the first time since I'd met her. Her smile put a gleam in her eyes, and it struck me that she was even prettier than I'd thought.

"Sometimes I take Paris Hilton to the park, but for the most part, she's stuck in the car all day," she commented.

Although her words came out drowsily, she seemed to be in a talkative mood. I would have preferred to sit quietly and enjoy the feeling of the sun shining down on me, but I didn't want to be rude.

"It's a shame that the dog can't get out more," I muttered, not really giving a damn about her dog. I was beginning to feel antsy as my mind wandered to the pebble-sized piece of heroin that was inside my jacket pocket. I reached inside my pocket and fondled it comfortingly.

"My dream is to buy a home in a rural area with lots of acres surrounding it. I want to provide a safe haven and a good environment for as many neglected animals as possible." Kaloni scratched her arm and spoke in a slurred voice as she communicated her ideal life.

"Any idea how you'll fund your altruistic endeavor?" Sarcasm colored my words, but she didn't seem to pick up on it. I noticed that Kaloni was less hostile than she'd been when we rammed into each other at the pawnshop. Being under the influence had removed the chip from her shoulder, and I preferred this softer and gentler version of her.

"I make good money on my job," she confided.

"Oh, yeah? What do you do for a living?" I inquired, although I doubted if she had a job.

"I dance at a club."

"You strip?" I was careful not to sound judgmental, but I wanted her to be more specific.

She nodded. "The pay is amazing. But I'm broke because I've been on suspension for a couple of months."

I raised my brows. *That's a long time for a suspension.* "Are you sure you still have a job? When is the suspension over?"

"I have another month to go. I got suspended for ninety days."

"That's a long-ass suspension."

"My boss wanted me to have enough time to get clean."

"Are you gonna make an effort?"

She shrugged. "It's hard to focus on getting clean when shit is falling apart all around you."

"Can't you work at another club?"

"No. Word is out that I'm unreliable, and I'm pretty much blackballed at all the clubs in the city."

"You could move to another city," I suggested.

She made a sour face and shook her head. "I can't move. I have a relationship with several dealers here in Philly."

"I feel you," I said.

As fucked up as my own life was, and in light of the fact that I'd also been fired over drug use, I had no business whatsoever offering advice to Kaloni or anyone else. But I was merely making small talk until I got back to the motel room and could block out my problems by snorting more lines.

"Getting suspended from work fucked up my life worse than it already was," she explained.

I didn't want to encourage her to keep talking, so I didn't comment. She was being annoyingly talkative, and I wanted her to revert back to her quiet, hostile persona.

"With no steady income, I got evicted from my place. Making matters worse, my boyfriend, Donnie, got locked up for shoplifting dog food for Paris Hilton. With his outstanding warrants, he's looking at twenty months." She dropped her head woefully. "I miss him so much; he was my soul mate. Without him to keep me straight, I've been making the worst choices ever, and I feel so alone."

I rubbed her shoulder consolingly.

"I racked up a big tab with one of my dealers. I've been ducking the dude for weeks, and it's only a matter of time before he catches up with me. If only I could get my job back, I could pay him the money I owe."

It was obvious that she wasn't going to shut up, so I reluctantly engaged in the discussion. "What did you do to get suspended from the strip club, if you don't mind my asking?"

"I got caught shooting up in the bathroom. I should have gone straight to rehab like I promised, but I couldn't leave Paris Hilton alone."

I was growing bored listening to Kaloni's long list of problems. Shit, I had my own issues. "You could have put her in a kennel," I said, allowing myself to be lured back into a conversation that I wasn't interested in.

"I planned to put her in a kennel, but after Donnie got locked up, I sort of lost my way. I wasn't thinking straight when I ran through my money before I could get my dog situated in a decent place." Her voice cracked a little, revealing that she was genuinely remorseful for not making wiser money decisions.

I could completely relate to recklessly blowing through money, and I squeezed her arm in understanding. She looked at me and I could see the pain in her eyes. In that moment, something clicked between us and we held each other in a long gaze. It wasn't about lust or anything sexual. It was about recognizing ourselves as two lost souls. Two human beings who were slaves to a drug that would eventually cause our demise if we didn't get help and kick it for good.

"Don't worry, we'll figure this shit out together. After we get high one last time, maybe we should both think about checking into a rehab facility," I said with a weak smile.

"Yeah, something has to change because I'm so tired of living like this." She sighed and then rested her head on my shoulder. Being an addict was all-consuming and draining, and it was obvious that she was exhausted.

We sat in silence for a while. After a few moments, she stood up and called for Paris Hilton, and the dog excitedly ran to her and leapt into her arms.

Back in the motel room, we got high again. Later, we ordered pizza but barely touched it. After going through the motions of watching TV, we went to bed. At some point during the night, Kaloni got out of her bed and crawled into mine.

We cuddled at first and then we fucked. She was open-minded and did freaky things that Elle would have never dreamed of doing, nor would I have expected her to. Sex with Kaloni was angry and rough, yet awesome. However, she wasn't the person that I wanted or needed. Despite the sexual chemistry between us, I found myself missing Elle terribly, and the moment I climaxed, I felt utterly hopeless and all alone.

Until that moment, I hadn't allowed myself to deal with losing Elle, and the pain that I'd been keeping at bay, tore through me with razor-sharpness and was unrelenting.

CHAPTER 3

In the morning the first thing I reached for was my drugs. Still lying down with my eyes closed, I blindly groped the top of the nightstand. Finding nothing, my eyes popped open and I sat upright. I shot an accusing look over at Kaloni's bed, which was empty.

Assuming she was in the bathroom, I angrily yelled her name. The response was deafening silence. When it occurred to me that Paris Hilton wasn't yapping and barking as she usually did, I became alarmed and jumped out of bed to check my pants pockets. To my horror, my pockets were empty. Every dollar of my money was gone.

Maybe she took the dog for a walk, I reasoned, and then raced to the window and looked out. I'd hoped to see her hooptie sitting in the parking spot in front of our room, but of course it wasn't.

That bitch! I should have known better than to trust a junkie, and I was pissed with myself for letting my guard down. Infuriated, I punched a wall and put a dent in it.

I gingerly ran my fingertips over my scraped-up knuckles and then flopped down on the bed in disgust. I glanced at the time and scowled. Only an hour and a half until check-out time.

What the hell am I going to do? I couldn't go crawling back to my parents. Over the past few years, I'd caused them enough grief to last a lifetime, and they deserved to live peacefully without having to worry about their adult son.

Like anyone else, I'd made my fair share of mistakes, but the biggest mistake of my life was my decision to undergo back surgery after suffering a ruptured disc in a car accident. That first failed surgery led to my having to go under the knife a second time, and in order to deal with the constant headaches and chronic back pain, I was prescribed OxyContin. A dependency on pain medication led to my current circumstances.

If I had known then what I now knew, I would have opted for rehab, yoga, meditation, medical marijuana—anything except back surgery.

While in the midst of wallowing in self-pity and fighting off the beginning sensations of drug cravings, I heard the loud motor of Kaloni's car. I threw on my sweatpants and Nikes, raced to the door and threw it open.

Kaloni opened the car door and let the dog out, but she remained inside the car, her body twisted around as she rummaged through trash bags in the backseat.

Having bonded with me the day before, Paris Hilton was excited to see me. She scampered up to me, greeting me with shrill barks as she nipped happily around my ankles. In no mood for the frisky little Chihuahua, I pushed her aside with my foot, and then stormed over to the driver's side of the car.

"Give me my fucking money and my fucking dope!" I snarled.

"I got you," she said nonchalantly with her back to me as she continued searching through the trash bags that were piled up in the back.

I bit down on my bottom lip and made growling sounds as I tried to control my fury. I had never put my hands on a woman in my life, but I was seconds away from snatching the raggedy car door off the hinges and grabbing Kaloni by the neck and choking the shit out of her. Although I was furious over her audacity to steal from me, my rage was heightened by the fact that I was feening for drugs.

Kaloni pulled something out of a trash bag and tossed it to me. Instinctively, I caught it and was pleasantly surprised to find myself holding a thick roll of bills secured by a rubber band.

"That's twice the amount I borrowed from you," she said and then tossed me a baggie.

I could feel myself getting a slight erection as I fondled the baggie that contained white powder. I had no idea how Kaloni had acquired the cash and drugs, and I didn't care.

She popped the trunk and slowly got out of the car. "I bought Paris Hilton some gourmet dog food. She's gonna be so happy," Kaloni said with a sluggish smile. "Paris Hilton!" she called out and her dog ran to her, barking happily.

It was obvious by Kaloni's slowed speech and lethargic movements that she'd already hit before driving to the motel. She had a habit of endlessly rifling through the contents of the bags in the backseat of her car and the piles of junk she kept inside the trunk when she was high. I had no idea if she was looking for the expensive pet food she'd bought or if she was searching for a change of clothes, and I couldn't care even less. As she continued fiddling around inside the trunk, searching for God knows what, I stepped away from the car.

Anxious to snort the white powder, I returned to the room and closed the door.

It seemed as if Kaloni had been outside for a hell of a long time, but in my hazy state of intoxication, I was oblivious as to whether minutes or hours had elapsed. I snorted some more lines and when I finally heard Kaloni swiping her keycard, I was so high I could have sworn that I heard the low rumble of male voices.

Curious to learn if I'd imagined hearing the voices, I fixed my eyes on the door as it opened. My high was instantly blown when I spotted two dudes creeping in behind Kaloni. One was holding Paris Hilton and the other was holding a gun with the barrel pressed into Kaloni's back. Kaloni's eyes were wide with fear and Paris Hilton was whining and squirming in the dude's tight grip.

"Whoa! What's going on, fellas?" I held my hands up in the universal gesture of confusion.

"Shut the fuck up and hand over the cash," said the dude who was holding the dog.

"And hurry the fuck up," his cohort added, waving the gun in my direction.

How the hell had Kaloni managed to get us involved in a stick-up! My drug-addled mind frantically tried to think of ways to reason with the young thugs. I tried to force my lips into a friendly smile, but my mouth wouldn't cooperate. Instinct told me there was no point in trying to reason with them. Although they appeared to be no older than eighteen or nineteen, I could tell by their cold, dead eyes that life had already hardened them, and they were left without a shred of humanity in their hearts.

The gunman glowered at me. "You hard of hearing, muthafucka? Gimme the fuckin' money!"

Reluctantly, I reached under the mattress and pulled out the roll of cash. It broke my heart to surrender the money, and I considered making a run for it. But, realizing that I couldn't outrun a bullet, I handed it over.

Dude counted the money and with a look of satisfaction, he stuck the roll in his pocket. Figuring that we were square, I bent over the screen of my phone and snorted a line. I had to do something to calm my nerves.

All of a sudden, the gunman knocked the phone out of my hand, and white powder swirled in the air before scattering onto the floor.

"Gimme the rest of the drugs this bitch stole from us."

"That's it…that's all I have left," I lied.

He put the gun to my head and cocked it.

"Don't hurt him, Saint," Kaloni pleaded. "He doesn't have any-thing to do with this." She turned her gaze on me. "Give him what he wants, Malik."

I pulled the baggie out of my pocket and grudgingly gave it to the thug named Saint.

Satisfied, he smiled. "It's a good thing this bitch decided to stop at the pet store, allowing me and my man to catch up with her and follow her here. Otherwise it might have been weeks before our paths crossed again."

I was disgusted with Kaloni for being so foolish. If you steal from drug dealers, you don't make pit stops…you get far away from the scene of the crime.

"All right, man, give her back her mutt and let's roll," Saint said to his partner.

"Nah, I'm holding this little mutt hostage until she takes care of me. The bitch owes me some top."

"I don't owe you anything," Kaloni said in a high-pitched voice.

"Time is money, bitch, and you wasted mine. Now, take care of me." He put Paris Hilton down and she quickly scurried underneath a chair. When he began to unbuckle his belt, I felt compelled to intervene.

"Man, you got what you came for—"

Before I could get another word out of my mouth, Saint charged toward me and whacked me upside the head and both sides of my jaw with the butt of the gun. I saw a burst of bright light before the room grew dim.

"Mind your business, muthafucka," he hissed at me as I lay moaning after being brutally pistol-whipped. Blood trickled down my face and my head throbbed.

"Let's go, Paris Hilton. Come on, girl," Kaloni said, clapping her hands in desperation.

I heard the sounds of a scuffle, but was too lightheaded to sit up and see exactly what was going on. I surmised that Kaloni had tried to escape with her dog, but the two drug dealers had blocked her path. I could hear them taunting her.

Next I heard Paris Hilton let out a painful cry.

"No! Oh, my God. Why'd you stab her?" Kaloni shrieked.

"If you don't stop running your mouth and start putting those lips to good use, I'ma stab your ass, too."

I could hear Kaloni sniffling and crying, but there was nothing that I could do to help her. Pitch darkness eased over me and I welcomed the loss of consciousness.

I was brought out of my stupor by the shrill sound of the desk phone ringing. Sitting up was painful, but I managed to position myself upright. Rubbing my throbbing head, I answered the phone.

"Check-out time," said a cheerful voice on the other end of the phone.

"Right. We'll be out in a minute," I mumbled. I hung up the phone and looked over at Kaloni.

She was sitting on the floor crying, with her face buried in her hands. Sprawled out next to her was the lifeless, bloody body of her dog. I knew how much she loved Paris Hilton, and I felt bad for her.

Despite my sympathy, I was ready to get away from Kaloni. I could wind up dead if I hung around with her much longer. But I wanted to at least help her bury the dog before I cut ties.

"We need to bury her," I remarked. "We can take her to the woods after we clear out of the room."

"Why do we have to leave?" Kaloni asked, sniffling and wiping her eyes.

"I only paid for one night."

"Can't we stay one more day?" she asked.

Annoyed by the dumb question, I frowned at her. "I don't have any more money…do you?"

"No," she whispered in a meek voice.

Disgusted by the predicament she'd put me in, I dropped my head in my hand and let out a long sigh. Then, I looked up at Kaloni. "They say that a junkie has to hit rock bottom before getting help. I don't know about you, but I'm at rock bottom and I'm ready to get some kind of help. I believe I still have health insurance from my old job, and it's time to put it to use."

"My parents offered to pay for my treatment," she commented.

"You should take advantage of their offer," I said as I stood up.

My eyes landed on Paris Hilton and I flinched. The little pooch had begun to grow on me, and I hated seeing her small body covered with multiple stab wounds. What kind of savage would viciously murder a little animal? If this wasn't an indication that my life was in the toilet, then I couldn't imagine what kind of tragedy it would take for me to realize that I couldn't go on living this way.

"Come on, Kaloni," I said, reaching for her hand. "Let's bury her."

Cradling the dead dog like it was a fragile infant, Kaloni cried openly as we trudged toward the wooded area behind the motel. Without access to a shovel, all we could do was cover Paris Hilton with branches and twigs. After we covered her sufficiently, I turned to leave, but Kaloni wouldn't budge.

"Come on, let's go," I said impatiently.

"I can't leave her like this. Suppose wild animals find her and tear her to shreds."

"What wild animals? We're in Philly, not the jungles of Africa," I scoffed.

"I know…but, squirrels and raccoons could find her and eat her.

We have to get a shovel and bury her, Malik. We can't leave her out here like this." She paused in thought. "Maybe the desk clerk has a shovel."

"I doubt if the desk clerk will give us anything if we don't pay the bill. And how are we gonna do that?" Anger began to build and I gazed at Kaloni accusingly. "If you hadn't been so sneaky, waking up and fucking with my money and my stash, none of this would have happened."

"I know, I know," she said, shaking her head regretfully. "I fucked up and I'm sorry." She covered her face with her hands, sniffling and crying. The sounds that emerged from her were so pitiful, I couldn't continue my verbal tirade.

I put my arm around her frail shoulders. "Don't cry. We'll figure this out. But, I can't look for a shovel or anything else until I get another hit. My head and my jaw...everything hurts," I complained, rubbing the sore and swollen areas where I'd been pistol-whipped.

"I kept something for us," she said, bending over and patting her right boot. She stuck her fingers into the top of her boot and pulled out a baggie that she'd hidden from the two drug dealers.

My eyes lit up and I nearly salivated at the sight of the baggie that bulged with white powder. I reached out a desperate hand. Since we no longer had a room for privacy, I was prepared to sit down on the ground and do lines right there in the woods.

"This is all we have until we can get some money, and I can't let you waste these good drugs by snorting them," Kaloni said.

Getting high by snorting required a larger quantity than shooting, but I wasn't willing to become a mainliner.

"No, I can't do that," I said firmly.

"It won't hurt you to shoot up just this once," she cajoled.

"No!" I insisted and then yanked the baggie from her hand.

While I snorted lines from the cracked screen of my phone, she began walking toward the car where her works were stored in the console. I didn't rush to catch up with her. I took my time, enjoying the euphoria that came with the rush. When I finished, I made my way out of the woods and headed to the motel's parking lot.

After she shot up, we both sat in the car, nodding for an indeterminable amount of time. As soon as we came down, she immediately started bugging me about getting a shovel from Home Depot.

"We don't have any money to buy a shovel," I reminded her with annoyance in my voice.

"But, you promised we'd give Paris Hilton a proper burial."

I groaned inwardly. At that point, I should have told her to drop me off at my parents' house. From the shelter of my childhood home, I could have made arrangements for rehab. But feeling a sense of responsibility toward Kaloni, I allowed her to talk me into going to Home Depot to steal a shovel.

Had I been in my right mind, I would have realized that with a big knot on my head and a swollen face, I stuck out like a sore thumb. But I wasn't in my right frame of mind. My entire body hurt, especially my head, and rational thought wasn't easy.

Two bumbling fools, Kaloni and I brazenly walked into the store.

While I browsed the aisle that contained shovels, she wandered to another part of the store. I located the shovels, looked them over, and selected a small one that seemed like it would be easy to sneak outside.

I waited a while for Kaloni to join me, but she was taking forever. Impatient to get the shovel out of the store, I slipped past the person who was checking receipts at the exit. I made it to the car without anyone from security running up on me, and I was relieved that Kaloni had forgotten to lock the car doors. I reached inside, popped the trunk, and then squeezed the shovel inside the area that was crammed with everything from household items to clothes, and a bag of dog food.

My heart clenched at the sight of the dog food. If only Kaloni had stuck to the regular dog food she had on hand and hadn't decided to splurge on the gourmet brand, Paris Hilton would've still been alive. I swallowed down a lump of sorrow and then closed the trunk. I slid into the passenger's side of the car and waited.

I had no idea why Kaloni was taking so long, and I was growing more and more agitated.

Alone with my thoughts, I was filled with regret about Elle. Cancelling a wedding had to be a painful and a huge embarrassment for her. She believed in me and I'd let her down. I hoped that my failings wouldn't cause her to lose her belief in love.

With the seat reclined, I was briefly at peace as I imagined Elle one day recovering from the hurt I'd caused and living her best life.

But the peace I felt was short-lived.

Seemingly out of nowhere, the car was surrounded by the flashing lights of police cruisers. Guns were pointed at me and I heard a booming voice demand that I get out of the car with my hands up.

I immediately obeyed, wondering why the cops were acting so dramatic over a stolen shovel.

I found out later that Kaloni had stupidly tried to rob a cashier, threatening the woman with a box cutter she had picked up in an aisle near the shovels. She was charged with attempted armed robbery.

They had me on camera entering the store with Kaloni, and I was charged with accessory to the crime.

Kaloni and I had separate trials and I never saw her again. I was convicted and sentenced to four years in prison. I heard that she was given ten years for armed robbery. It seemed like a stiff sentence for an underweight young woman who didn't have the strength to hurt a fly.

CHAPTER 4

After seven months of incarceration, I was pleasantly surprised when Elle came to visit, and I was even more surprised to see that her stomach was swelled with child. Pregnancy agreed with Elle. She had that glow that I'd heard about but had never actually witnessed with my own eyes. When I sat across from her at the table in the visitors' room, she reached out and grasped both my hands.

"It's good to see you, Malik," she said with a faint smile.

"Good to see you, too." I examined her face closely…questioningly. I nodded toward her stomach and lowered my voice to a whisper. "Is it mine?"

"Of course, it's yours," she said with indignation.

"How far along are you?"

"Seven months."

"Why didn't you tell me sooner?"

"What good would that have done? I'm here now because I wanted you to know before he's born."

"We're having a boy?" I asked joyfully.

She nodded and I was filled with a sense of hope that I hadn't allowed myself to feel for a long time. Suddenly I had a reason to look forward to the future, and I quickly convinced myself that Elle had a change of heart. She'd come to tell me that she was willing to do this bid with me and still wanted to get married.

Happiness washed over me as I imagined going home to my wife and child one day. My son would be approximately four years old when I got out, but I was hopeful that Elle would bring him to see me on a regular basis, allowing us to establish a close father and son relationship.

My gaze wandered downward and I noticed Elle's bare finger. Reminded that I'd pawned her engagement ring, I felt a sharp stab of guilt. Even if I were a free man, it was too late to get the ring out of hock, so I vowed to myself that one day, I'd replace it with an even bigger diamond.

"Elle, baby…you're giving me a new lease on life; I'm not going to mess up again. I swear! I went through horrible withdrawals in here, and I'm clean now. And I'm going to stay that way. I know I've said that before, but since I've been behind bars, I've been attending Narcotics Anonymous meetings, and I've learned that maintaining sobriety requires sticking to the program for the rest of my life. I'm willing to do whatever it takes to have you and our child back in my life. I'll fight with everything I've got," I said with earnestness.

Waiting for her response, I stared at her fixedly.

She looked away uncomfortably, and when she finally returned my gaze, her features were arranged in an unreadable mask.

I gave her a searching look.

"I didn't come here to make future plans, Malik. I came to tell you about the baby and to ask you to give up your parental rights."

Believing I'd heard wrong, I cocked my head to the side. "You want me to do what?"

"It's for the best. You're going to be serving time for three and a half more years, and our son is going to need a positive male role model in his life."

"I can be a role model when I get out of here."

"He'll need a father figure sooner than that. And that's part of the reason why I've decided to marry Everett Wilson. We're having an intimate wedding ceremony in two weeks."

Feeling as if all the air had left my lungs, I gasped. "Everett Wilson! You're fucking around with your boss?"

"I wouldn't put it that crudely," she replied.

"How long have you two been involved?" I asked, frowning excessively as I envisioned my fist knocking out his front teeth.

"A few months."

"I always suspected that that sneaky bastard had the hots for you, but every time I mentioned it, you always downplayed my suspicions."

"That's not important anymore, Malik. What's important is that Everett is a good man. He's dependable, financially stable, and he loves me. He has stuck by my side at my lowest point when I had to deal with the hurt and embarrassment of canceling our wedding. And when I found out I was pregnant, and didn't know where to turn, he was there for me. He's never missed any of my doctor's appointments, and it was Everett who rejoiced with me the first time I heard the baby's heartbeat."

I felt like standing up and flipping the table over, and I would have if it weren't soldered to the floor. The next best thing was to pound on the table in outrage, but that kind of outburst would have brought our visit to a quick end and would have landed me in the hole. As I tried to suppress my anger, I could feel the pulse beating in my temples.

I took a deep breath and tried to reason with Elle. "It's not like I'll be serving time forever. I can be a good role model for my son when I get out," I said with desperation breaking into my voice.

She stared at me with her mouth pressed into a tight line, letting me know that she wasn't budging from her position. Frustrated, I raked my fingers down the side of my face.

"I can't do it. There's no way I would ever willingly sign my child over to another man," I said firmly.

"You've made a wreck of your life, and I don't want your bad decisions to impact our child in any way." She paused and gazed at me, as if waiting for me to agree with her.

I gave her a hard stare, letting her know I wasn't budging from my position, either.

She sighed again. "Whether you agree to it or not, Everett will be raising your child. I don't need your signature for that. I'm putting his name on the birth certificate, ensuring that he'll be the child's legal father."

"I have rights, Elle. You can't do this to me," I said with seething anger.

"You should put your pride aside and think about what's best for your son. I know you didn't deliberately blow up my life, but you did. I know you possess the capacity to love your child, but you and I both know that all you'll ever do is disappoint him. If you love him and if you ever loved me, do us a favor and stay out of our lives."

"You can't keep my son away from me," I snarled. "I'm gonna fight for my son. I'm gonna sue you and your bitch-ass boss. I have rights!"

"I had hoped we could discuss this like rational people, but I see that we can't," she said with a tone of finality.

The idea of her and her arrogant boss trying to take away my parental rights had me clenching my fist under the table. I would have felt so much better if I could've punched something: the table, a wall, anything!

But I had to get a grip on myself or risk being put in isolation for thirty days. I'd heard horror stories about solitary confinement and I definitely didn't want to spend any time there. Realizing I had to get far away from Elle before I lost control of myself, I stood up and beckoned the guard.

As I was being escorted from the visitor's room, I looked over my shoulder and gave Elle the dirtiest look I could muster.

Back on my cell block, the more I thought about what Elle had asked me to do, the more depressed I became. Most women wanted their child's father to be active in the kid's life, but she thought of me as such a lowlife that she didn't want my child to know that I existed.

My sense of hopelessness was all-consuming, and I could feel tears starting to well in my eyes. But I couldn't permit myself to cry around a pack of hardened criminals.

The C.O. escorted me back to my cell and locked me in, and my way of warding off the tears that threatened to fall was to haul off and bust my cellmate, Louie, in the mouth.

I released a vile outburst of profanity and swung another punch; this one landed in his gut, doubling him over. Although my tears were imperceptible to the human eye, the intense pain in my heart manifested in an unwarranted act of rage.

"What's wrong with you, man?" he sputtered, staring at me in disbelief as blood poured from his lips.

"I told you about sitting on my bed, motherfucker," I growled, pointing to a slight crease in the thin blanket that covered the bottom bunk where I slept.

I wanted to fight, and so I hit Louie with some body blows, but instead of fighting back, his punk-ass yelled for the C.O.

Ironically, I ended up in the hole for thirty days, after all.

Thirty days inside a small, crypt-like cell was pure torture. I craved a TV, a radio, a magazine…even one page of a newspaper would have helped to ease my boredom. During my time in the hole, my drug cravings returned—full force. With nothing but time on my hands and nothing to distract me, all of my waking hours were filled with thoughts of getting high again. When I slept, I was tortured with nightmares of my future son calling another man, "Daddy."

I emerged from solitary as a broken man, and desperately needed something to ease my emotional suffering. Drugs were rampant in prison and all I had to do was put the word out. I traded my commissary bag for my first hit. I conned my mother into sending me extra money to fund my addiction, telling her that I needed to purchase books and spiritual material to enhance the in-house treatment program.

Each time I got high, I told myself that I was only doing it to be able to cope with prison life. I also told myself that nodding all day helped me forget my surroundings and made time move faster. After a while, my weight started falling off, and I was walking around with a vacant look in my eyes. Before long, I overdosed on some bad shit.

Miraculously, I survived again. But after yet another brush with death, this time I had an epiphany.

I wasn't fit to be a father.

A feeling of acceptance washed over me, and I contacted Elle and agreed to sign the papers to give up my parental rights.

CHAPTER 5

I went cold turkey in prison and traded my drug habit for a punishing workout regimen in the prison gym. A loner at heart, I kept to myself and stayed out of trouble.

Three years later, I was released.

Blending in with joggers, mothers who pushed their babies in strollers, and others who were enjoying a leisurely spring day in the park, I pretended to be engrossed in feeding the pigeons. I was bigger and bulkier from thirty-six months of pushing iron, and with the brim of my cap pulled down to conceal my face, I felt certain that no one would be able to identify me as Malik Copeland, ex-con.

I checked my watch and at exactly two-fifteen, I turned my attention to the entrance of the park. Like clockwork, three staff members from a prestigious preschool shepherded a group of three-year-olds into the area.

My son, Phoenix, was among them and I watched him from my peripheral vision.

For the past two weeks, I'd been stalking him, his mom, and even his so-called father. I knew their routines, and today was a perfect opportunity to snatch my son.

Phoenix looked so much like me; I could have picked him out of any crowd. And even though he called another man, "Daddy," I had no doubt that he and I would develop a natural bond.

I'd been at my lowest point, both mentally and physically, when I'd signed over my parental rights. Now drug free and of sound mind, I had no choice but to forcibly claim my son. Fighting Elle and Everett in court would be pointless; no judge would rule on the side of a former addict and ex-con.

My rental car was parked a half-block away from the park. All it would take to start a new life with my son was to take the teachers off guard with a quick grab and a swift sprint to the car.

With my back to the teachers and the toddlers, I sprinkled bread crumbs on the ground as I slowly inched backward with pigeons following me. Suddenly, I was swarmed by an army of squealing little kids who were fascinated by the birds I was feeding.

"Look at the birds! Can we feed them?" The children's voices were a joyful chorus as they scampered around me with out-stretched hands.

Apologizing to me, the teachers hurriedly began gathering up the high-spirited children.

My plan was foiled and I had no choice but to postpone the abduction of my son. The teachers had their guards up now, and without the element of surprise, my plan wouldn't work. The teachers were in full "protect the kids" mode and would have screamed their heads off and viciously attacked me if I had attempted to run off with Phoenix.

"Wait! I want to feed the birds," insisted a little guy with coconut-brown skin and facial features that were exactly like mine. I didn't see any of Elle's characteristics in our son's face. It seemed as if her genes had been completely obliterated by mine.

"Please, mister; may I feed them?" he asked politely and articulately.

Before his teachers could protest and spirit him away, I quickly dug inside the plastic bag that contained the birdfeed and scooped out a handful. I carefully placed the bread crumbs into his small palm.

That's when it dawned on me that the bread crumbs were symbolic of what I had to offer him—nothing but crumbs. It would be selfish of me to remove him from his stable lifestyle and force him into the harshness and uncertainty of living life on the run. I had allowed my pride and my ego to get the best of me, but I now realized that the best thing I could do for my son was to walk away.

Misty-eyed, I gave Phoenix a pat on the head and walked away. When I looked back at him, I saw the most pitiful sight I'd ever seen. My son was standing still with an arm outstretched, like he wanted me to come back and pick him up. He stared at me with tears running from his eyes, crying silently, while sucking his thumb.

As I turned my back to him and quickly exited the park, I could feel my heart breaking into a thousand pieces.

During my first few months out of prison, I did odd jobs. I drove a delivery truck, worked in the factory of an Italian bread company, and transported disabled people to their medical appointments, but there was no meaningful work for an ex-con. Nothing that paid well or presented a mental challenge.

I continued to secretly stalk Elle and Phoenix. I couldn't help it. I needed to know that he was all right and was being treated well by his stepfather.

One day when Elle caught me spying on her and Phoenix during an outing at the zoo, I had hoped she'd introduce me to my son and allow me to join them.

But she recoiled and tightly clutched Phoenix's hand. She threatened me with a restraining order, making it clear that she considered me an irredeemable monster, unfit to come anywhere near her or our son.

I didn't need any trouble with the law, and I knew that as long as I was in Philadelphia, I wouldn't be able to stop myself from checking on Elle and Phoenix—the family that should have been mine.

It was definitely time for me to move on. I remembered that one of the inmates back in prison, a Mexican guy from Arizona named Elias, constantly raved about the great weather there, and he'd told me he could hook me up with a job working for his uncle's roofing company if I ever thought about relocating.

I found Elias on Facebook and in-boxed him, asking if the offer still held.

He assured me that he had a job for me, and a week later I was on a flight to Phoenix. I took it as a good sign that I was relocating to the city that bore my son's name. I didn't know anything about roofing, but I'd always been a quick study and was sure I'd catch on easily.

Phoenix was as good a place as any to try to rebuild my life. Also, living in a place where it didn't snow was a plus.

I arrived in Phoenix and quickly found a cheap, furnished apartment. For some unknown reason, the place came equipped with potted plants that I unwittingly agreed to maintain when I signed my lease. It was a good thing the plants were a variety of cacti that required minimal care because I didn't know the first thing about greenery.

For the first time in a long while, I felt hopeful that I could put my dark past behind me and look toward a bright future. I was getting yet another second chance, and I made a promise to myself that this time I wouldn't screw it up.

I spent my first day sightseeing and getting to know my new city. Although I wouldn't get to watch my son grow up or participate in his upbringing, I planned to reach out to him when he turned eighteen and let him know that I was his real father. Meanwhile,

I had to ignore the ache in my heart and strive for a small amount of personal happiness.

Before I could even think about starting work with Elias and his uncle, I had to find a nearby Narcotics Anonymous meeting. Drug addiction had taken me to hell and back, and although I'd miraculously survived both death and prison, I dared not take my sobriety for granted. Realizing that I needed support, I did a quick search online and found a meeting at a church that was within walking distance of my apartment.

At the meeting I took a seat among the group and found myself sandwiched between a skinny, Caucasian teenage boy and a fifty-something Native American man who gave me a head nod while maintaining a stoic expression.

At nineteen years old, the teenager wasn't old enough to legally purchase liquor, yet when he shared his story, he admitted that he'd been abusing drugs and alcohol since he was eleven years old. I wondered how in the hell an eleven-year-old kid had gotten access to alcohol and narcotics on a regular basis.

After the teenage kid finished sharing his sad story of how his addiction had resulted in stints at detention centers and mental health facilities throughout his young life, I immediately thought of Phoenix and prayed that he would have a normal childhood and adolescence, free of addiction. Some said addiction was genetic, and I could only hope that I hadn't passed on any addict-genes to my innocent child.

When it was my turn to share, I reluctantly stood up and introduced myself. I intended to keep my story short and only talk about how my addiction had led to my involvement with Kaloni and turned me into a petty thief who stole a lousy shovel and ended up doing hard time. But once I started talking, I couldn't stop, and I wound up speaking about the education and career that I had thrown away. And I didn't stop there. I surprised myself when I divulged my painful innermost feelings about losing my fiancée, and signing away the parental rights to my son. I even admitted to relocating, so that I wouldn't be tempted to kidnap my son. I exposed so much about myself that when I finished sharing, I felt embarrassed for myself.

The meeting ended and people began to mingle in clusters. Some hovered around the coffee and doughnuts table while others darted outside to take a smoke. Choosing not to hang around, I made a beeline for the exit sign. Someone tapped me on the shoulder and when I turned around, I was surprised to see the Native guy I'd been sitting next to. He was medium height and stocky. A real sturdy-looking, older guy with long black hair that he wore in a ponytail that hung down his back.

We hadn't exchanged more than a head nod, and I was curious to know what he wanted.

"Yeah?" I asked with raised brows.

"Hello, Malik; my name is Ahiga Greystone," he said, extending his hand.

We shook hands and he smiled at me with warmth.

"Thank you for sharing your story. Listening to the experience of others is tremendously helpful to everyone in attendance, so please don't feel as if you made a fool of yourself."

"Are you a mind reader?" I asked, chuckling nervously.

"No, it's a typical reaction after spilling your guts to a roomful of strangers." He smiled and crow's-feet gathered at the corners of his eyes, giving him the look of a wise elder. Something about his calm demeanor put me at ease, and I accepted his invitation to stay a while and have a cup of coffee.

We began a conversation and he asked in a fatherly way about my financial situation.

"I'm okay. I start a new job in the morning with a roofing company, and I'll get paid once a week—under the table."

"Good for you," he said, patting me on the back as he ushered me around the room, introducing me to other members of the group.

Before I left for home, Ahiga gave me his phone number. "I'm not your official sponsor, but if you ever need to talk, I'm always available to listen."

"Thanks, man," I said, stuffing the piece of paper inside my pocket.

CHAPTER 6

The perpetual warmth of Arizona was enjoyable during normal daily activities, but with the sun beating down on my head while climbing up and down a ladder, I felt like I was in hell. I thought the job that Elias had offered would require nailing down a few shingles, but there were a lot more components in replacing a roof than I had ever imagined. It was backbreaking labor and there was a lot of grueling prep work before we even got started.

Elias, his uncle, and his cousin were accustomed to the heat and weren't fazed by it. By all appearances, I was in better physical shape than the three of them, but while they joked and laughed as they worked, I gasped and panted from the intensity of the heat. Even though I guzzled down one bottle of water after another, I couldn't seem to quench my thirst.

My coworkers spoke in Spanish to each other throughout the course of the day. I occasionally recognized a word or two, but I was no linguist. Unless someone was barking an order to me in English, I was basically left out of the conversations. By the end of the workday, I was sunburned, thirsty, sore, and my head ached from listening to conversations delivered in rapid-fire Spanish that I couldn't comprehend. My misery was compounded when I was tasked with cleaning up after the job was completed.

As soon as I got home, I switched on the AC and then trudged to the kitchen. I opened the fridge and stood with the door open as I drank straight from the container, trying my best to down a full gallon of cold water. I wiped my mouth with the back of my hand and made my way to the bathroom and ran hot water in the tub. I slid inside the scalding water to soak my aching muscles, and I knew with certainty that I wasn't going to make it as a roofer—not for very long. As soon as something else came up, I was out of there. But being an ex-convict, my options were limited, and I'd most likely have to tough it out with the roofing job for much longer than I preferred.

Later in the evening, I got dressed and dutifully went to my recovery meeting. Having that extra support was like being thrown a lifeline, especially while I was feeling down and out. Addicts used any excuse to get high, and depression was at the top of my list of triggers.

When I entered the basement of the church, I was surprised to find it much more crowded than my first visit. I scanned the room and spotted Ahiga. He gave me a wave and nodded toward the seat beside him where a black hat was resting.

I approached and he lifted the hat, placing it in his lap.

It was a worn black Fedora with a band made of Native American beading and a bright blue feather tucked on the side.

"Cool hat," I complimented.

"Thanks," he responded. "It belonged to my father and I wear it to keep his spirit close to me."

"Hmm, that's deep," I uttered, not knowing what else to say.

"How was the first day on the job?" Ahiga asked.

I shook my head glumly. "Brutal, man. Absolutely brutal."

"I'm surprised you do manual work. You struck me as someone

who was more analytical…" His voice trailed off as we both noticed a cute white chick that was sending a sultry smile in my direction. She was wearing jeans and a close-fitting crop top that showcased her big boobs and exposed a lot of skin.

Imagining the two of us twisting up bedsheets, I inadvertently licked my lips as I returned her smile, and I made a mental note to strike up a conversation with her during the break. I hadn't enjoyed the company of a woman since arriving in Arizona, and I was eager to make her acquaintance.

Ahiga nudged his chin toward the sexy white chick. "They say it's best to socialize with people in recovery, but from my experiences, when it comes to members of the opposite sex, it's not a good idea unless the woman has been in recovery for over a year. She's only been clean a few months, son. She may not be your best choice for female companionship," he said sagely.

I instantly felt the heat of annoyance, and it was on the tip of my tongue to tell Ahiga that he wasn't my damn father and to mind his own fucking business. But thinking back to Kaloni and the destruction she brought to my life, I reeled in my raging hormones.

Elias's uncle never bullshitted me about my money. He paid well and delivered my pay in cash every Friday—on time. But the job was not only labor-intensive; it was dangerous. During my third week on the job, I fell off a roof and luckily didn't sustain any broken bones. But two weeks later when I was accidentally splashed with hot tar, I decided it was time to rethink my career choice. After a trip to the ER where my burned left forearm was treated and bandaged, I was sent home with the strict order to stay off roofs for two weeks. Although my arm hurt like hell, my burns weren't as severe as they could have been, so once again, I was lucky. But how long would my luck last?

I searched online for menial jobs that I didn't think would do a background check on me, and after turning up nothing, I decided to call Ahiga and find out if he knew of any job leads.

"Uh, hello?" he said, sounding distracted when he answered the phone.

"Hey, Ahiga. It's Malik. I had a little accident at work, and uh, I don't think working with roofing is gonna work out for me. So, I was wondering if you knew of any job leads. Something that doesn't require a background check."

"I'm in the middle of something, son. But we can we discuss this at the meeting Wednesday night. I may know someone who's hiring, but I can't talk right now."

"Sure, man. Okay, I'll see you on Wednesday." I hung up with a feeling of optimism. Ahiga didn't appear to be prone to hype, and I felt hopeful that he might be able to put me on with a reliable gig.

With time on my hands until I could get back to work, I resorted back to my old habit of checking on Elle. But instead of physically following her, I cyberstalked her, obsessively monitoring her social media accounts like I was the administrator of her pages. Viewing photos of her and Phoenix warmed my heart, but whenever I came across photos or videos that involved interactions between Everett and my son, I felt my pulse throb as my mood shifted from joy to rage.

Cyberstalking wasn't healthy behavior, and I made a mental note to talk to a professional if and when I ever got access to health insurance.

Wednesday finally rolled around and with rent to pay and other bills starting to pile up, I was eager to get more information on the job lead Ahiga had mentioned over the phone.

I entered the church basement fifteen minutes before the meeting started. Moving my head from side to side, I surveyed the crowd and spotted Ahiga across the room, engrossed in a conversation with Steve, the white dude who facilitated the recovery meetings.

Ahiga hadn't noticed me in the background, and I quietly observed him. Although he was middle-aged, he looked strong as an ox. He carried himself with a quiet dignity and gave the impression of being a strong-willed individual. I wondered what kind of demons had penetrated his steely resolve and led him down the destructive path of illicit drug use.

I hadn't heard him stand up and give a personal testimony yet, and I was curious about his story.

When his conversation with Steve ended, he meandered over to the coffee station.

I approached him and extended my hand. "Hey, man, what's good?" I said with a smile. My jovial demeanor was merely a front; inside I was starting to panic about my employment situation.

"Hey, Malik. You caught me in the middle of a complex job the other day, which was why I couldn't talk."

"Oh, sorry about that."

"No problem. When you gave your testimonial, you mentioned that you installed generators on your last full-time job."

"Yes and I was surprisingly good at it considering my background is in African American history."

"Are you computer savvy?"

"Absolutely," I said with confidence.

"Then I have a job for you. You'll be working with me."

"Really?"

He assumed a serious expression. "I used to work for a company that maintained huge data centers for major companies, like Walmart and Wells Fargo bank. Due to my troubles with addiction, they had to let me go. That was seven years ago. In the past few years I've been doing independent jobs with small business owners within the Native community. Lately, business has started picking up and I've been getting contracts outside of my community. I'm getting overwhelmed and could use some extra help."

I couldn't believe my luck. A job where I could use my brains instead of brawn and I'd be working for someone who wouldn't judge me. I broke into a smile and spread my arms wide. "I'm your man…when do I start?"

"There's extensive training involved. I had to train for six months when I worked for the company. But you're lucky that you can learn on the job, working alongside of me. I can start you at thirty an hour while you're training, and we'll discuss a pay increase after you've satisfactorily completed the training program."

"Sounds good," I said, nodding briskly.

"Can you start tomorrow?"

Hell, yeah! "Yes."

"Good, I'll text you the address of the job. Meet me there at six-thirty p.m."

I arched a brow. "The job is at night?"

"Is that a problem?"

"Not at all," I assured him. "I'm a little surprised, that's all."

"In some instances, I have to turn off the power and most companies don't want to interrupt the flow of the workday."

"That makes sense."

Steve called the meeting to order, and Ahiga and I took our seats in the circle of metal folding chairs.

I met up with Ahiga at a dental office in the suburbs at six-thirty sharp. He was carrying a sturdy laptop in one hand and a heavy canvas bag in the other. A security guard let us in and escorted us to the data center, which was actually a small electrical room with one server.

"We're only here to do monthly preventative maintenance," Ahiga explained. "But remember, preventative maintenance is the bread and butter of this operation. It's how we keep the business running."

I nodded.

"Now, this Panasonic Toughbook is my lifeline." He nudged his chin toward his laptop. "I'll make sure you have your own Toughbook. It'll contain all the instructions, codes... everything you'll need to do a job. I'll also make sure you have all the tools you need to get inside the equipment. Screwdrivers, wrenches, drills, voltage radar, and of course you'll need to carry your protective work gear in cases where you're working directly with electricity."

I frowned at the idea of working directly with electricity.

"It's not typical to have to protect one's self against an arc flash during a maintenance job, but in other situations—for instance, when you're doing a repair—it can happen. During an arc flash, electricity will swiftly travel through the air and connect with your body. Believe me, you don't want to feel the jolt of five hundred and eighty volts," he said grimly. "During repair jobs, it's mandatory that you wear head-to-toe protective gear."

"We always turned off all power supplies when installing or servicing generators, and I never had to worry about arc flashes," I said.

"This is different. But you don't have to worry about an arc flash happening on this particular job. Basically, all we have to do here tonight is open up the equipment, change the filters, check the wires, and check the temperature."

I didn't have a clue about changing filters or checking wires in a computer system, but I gave a head nod. I was totally in the dark, but I intended to study and learn everything I could about my new job.

Ahiga opened his bag and took out a large screwdriver and opened the back of the unit. "Tonight, I want you to watch me closely and feel free to ask questions."

"Okay, boss."

"This small job is good practice for you. Some of our clients have massive data centers that are located in a separate building from the business site. Those off-site centers are equipped with rows and rows of server cabinets. It can be somewhat intimidating," he said as he began to tinker with the small server.

I hovered over Ahiga, listening intently as he explained what he was doing.

"This small server is essential to this business's daily operation, which includes accessing patient records, retrieving medical insurance information, email communication, financial information, and much more. It's vitally important that we do everything we can to keep the system from going down."

"Got you," I said, trying to inject confidence that I didn't feel into my tone.

There were two soft raps on the door. Thinking that only the security guard was on the premises, I was surprised to see a young black woman enter the server room. She was medium height, slender and had smooth walnut brown skin. And she was wearing a lab jacket with her name stenciled in red. She was pretty in an understated way.

"Good evening, Dr. Ravony. I didn't know you were still here," Ahiga greeted with a smile.

"Yes, a pile of paperwork has kept me chained to my desk," she quipped with a melodically beautiful French accent.

I'd never met a black person with a French accent and I was so intrigued, I inadvertently gawked at her.

"This is Malik Copeland, my new coworker," Ahiga introduced.

"Hello, Malik," she said in her musical voice. The way she pronounced my name made me feel special, and I would have loved to hear her say it again and again. Her dark eyes were doe-shaped and expressive, and I could have stared into them forever. But the way my heartbeat sped up and began to pound like a drum, I was forced to look away in embarrassment.

No other woman except Elle had ever ignited that kind of reaction in me, and I wondered if my physiological responses indicated that I was finally over the woman I had intended to marry.

"Nice to meet you, Doctor," I said with a smile that I hoped looked respectful and friendly rather than flirtatious.

"So, how's the little one doing?" Ahiga asked.

Little one? I felt instantly deflated. My dream girl was married with a kid. Oh, well, she was out of my league, anyway.

At the mention of her child, Dr. Ravony's eyes lit up. "Zoe is doing great. She's only three months old and she's trying to sit up on her own. She's starting to sleep a lot longer during the night, which is great for me."

Ahiga's brows furrowed. "What happened to the two nannies that were helping you take care of the baby?"

"Having child care help around the clock was a temporary arrangement until Zoe got a little older. But I still have Lucinda, my full-time nanny who takes care of her while I'm at work. When she leaves in the evening, I'm on my own. Motherhood can be challenging, but I don't want to give the impression that my daughter is a handful because she's not. She's the sweetest, most angelic baby in the world."

"I'm sure she is, and she gets her disposition from her mother," Ahiga chimed in, wearing a paternal smile.

"Thanks, Ahiga. I'll get out of your way so you can get back to work. I just wanted to pop in and say hello before I left for the night."

"All right. Take care of yourself and little Zoe."

"I will." Dr. Ravony exited the room, leaving behind a floral scent that suited her perfectly. Her husband was a lucky man. For some inexplicable reason, it annoyed me that the doctor's husband got to sleep through the night while she had to walk the floor with their child. I wondered what kind of work he did that entitled him to a peaceful night's sleep.

Ahiga walked me through the required steps for maintaining the system, but I was only half-listening. I couldn't stop thinking about Dr. Ravony. Although her eyes lit up when she talked about her infant daughter, I detected something sad behind her smile. I wondered what was troubling her.

CHAPTER 7

After four months of intense on-the-job training, Ahiga decided that I no longer required direct supervision and was capable of working independently. I bought a used truck that allowed me to get to my assignments on one part of town while Ahiga drove his truck to a different work site. He was only a phone call away if I ran into a problem that I couldn't resolve, but I figured out most issues on my own and rarely had to ask for help.

I stayed out of trouble by working long hours and regularly attending recovery meetings. Dating apps kept me occupied with plenty of female companionship, and I convinced myself that although my life wasn't perfect, it was as good as it gets for someone with a troubled past like mine.

I didn't realize how much I missed being in a loving relationship until I'd made a solo trip to Dr. Ravony's dental practice. Once again I arrived at six-thirty and was escorted to the server room by the security guard. I hoped that Dr. Ravony would stop in to say hello, but after thirty minutes elapsed, I figured she had left for the evening. Disappointment swirled around me like a dark cloud, but I pushed past the letdown by reminding myself that I was there to check on the system and not to gawk and drool over the pretty dentist.

Hunched over the system and in a zone where I felt like I was one with the equipment, I didn't hear the door open. Her presence was announced by her sweet fragrance, and when I heard her voice, my heart literally skipped several beats.

"Good evening, Malik. How are you?"

Instead of experiencing the sensation of butterflies fluttering around, it felt like giant bat wings were flapping inside my gut. I couldn't trust myself to speak in an even tone, and so I cleared my throat as I turned to face her.

"I'm doing well, and you'll be glad to know that your system is running great. Everything seems to be up to standard."

"That's good to know." She gave me a smile that warmed my heart and then quickly began heating up my loins.

Getting an erection while she innocently smiled at me was embarrassing. I tried to focus on her neck instead of her mouth, but I quickly discovered that her long, delicate neck was sexy, also. I couldn't risk offending her with the way my quivering dick was pointed in her direction like a missile, so I turned back to the server and began tinkering with the wiring.

"Well, it was good to see you again, Malik."

I looked over my shoulder. "Likewise," I said, feeling like a complete asshole for lusting over a woman who had a husband and a newborn at home.

I stole another glance as she walked toward the door, and when her knees suddenly buckled, I rushed to her side.

"Are you okay?" I asked, holding her up.

"I feel lightheaded," she said as I steadied her with an arm around her waist.

I led her to a chair and hovered over her as she sat down.

"It's been a long day. One patient after another, and I forgot to eat. I'm probably dehydrated, too," she explained.

"I'll get you some water," I said, gesturing toward the water cooler outside the door.

"I'll get it myself. I didn't mean to disturb you."

"You're not disturbing me. Now, sit still," I insisted as I made my way to the corridor. I filled a plastic cup with water and brought it to her.

"I feel so foolish," she said as she accepted the cup of cool water.

"No reason to feel foolish. Drink," I said firmly.

She turned the cup up to her lips and drained it.

I studied her, wondering if she was really okay. "You probably should eat something," I suggested.

"I was about to leave, and so I'll pick up something on the way home."

I glanced at her with concern. "Do you think you're okay to drive yourself?"

"Yes, I feel better already." She tossed me a reassuring smile.

"It's not a problem for me to drive you if you need me to."

"No, I'll be fine. Besides, you're still working."

"I'll be finished in a few minutes." It suddenly dawned on me that her husband might not appreciate his wife being dropped off by a strange man. "Maybe you should call your husband and ask him to pick you up." As I spoke, my eyes zoomed in on her ring finger, which was bare.

"I'm not married," she divulged.

"Oh." I was pleasantly surprised and concluded that she was a progressive single woman who didn't want to wait around for the perfect man to materialize before having a child. Discovering that she was single gave me hope that there was a remote chance that I could get to know her better.

She accepted my offer and we left her dental practice together. She gave me her address as I helped her into my truck. I was glad that I kept it spotlessly clean. My F-150 was a source of pride. It was my first major purchase in a long time, and it represented my drug-free lifestyle, accountability, and a fresh start in life. For those reasons, I was obsessive about the appearance of my truck, constantly wiping away every little speck of dust.

Ahead, I noticed the McDonald's arch and asked if she wanted to pick up something from there.

"Yes, that's fine," she replied.

We drove through the drive-thru and we both ordered from the menu. When she pulled out a twenty, I refused to take it. "I got this."

"No! You've done so much; I can't let you pay for my food," she protested.

"It's a small thing, Doc. Don't worry about it."

"Okay, if you insist," she said with a cute smile.

Once again, I detected sadness behind her smile. I continued watching her from my peripheral vision and wondered about the source of her pain. She looked so vulnerable, I had to restrain myself from taking her hand and assuring her that everything would be all right.

She opened her bag and began munching on the fries. We drove along in silence for a while and then I inquired about her French accent.

"Are you Haitian?" I asked.

"No, I'm Malagasy."

"Mala-who?" My brows furrowed in confusion.

"I'm from Madagascar, an island country in the Indian Ocean, off the coast of East Africa. We speak our native tongue, Malagasy, and we also speak French."

"Your accent is beautiful."

"Thank you. I came here fifteen years ago to attend the University of Arizona and fell in love with the area…and I made a new life here."

"It's easy to love this area of the country. Can't complain about year-round good weather."

"Yes, the weather reminded me of home. I couldn't deal with cold weather or snow. Are you originally from here?"

"No, I'm a newcomer; I've only been here six months. I'm originally from Philadelphia, but I don't miss the cold or snow."

"Have you visited any of the popular tourist attractions?"

"Not yet. Been too busy working, but I do plan to visit the Grand Canyon one of these days."

"That's on my bucket list also. I'm ashamed to say that after all these years I've never taken the time to see it."

Maybe one day we could see it together. "Hopefully, you'll get around to it."

"Yes, but no time soon. That's a trip that I'll take with my daughter when she's old enough to appreciate it."

When we reached her lovely, yet modest, one-story, Pueblo-style home, I offered to give her a ride to work in the morning.

"Thank you, Malik. That's really nice of you."

"What time should I pick you up?"

"Is eight o'clock okay?"

"It's fine. See you then, Dr. Ravony."

"Please. Call me Sasha."

"All right, Sasha. See you in the morning."

I made sure she entered her home safely and then drove off. Tomorrow couldn't have come soon enough. I looked forward to seeing Sasha again and being in her presence, even if I had to play the role of her personal driver to make it happen.

I was excited to have an opportunity to be with her again. So excited, I had a hard time falling to sleep, but despite my lack of slumber, I was up at the crack of dawn. By six-forty-five, I was sitting in the barber's chair. I didn't actually need a cut, but wanting to make a good impression on Sasha, I decided to get a fresh lineup and a professional shave. At eight sharp I studied my reflection in the rearview mirror. I debated whether I should walk up to her door and ring the bell, but I didn't want to overstep my boundaries. Calling her to announce my arrival was out of the question since I didn't have her number, so I had no choice but to gently honk the horn.

She came out a few moments later, looking slim and lithe in dark slacks and a buttoned, peach-colored top. Her conservative style of dressing couldn't hide her sex appeal, and my gaze ran up and down her body as she approached my truck.

"Good morning, Malik. I can't thank you enough for your kindness."

"Oh, it's nothing."

"Yes, it is, and I have something for you." She reached inside her purse. Thinking she was going to offer me money, I felt my jawline tighten. To my relief, she pulled out a set of tickets instead of money.

"One of my medical suppliers gave me these tickets to the Phoenix Suns game, and I want you to have them. They're for tomorrow night's game. Take a buddy or…uh, your significant other," she added with a shrug.

"I don't have a significant other. Besides my boss, Ahiga, I haven't made any friends yet."

"Maybe Ahiga would like to go," she suggested.

"Ahiga's a good guy and all, but I see enough of him on the job and socializing with him would be too much," I said with a chuckle. I wanted to add that I also saw him a couple evenings a week at recovery meetings, but I kept that information to myself. I wasn't ashamed of attending NA meetings, but it wasn't my place to put Ahiga's business out there.

"Would it be too much to socialize with me?" Sasha smiled mischievously and I wasn't sure if she was being playful or if she seriously wanted to go to the game with me.

"Do you like basketball?"

"I don't know anything about the sport, but I'm sure I'll enjoy your company."

It wasn't clear if she was hitting on me or merely being friendly. Maybe she felt sorry for me, a stranger in a strange land. Whatever the case, I was glad she had agreed to attend the game with me.

Although the Phoenix Suns lost the game, Sasha and I still had a good time. We had such a good time that the basketball game led to a brunch date the following Sunday. Then, on the first Friday of the month, we strolled along Roosevelt Row. Known for its art galleries, impressive murals, award-winning local restaurants, trendy boutiques, and live music, the Roosevelt Row served as a central hub for art and culture in downtown Phoenix.

As we strolled along with other pedestrians, gazing at the plentiful street art, Sasha's hand found its way into mine, and I stroked her soft skin with my thumb. At one point, we stopped to admire a mural painted by a young Native American artist. In that moment, genuinely happy and at peace, I raised Sasha's hand up to my lips.

"Thank you," I said as I kissed the top of her hand, and allowed my lips to graze against her soft skin.

"Thank you for what?" she asked.

"For this unexpected joy. I haven't been happy for a long time, and even if you never go out with me again, I'll be grateful for this night."

In the midst of a crowded pavement, everyone else faded into the background. Oblivious to the throng of pedestrians, Sasha moved into my arms and raised her lips to mine as if we were in a private space.

Two days later, she and I, along with her daughter, Zoe, enjoyed a tranquil Sunday in the park. Before long, I became a regular household guest, frequently staying overnight. Our lovemaking was always tender, as if we were both afraid to give in to unbridled passion.

"What's wrong, Malik?" she asked one night as I lay beside her, lazily running a finger over her shoulder and down her arm.

"Nothing's wrong. I couldn't be happier."

"So you say, but your sad eyes tell a different story."

I shifted my position, surprised that she saw the sorrow that I thought was buried deep inside my heart. Wanting to be forthright, I cleared my throat and began telling her my story. I didn't leave out anything. I told her about my drug history, my prison stint, and the great loss of my ex-fiancée and my son.

Being in a relationship with Sasha had always felt like a temporary gift from the universe. She was too good to be true. Perhaps that was why I always held back when I made love to her. It sometimes felt as if we were both made of glass that would shatter if we truly let ourselves go.

Prepared to be banished from her bedroom—from her life, I took a deep breath, waiting for the ax to fall. Surprisingly, she took my hand and squeezed it.

"We all have a past, Malik. Zoe's father wants nothing to do with her or me, and it hurts me to the core."

"Her father?" I said with bafflement. "You never mentioned him, and I assumed that Zoe was the product of an anonymous sperm donor."

"No, I was foolish enough to get involved with a married man."

I gave her a look of surprise.

"Even seemingly smart, professional women make stupid mistakes. He pleaded with me to get an abortion, but I couldn't do it. I was so offended by his request that I angrily told him that I didn't need him to help me raise my child. He eagerly took me up on my offer to let him off the hook, and he has never set eyes on Zoe. He pays child support, but that's it." Tears filled Sasha's eyes and she sorrowfully shook her head. "He doesn't want a relationship with his own daughter. How cruel is that?"

"It's pretty fucked up," I replied, marveling at the irony of our backstories.

Our shared sorrow was so intense, it was palpable. Following our primal instincts, we turned to each other for solace. Throwing back the bedcovers, we pounced on each other like animals. It was nothing like our lovemaking in the past that was always careful and tame. We were like savages—thrashing, grunting, and groaning as our sweaty bodies slapped together harshly. For the very first time, we felt unguarded enough to allow our true feelings to show.

CHAPTER 8

I waited until I was sure that my relationship with Sasha was solid before I mentioned it to Ahiga. It didn't matter whether he approved or not, but I thought he should know. We were sitting next to each other at a recovery meeting when I told him, and I expected him to say something like, "You should only get involved with women who are in recovery…women who understand what you're going through." Or "It's not a good idea to mix business with pleasure."

I was prepared to tell him to keep his advice to himself, but he surprised me by smiling and nodding his head. "Dr. Ravony is a good woman. Very smart and focused. You two make a nice couple. I'm happy for you, man," he said with sincerity.

I knew that he was divorced and had a grown daughter and two grandchildren, whom he adored. He never mentioned what had happened with his marriage, but I'd gotten the impression that the demise had a lot to do with his former drug habit. I had no idea if there was a special lady in his life. He wasn't very talkative about his personal life and I didn't pry into his business.

I hadn't imagined myself becoming adept at changing diapers, strapping in car seats, and certainly hadn't pictured myself singing lullabies. But as the new man in Sasha's life, I became a surrogate father to Zoe, and I performed all sorts of parental duties that I'd never done before.

At first, I'd tired not to get too close to Zoe, in case my relationship with her mother was only a fling. But she was such a sweet baby, I was helpless to stop her from stealing my heart.

Sasha and I never had a discussion about me officially moving in, but I was there much more than I was at my own apartment. The cactus plants that I had promised to nurture and maintain had become sickly-looking, a testament to how little time I spent at my place.

My love for Sasha increased with each passing day, and loving her meant loving her daughter, and I put down my guards.

As time went on, I was there for all of Zoe's important milestones: sitting up, teething, and crawling. And although we became as close as any blood-related father and daughter, it was a big shock when one day while in her mother's arms, she reached for me, calling out, "Da-Da!"

Soon after she began referring to me as Da-Da, I asked Sasha to marry me, and she said, yes. We both decided that after we were married, I would adopt Zoe and give her my last name.

I called my parents and shared the good news with them. They were both happy that my life was going well and that I had found love. Although they were impressed that Sasha was a dentist with a thriving practice, my mother was not too pleased about me parenting another man's child.

In an attempt to spare them from heartache, I never told them they were grandparents. It would have been pointless and cruel to make them aware of the existence of a child they could never have physical access to. Due to my failings, they too had been stripped of their legal rights of ever having a relationship with my son. Although I felt that they had a right to know, I simply couldn't bring myself to hit them with such hurtful news. It wasn't right to put them through any more trauma than I already had.

"What do you know about being a parent?" my father asked, unable to keep the irritation out of his voice. "Do you expect your mother and me to pretend that this strange baby you plan to adopt is our own flesh and blood?"

"That's up to you, Dad," I replied with a sigh. In that moment I knew I couldn't invite my parents to the wedding. It was going to be a small, intimate affair, anyway, and there was no point in giving my dad an opportunity to spoil our special day with his negativity.

Sasha tended to be very sensitive when it came to Zoe, and all I needed was for my father to hurt her feelings with an off-the-cuff comment.

"I hope you and Sasha plan to have a baby of your own very soon," my mother chimed in. "If you gave your father and me a biological grandchild, it would make it easier for us to accept the other child."

"The *other child's* name is Zoe," I reminded her, feeling protective toward Zoe and annoyed over my parents' narrow-mindedness.

Pretending that something came up, I abruptly ended the call. My mother probably would have been amenable to coming to the wedding and meeting Sasha and Zoe, but there was no way my dad would want to be bothered with fawning over a baby that was no kin to him. Most likely they wouldn't want to make a trip to Arizona until Sasha and I gave them a biological grandchild.

Sasha's small family consisted of two elderly aunts who were both too sickly for international travel. Both of her parents had died when she was a child, and on our wedding day, neither of us had any family members in attendance. Ahiga stood as my best man and Sasha's dental assistant, Caroline, was her maid of honor.

There were no other guests.

We only had each other and Zoe.

Sasha looked timeless and elegant in a simple white dress and a floral headband. From the way she kept smiling at me, I gathered that she liked how I looked in my black suit. After we exchanged our vows, we left the chapel and enjoyed an intimate dinner with Ahiga and Caroline. We postponed our honeymoon due to our work obligations. Besides, neither Sasha nor I were willing to leave Zoe behind, not even for a quick weekend getaway or a one-night mini-moon.

The day after the wedding, I replaced the cacti that I'd neglected with brand-new plants. I packed up my meager belongings and officially moved out of my apartment.

But before I drove my belongings to Sasha's home to begin a new life with her and Zoe, I had to check on Phoenix, one last time. I had come to realize that the gaping hole in my heart would never mend if I continuously watched him, even if only from afar.

Unfortunately, Elle had changed all her social media accounts to private, so I could no longer view the voluminous amount of pictures and videos that she tended to share. But luckily Everett kept his Facebook page public. Spying on Everett's page and seeing him interacting with my son was a form of self-torture that tended to leave me in a depressed state, but I had to be certain that Phoenix was in good hands before I cut my emotional ties to him.

Sitting in my truck with the engine idling, I pulled up Everett's Facebook page on my phone. There were mostly photos of sporting events with his colleagues, silly reposts, or stupid GIFs. I kept scrolling through crap until I came across a video of Phoenix taking swimming lessons in the family's large backyard pool.

Through dedicated online detective work, I discovered that Elle and Everett had bought a home in the suburbs that was equipped with a pool and an outdoor sauna.

"Look at me, Daddy! Watch me swim in the arrow position," my son called to Everett, flashing a big smile.

Wearing goggles, Phoenix pointed his arms straight over his head and slid into the sparkling blue water. Arms stretched out, face underwater, he kicked his little legs powerfully as he propelled a few feet forward.

Pride swelled my heart as I watched him showing off his swimming skills, but that feeling was quickly followed by pangs of guilt over my absentee-father status.

"You're doing great, son," Everett replied off-camera.

I watched Phoenix show off his backstroke and breaststroke before the video cut off. Oddly, my anger at Everett diminished and for the first time, I felt relieved that my son was being raised by a decent man who obviously loved and wanted the best for him. Although I never cared for Everett, I couldn't deny that he was a doing a great job of raising Phoenix.

I came to the conclusion that the universe had a weird way of showing people what they needed to learn. Had I not met Sasha and grown to love her daughter, I would have never realized that the true parent is the person who puts in the time to lovingly shape and mold the child. Through my own fault, I'd been imprisoned during the first three years of Phoenix's life. It was time for me to stop sulking and appreciate the fact that Everett had been there, a hands-on parent, filling the void.

I arrived home and set my boxes down in the entryway.

Carrying Zoe, Sasha came into the living room to greet me. We both laughed when Zoe flung herself out of Sasha's arms and into mine and then cupped my face with her tiny hands.

"How's Daddy's girl?" I asked, holding her high in the air.

CHAPTER 9
NINE YEARS LATER

"Oh! A deer," Zoe exclaimed, scooting closer to the window of our rented minivan for a better look. Holding up her cell phone, she began to get a picture of the animal as it grazed in the forest on the right side of the road.

"Look, Zoe! Two more deer are behind the trees. Did you get a picture of them, too?" Sasha asked, pointing excitedly.

"Yeah, I got 'em." Zoe leaned forward and handed her phone to Sasha.

Sasha peered at the photos. "They're beautiful, sweetheart. You're quite the photographer."

The three of us were all smiles as we rode through Grand Canyon National Park on our long-anticipated family road trip to the iconic landmark.

Nine-year-old Zoe was equally excited about visiting the kid-friendly Yavapai Museum of Geology and attending the Discovery Pack Program where children learned about the park's ecology and wildlife. Surprisingly daring, Sasha planned to zip line across the Grand Canyon. I, on the other hand, preferred something a little more sedate, like a helicopter flight over the mile-deep canyon.

"This is taking forever. How much longer, Daddy?" she whined, finally losing patience. After being cooped up inside the van for four hours, her crankiness was understandable.

"Only a few more miles, Zo-Zo," I assured her, using her pet name and adding a placating tone.

After the four-hour ride from our home in Springfield Hills (which was outside of Phoenix) to Northern Arizona, where the Grand Canyon was located, none of us had banked on having to endure even more travel time. After finally reaching our destination, we thought we'd be able to simply roll up on the Grand Canyon, but unfortunately, we had to drive a considerable distance through the national park to get to the main attraction. And it didn't help that the Internet connection started going in and out the moment we were inside the national park.

Finally, after an endless road trip, we made it to the South Rim and were rewarded with the visual of the most magnificent and breathtaking sight we'd ever beheld. It was no wonder that tourists from around the globe flocked every year to view the Grand Canyon, with its red-rock cliff walls that were set against a clear blue sky.

"This is incredible! Look at God's creation," I said with awe as I stretched my arms around both Sasha and Zoe who stood on either side of me.

"It's spectacular," Sasha agreed. "I never imagined it was this large when we were driving up to it."

"Was it worth the long ride, girls?" I asked my wife and my daughter.

Beaming, Zoe nodded. "Yep, it was worth it, Daddy."

"Are you gonna zip line with your mother across the Grand Canyon?" I teasingly asked Zoe.

Making a face, she gave the idea a thumbs-down. "I'll cheer Mom on, but my feet have to be planted on solid ground."

I laughed and tickled Zoe's side, causing her to giggle and squirm.

Tall and lanky, Zoe stood almost shoulder-to-shoulder with her mother. As she approached puberty, she was all elbows and knees. While many of her school friends had already begun to mature physically, Zoe still had a child's body and I was relieved. I wanted her to remain a little girl for as long as possible.

"Should we check into our cabin or eat first?" Sasha asked.

"Eat first!" Zoe and I shouted in unison.

There were quite a few dining possibilities, but we selected a cafeteria-style eatery that had a wide array of options and no waiting time, unlike the higher-quality restaurants in the area that had up to an hour wait times.

Best of all, there was reliable Internet service, which prompted the three of us to peer at our phones.

While Zoe posted the photos she'd taken of the deer to her Instagram page and Sasha checked emails, I peered at my phone's screen, puzzling over seven missed calls. The calls were from a number I'd never seen before.

A number with a Philadelphia area code.

"What's wrong, Malik?" Sasha inquired, sensing a change in my mood.

"Nothing, babe," I muttered as I rose from the table.

"Is Daddy okay?" Zoe inquired.

"Yes, he's fine, sweetheart. Something with work probably came up," Sasha reassured her.

My wife's and daughter's voices became distant as I numbly made my way across the room, hurriedly weaving through the jammed tables.

Instinctively, I knew who the call was from and the knowledge left me breathless and barely able to stand up. In a private area of the food court, I leaned against a stone pillar, using it for support.

Although I hadn't allowed myself to consciously dream that this day would come, a part of me realized it was inevitable that my son would reach out to me. But I hadn't expected it to happen this soon. I thought he'd be a full-grown man when he found out the truth and wanted a relationship with me.

My finger hovered over the number. What would I say to him? How could I make him understand that I never wanted to abandon him? But there was proof that I had willingly given him up. With my signature on the dotted line, I didn't have a leg to stand on.

I anxiously pressed on the screen without giving any thought to what I'd say to him. As I listened to the phone ring, I practiced my opening line: *Hey, buddy. Hi, Phoenix. Hello, son.*

"Malik! What took you so long to return my call?" Elle asked.

I was shocked to hear her voice instead of Phoenix's. He was thirteen now and I couldn't imagine what his teenage voice sounded like. "I'm in the Grand Canyon and cell phone service hasn't been great."

"The Grand Canyon! I thought you'd be halfway to Philly by now. Didn't you listen to my messages?" Elle asked in a frantic tone.

"I didn't know you left any messages. What is it? Did something happen to Phoenix?" My stomach twisted in panic as I waited for her to respond.

There was a long stretch of silence on the other end.

"What happened?" My voice emerged loud enough to arouse the curiosity of nearby diners who openly gawked at me.

I turned my back to them. Lowering the volume of my voice by several decibels, I asked, "What happened? Is he all right?"

"He tried to kill himself," she blurted in a trembling voice.

"What! Why would he do something like that?" It was horrifying to hear that my thirteen-year-old son had attempted suicide.

And I was also extremely guilt-ridden.

"He used heroin. He tried to overdose on heroin. He wanted to hurt me by mimicking the way you almost died," Elle confided, sniffling quietly.

Her words struck as forcefully as a hail of bullets riddling my body, and I felt myself go limp.

Elle's sniffling escalated to open sobbing, and I couldn't think of a word of comfort.

"How does a thirteen-year-old get ahold of heroin?" I asked accusingly.

"With the Internet at their disposal, kids today can get anything they want. Besides, Phoenix is not your average child. He's extremely intelligent and very resourceful."

I scratched my head. "Well, what the hell is going on in his life that would make him want to end it? Was he being bullied at school? Girlfriend problems?"

"No! He's one of the most popular kids in his class. Girls adore him, but he basically ignores them."

"Well, something's terribly wrong. Is it Everett? Does he mistreat my son? I swear to God, I'll kill your fucking husband if he has anything to do with this." My voice grew loud and I reined myself back in, speaking in a harsh whisper. "I should have never listened to you. You took advantage of me when I was at a low point. If Everett hurt my boy in any way…mentally or physically, I'll fucking end his miserable existence!"

"Everett didn't do anything to him," Elle cried. "All he ever did was love Phoenix."

Although I'd been trying my best to monitor my temper, I could no longer keep it reined in. "Then what the hell happened?" I exploded, startling the patrons who were trying to enjoy their meals.

There was a hush in the food court and people were staring at me. When I saw Sasha and Zoe coming toward me with confusion etched on their faces, I realized that I was causing a scene.

As Sasha and Zoe grew closer, I halted their approach by thrusting out my hand in the "stop" gesture. I could feel the muscles tighten in my face, forming an expression that was hard and unwelcoming.

Sasha squinted at me in bafflement. I instantly felt bad about my brusque demeanor, so I gave her an awkward smile that was meant to convey that I was in the middle of a crisis, and it was an inappropriate time for her to badger me with questions.

Sasha put a protective arm around Zoe and steered her back to our table. Guiltily, I watched them amble away.

"He found out about you, Malik," Elle said, her anguished tone forcing my gaze away from Sasha and Zoe.

"How did he find out?"

"He became suspicious because he didn't look like Everett, and when he started asking questions, I stupidly lied and insisted that he was Everett's biological son. He secretly did a DNA test on himself and Everett and sent it off to a lab."

"You should have told him the truth, Elle."

"I didn't know how. I'd lied about it for so long, it began to feel real. When he got the results, he confronted me. He looked at me with so much hatred, it was frightening. At that point, I had no choice but to sit down with him and tell him the entire sordid story. He didn't take it well. He started skipping school, hanging out with older kids. At home, he was disrespectful toward Everett and me. The three of us went to family therapy and it seemed to be working. Phoenix became more pleasant, his grades improved, and he appeared to be back to his former self."

"And what happened?"

"I found him in his bedroom, passed out...with a syringe next to him. It was so terrifying. I called for an ambulance and luckily they were able to revive him."

"Where is he now?"

"In the hospital. On the psych unit."

"You had him institutionalized? Why, for God's sake?"

"I didn't have a choice. You can't try to kill yourself and then waltz right out of the hospital. They detained him and put him on suicide watch because he keeps saying he wants to die. That's why I called you and left those messages, asking you to come to Philly as soon as possible. Phoenix needs you." There was a catch in her throat as she spoke those last three words.

"I'm on my way."

I ended the call, but instead of returning to our table, I remained slumped against the stone pillar, filled with regret over how badly I'd failed my son. I wondered how Elle had gotten my number, and concluded that she'd called my parents. They still had a landline with the same phone number we'd had since I was a kid. I also wondered if she'd told them they were grandparents. *Nah, they would have called me immediately if they'd heard that astonishing news.*

My heart ached for Phoenix. He had followed in my footsteps out of sheer desperation. I had stopped cyberstalking him many years ago because I thought it was an unhealthy activity—something that wasn't beneficial to him or me. Back then, he appeared to be extremely well-adjusted, but I obviously was wrong. Maybe I would have seen signs of his emotional distress and maybe I could have helped him if I had carefully watched his development over the years.

But what would pictures and videos have shown? People didn't post their disappointments and failures. They didn't post pictures of family fights and failing grades. They only revealed the most attractive aspects of their lives, giving the impression that their days were a string of accomplishments, accentuated with sunshine and rainbows.

I took a deep breath, trying to pull myself together before I delivered the shocking news to Sasha. With Sasha owning and running two dental centers and with me buying out Ahiga when he decided to retire four years ago, we were overwhelmed with work obligations.

Of my five employees, a young man named Weston Rogers was my right-hand man, and he was holding the fort down while I was away. Even though Weston was more than capable of running things efficiently, it took a lot of cajoling from Sasha for me to agree to leave my business for an entire week.

We both wanted to see the Grand Canyon with Zoe while she was old enough to appreciate it, yet young enough to be amenable to spending a week-long vacation with her parents, and so we both left our businesses in the hands of others.

Our visit to the Grand Canyon during spring break had been meticulously planned for months. A private tour guide had been hired in advance, a helicopter was chartered well ahead of time, and we'd signed Zoe up for several kid activities that she was looking forward to. I couldn't expect my wife and daughter to terminate our long-awaited vacation simply because I had to.

Wearing a grim expression, I made slow strides to our table, trying to find words that would soften the blow of me abandoning my family in the wondrous and awe-inspiring Grand Canyon.

I sighed heavily as I plopped down at the table.

"Don't tell me there's an emergency at work," Sasha said, shaking her head.

I opened my mouth to tell her about the shocking call from Elle, but before I could arrange my words, she continued talking.

"It's our vacation, Malik…and you can't run off to fix something at work. You hired Weston as your right-hand man, so let him handle whatever is wrong."

"All I need is a day—two days max, and I'll be back here with you and Zo-Zo," I said, going along with Sasha's version of my crisis. I hadn't intended to lie to her, but under the circumstances, it was more convenient to make her believe that I had a work thing to attend to rather than confiding that my long-lost son had tried to kill himself and desperately needed me.

Although we'd been honest with Zoe, telling her the truth about her heritage, we'd never informed her about Phoenix because I found it too painful to discuss. And now was not the time to burden her with grown folks' problems. I'd tell her everything when I returned.

"I'm gonna drive back to straighten something out, and if all goes well, I'll be back tomorrow evening," I said with an apologetic smile.

Sasha's face became thoughtful. "I'm not going to ask for details, but it must be important if you would disrupt our first major family vacation."

"It's really important." I kissed her and Zoe, and then dashed out of the food court.

CHAPTER 10

Rushing through Philadelphia International Airport with the strap of my travel bag slung over my shoulder, I trotted past the baggage claim area and exited through the sliding doors. My Lyft driver pulled up to the curb and I jumped in. The driver was going as fast as the speed limit allowed, but I still tapped my finger impatiently against the armrest.

I texted Elle to let her know that I was only minutes away from the hospital where Phoenix was being treated. While returning my phone to my pocket, a call came through from Sasha. It was bad timing and I couldn't take her call. I shut my phone off and the driver pulled up in front of the hospital. I jumped out of the car and hurried inside.

Elle was waiting in the lobby.

She came forward and hugged me tightly.

We broke our embrace and stared at each other. She knew about Sasha and Zoe, and I wondered if her inquiring eyes were trying to picture me as a dutiful husband and parent as opposed to the irresponsible addict I'd been when we were together.

"You look good, Malik. I can see that life's treating you well."

"Thanks. You look good, too," I replied.

Despite the signs of worry that creased the corners of her eyes, the years had been kind to Elle. She was as beautiful as she'd been when I last saw her…maybe more so. She was wearing a chic pair of wide-leg dark slacks that were paired with a simple white top. A string of pearls encircled her neck and a sleek blazer completed her look, which was a nice balance of elegance and business-casual.

I tore my eyes away from the woman who had hurt me to my core when she stripped me of my parental rights. "Can I see my boy, now?" I asked with my jaw set firmly.

"Yes. Also, we're scheduled for a family therapy session in a few hours. Is that okay with you?"

"I wasn't expecting that…but, yeah, it's fine. Will Everett be attending with us?" My question came out sounding bitter, which I hadn't intended.

"No, we've already had our session, and now the therapist wants to give you and Phoenix the space to express your emotions in a safe environment."

"Does Phoenix know I'm here?"

"He knows you're on your way from Arizona, but he doesn't know you're physically in the hospital.

"Are you ready to meet Phoenix?"

I took a deep breath and nodded.

We took an elevator to the sixth floor and marched briskly down a corridor until we reached an area that was locked off from the rest of the floor.

"They have him locked in like a criminal?" My voice rang with indignation.

"I don't like it either, but it's for his protection. The doctor feels he's still capable of doing harm to himself, and so…" Her voice drifted off and she pressed the doorbell of the Child Adolescent Psychiatry unit.

A nurse buzzed us in and Elle led the way to a vast and sunny activity room where adolescents engaged in various forms of recreation. They all looked lethargic and spaced-out. I glanced at two girls who were playing ping-pong and it was the slowest-moving ping-pong game I'd ever seen.

Some kids played checkers and others worked on jigsaw puzzles, but quite a few of them stood around staring blankly. On the far side of the large room, there was an exercise class going on, but the participants were moving like zombies, and I doubted if any of them were working up a sweat.

"There's Phoenix!" Elle pointed to a light-brown-skinned boy sitting in a chair and staring at an overhead TV screen.

We were at least thirty or forty feet away from him, and even from that distance and with only his profile on view, I easily recognized my son. Ten years had passed since I'd last set eyes on him, but I could have picked him out of any crowd.

With her lips stretched into a pained smile, Elle walked purposefully toward him.

I didn't accompany her. I remained near the locked door, frozen in place with my heart racing as I gawked at Phoenix from afar. This wasn't the way I'd imagined our first meaningful encounter since he was a toddler, and I wasn't prepared for the range of emotions that swirled throughout me, creating an internal storm.

I felt a tremendous amount of anger toward Elle for keeping my son and me apart, and I was disgusted with myself for rolling over instead of fighting her in court. But, beyond those negative feelings, I was stricken by a rush of love that powered through me so vigorously, I became physically weakened by the sheer force of it.

I watched Elle lean over, circle her arms around Phoenix, and kiss him on the cheek. She said something that caused him to pull away from her embrace as he jerked his neck in my direction.

I waved at him and tossed him a smile that was as cheerful as I could manage under such emotional circumstances.

Elle beckoned me and I crossed the room, moving toward my long-lost son.

"Phoenix, this is Malik, your biological father." Elle spoke in a voice that was as soft as a whisper as she struggled to maintain her composure.

It was a monumental moment, yet the tension in the air was thick enough to cut with a knife.

"Hey," Phoenix said without making eye contact with me.

"How are you feeling, Phoenix?" I asked with forced joviality.

He did a slight eye roll and I could imagine him thinking, *'How do you think I feel, dummy?'*

"Not feeling so good, huh?" I said, answering the question myself.

"I just want to get out of here," he mumbled. "My counselor thought it was a good idea for me to work out my issues with you, so…" He didn't finish the sentence, but I gave his arm a squeeze, letting him know that I understood.

I took a seat in the empty chair on his right. "I understand that you attend an exclusive school where the students and instructors only speak French," I said, trying to strike up a conversation.

"Oui," he uttered in a vaguely hostile tone that let me know he wasn't in the mood for small talk with me.

I had imagined that Phoenix and I would have a natural bond, but apparently he was going to make me work hard to establish a connection. Deciding not to bombard him with questions, I sat quietly, pretending to focus on the World War II movie he had been watching when we'd first arrived.

During the uncomfortable silence, I found myself stealing glances and marveling at his physical characteristics. He looked like a mixture of several of my family members. His top lip was shaped exactly like my mother's, and oddly, Phoenix displayed a few of my father's mannerisms without ever meeting the man. I saw a little bit of my uncles on both my mother's and father's side.

But despite the array of genetic traits that he had inherited from various family members, he favored me the most. It was obvious that I had "spit the boy out."

I could tell that Elle coddled him. It was apparent by the way she kept stroking his close-cut hair, despite how many times he leaned away from her motherly touch.

I regarded his haircut and was surprised that he wasn't wearing a high-top fade with sponge twists on top, the trendy style that many young guys wore today. Phoenix was sporting a buzz-cut, giving him an even more youthful and innocent-looking appearance than the average thirteen-year-old boy.

I was perplexed as to why Elle had portrayed him as a worldly sophisticate, a young man who was wise beyond his years. He seemed like a typical middle-schooler who should have been more comfortable riding a skateboard than consorting with drug dealers and purchasing their poisonous product.

What kind of heartless degenerate would sell hard drugs to an innocent child? I was fixated on that question and could feel my fists balling with the urge to beat the crap out of the scumbag whose actions could have cost Phoenix his life.

The three of us sat without speaking, each of us pretending to be absorbed in the war movie that played on TV.

"Mom?" Phoenix said, breaking the silence. "I gotta get out of here. This place is like a high-security prison. They don't let us have anything. No outside food or any kind of treats are allowed. I just want a freakin' pizza, mom! They consider something as innocent as a paper clip to be contraband. When are they gonna let me go home?"

"That depends," Elle answered.

"Depends on what?"

"On whether or not your doctor thinks you can manage your normal routines without self-medicating."

"I'm not an addict! It was a one-time event."

"A one-time attempt at suicide is not something to take lightly," Elle explained, stroking his arm soothingly.

"But I'm okay, now. Mom, can I please go home?"

"It's not my choice, Phoenix. I can't demand an early release for you simply because I want to."

"Can you do something, Malik?" He finally looked me in the eyes.

"You need to focus on the treatment program they're offering," I said resolutely while wishing I could whisk him out of there and take him back to Arizona with me, but of course, I couldn't.

Phoenix's attention drifted back to the TV, making it clear that I was of no use to him.

My first instinct was to try to reason with him, but being an outsider, I decided it was best to give him his space.

"I could use some coffee. What about you?" I said to Elle.

"Yes, caffeine is exactly what I need." She turned to Phoenix. "We'll see you at the therapy session in a half hour."

He shrugged indifferently, keeping his eyes glued to the TV screen.

Phoenix seemed like a totally different kid in the therapy session. He was animated and talkative, and extremely forthcoming. He easily articulated his feelings about discovering that Everett was not his father. He said that he felt betrayed and that it angered him when his mother wouldn't give him information about his real father.

"I just wanted information about my heritage, and my parents acted like my curiosity was a crime. My mom finally told me that she kept my dad out of my life because he did drugs, and when I asked her if he was still on drugs, she didn't have an answer for me. I told her I wanted to meet him, but she wouldn't allow it. What I did... shooting heroin was a drastic measure and also stupid...I realize that now. But at the time I was hurt and angry and probably suffering from abandonment issues," he said, glancing in my direction.

"I wasn't trying to kill myself," he continued. "I wanted to show my mom how much pain her decision was causing me. I'm ashamed and I'm sorry, and I'll never do it again. I want my life to go back to normal. I just want to go home."

By the end of Phoenix's heartfelt statement, he and Elle were both wiping tears from their eyes while I struggled with a lump in my throat that seemed like the size of a boulder.

"How do you feel about the recent events regarding your son?" the therapist asked me.

"Guilty. Like an absentee father. If it's at all possible, I want to establish a relationship with Phoenix and try to make up for lost time. I don't expect to replace Everett, but I'd like to have a role in Phoenix's life. I haven't used drugs in over ten years, and I've been a productive member of society for the same amount of time. If Phoenix could spend a week or so with me in Arizona during the summer, I think we could begin to build a bond."

"Visitation is for the courts to decide, Mr. Copeland," the therapist said.

"I'm thirteen, not three! I'm old enough to decide if I want a relationship with my parent," Phoenix interjected.

"How do you feel about Phoenix visiting his birth father during the summer?" the therapist asked Elle.

Elle fiddled with the hem of her jacket and then cleared her throat. "His father and I have talked about it, and if having a relationship with Malik will be beneficial to Phoenix, then we're on board with the idea."

Phoenix directed a smile my way that was bashful and boyish, endearing him to me. I smiled back. I gave him a big grin that expressed my inability to conceal my joy.

I wondered what had happened to the sullen teenager that barely opened his mouth when we were in the activity room. I told myself that therapy had a way of bringing out a person's true character, and I was now witnessing the real Phoenix, a normal kid who had tried to deal with complex problems and conflicting emotions that would have overwhelmed the average adult.

At the conclusion of the therapy session, Phoenix asked how soon he'd be discharged. Dr. Pitts shuffled some papers around on his desk and then looked at Phoenix. "I recommend a thirty-day treatment plan. If things go well, you'll be able to leave here at the completion of the program."

Disappointment was evident in the way that Phoenix's shoulders slumped. I half expected him to break down and cry, but he pulled himself together and said, "Okay, Dr. Pitts. Cool." He then produced a brave smile.

In that moment, I felt so proud of Phoenix. He was obviously disappointed, but he held it together.

After the therapy session, we returned to the activity room.

"How about a game of ping-pong," I said to Phoenix.

"Are you any good?" he asked.

"I was the ping-pong champ back in college," I bragged.

"That was what...forty years ago?" he teased.

"Not that long ago...I'm only forty-one."

"Only!" Phoenix laughed as he ragged on my age.

"Okay, you asked for it. I was going to show you some mercy, but not anymore."

"You're the former ping-pong champ, but I'm the current title holder. Tell him, Mom."

"He's really good, Malik," she concurred.

"Show me." I picked up the paddle, prepared to go easy on my son. But he put me in my place in a matter of seconds, showing off skills that far surpassed mine.

"Who are you?" I asked jokingly.

"Your son," he responded in a somber tone that melted my heart to such a degree, I put down the paddle and moved toward him.

Phoenix met me halfway. And in the midst of the activity room of an adolescent psychiatric unit, my son and I bonded as I held him in a tight bear hug.

CHAPTER 11

Sitting on the bed of my hotel room in downtown Philadelphia, I clenched my phone, dreading having to call Sasha and admit that I'd lied about having a work emergency. In all the years of our marriage, I'd never deceived her, and it was time to come clean.

I glanced at the clock. It was eleven at night here, but only eight in Arizona, which meant that Zoe was still wide awake. I didn't want her to know about Phoenix just yet. I wasn't trying to hide him, but Sasha and I needed to be on the same page when it came to how much information we shared with Zoe. Did we tell a nine-year-old about her daddy's former drug habit and prison stint? It seemed like far too much negative information for a child to process.

I let out a sigh and tapped the screen of the phone. Sasha picked up on the first ring.

"Hey, babe," I said in a gloomy tone that I would have preferred to disguise but was unable to.

"I've been so worried about you, Malik. Is everything all right?"

"It's a long story. Is Zoe nearby?"

"Yes, should I put you on speaker?"

"No!" I blurted frantically. "I don't want her to overhear our conversation. We need to speak privately."

"Oh, all right. Hold on." There was worry in her voice and I felt awful for causing her distress.

In the background I heard her tell Zoe that she had to step outside the cabin to speak with Daddy in private. Only a year ago Zoe would have been upset if she didn't get to talk to me, but she was getting older and I didn't hear a word of complaint out of her. In my mind's eye, I could picture Zoe preoccupied with something on her iPad or peering intently at the screen of her phone as she texted back and forth with one of her friends.

"I'm back," Sasha said. "What's going on, Malik?"

"I didn't leave over a work situation. The call was from my ex, Elle. She reached out to let me know that my son had attempted suicide…by overdosing on heroin."

"Oh, no! Is he going to be all right?"

"Yes, I believe so."

"That's a relief."

"Sasha, I'm sorry for lying to you, but I didn't know how to tell you without involving Zoe. I didn't want to upset her and ruin the vacation. I felt like I was between a rock and a hard place."

"It's okay, I understand."

"Thanks, babe. I appreciate it."

"Do you know why he tried to end his life?"

"Yes. I was included in his therapy session this evening, and he expressed himself quite articulately. According to Phoenix, he was desperate to find out the truth about his paternity, and the drug thing was a cry for help, not an actual desire to die."

"Did you two get along okay?"

"Not at first. He practically ignored me initially, but after the therapy session, we had a special moment—a really powerful moment," I said, my voice catching as a wave of emotion passed through me.

"What's he like?"

"He's a typical thirteen-year-old. Moody and incommunicative one moment and animated and talkative the next."

"I see. So, where do we go from here?"

"Well, he wants to spend a week with us during the summer, if that's okay with you. Are you comfortable with that idea?"

"Of course. How could you ask me such a question?"

"Just making sure. I don't want to be presumptuous."

"He's your son, and I'm thrilled that you're finally going to get to know him. And Zoe's going to be so excited to find out she has a big brother."

"After we tell her about Phoenix, we're going to have to tell her my story also…the whole ugly truth about my past."

"Zoe loves you and nothing you tell her will change that."

"I know. But I wish she were a little older. Nine is so young for her to try and comprehend the meaning of drug addiction."

"She's not as unenlightened as you seem to think. She knows that your NA meetings are a big part of your life, and she's aware that you had a drug problem before she was born."

"I had no idea that she knew."

"That was a little secret between Zoe and me," Sasha said with a chuckle.

"Does she know that my drug of choice was heroin?"

"Yes. And as far as she's concerned, it was a different lifetime and has nothing to do with who you are now."

"Well, I don't think we should tell her about Phoenix's incident. She doesn't need to know that, Sasha," I said firmly. "It was a stupid mistake and I don't want him judged by it."

"I won't say a word about it," Sasha promised. "How long will you be in Philly?"

"I want to spend as much time with Phoenix as possible, so I probably won't make it back to Arizona until the vacation is over."

Sasha was briefly silent and I could feel her disappointment as my words sunk in.

"I'm sorry, Sasha. But…"

"It's fine, Malik. You don't have a choice. Your son needs you; you're exactly where you need to be."

I let out a sigh of relief, silently vowing to make this up to my wife. I couldn't ask for a more understanding woman during this very difficult time.

"Hey, Bio-Dad," Phoenix greeted cheerfully when I arrived for my first solo visit with him at the hospital. We embraced and stared at each other for a long moment, both keenly aware of how eerily similar we looked.

"The only difference between us is our build," he commented as he observed me. "Am I going to magically grow muscles like yours one day?"

I laughed. "I used to be slim, too, but I put in a lot of hours at the gym, pumping iron. But that's not something you need to be concerned with at your age."

"Don't worry; I'm not. I'm okay with the body I have. Besides, lifting weights seems boring, and I'm more cerebral," he said, tapping his left temple.

"So I've heard. Your mother told me that until recently, you'd always been a straight-A student, always on the honor roll. Do you plan on hitting the books again and bringing your grades up?"

"Yeah, but I don't need to hit the books to do it. All I have to do is start showing up for my classes again, and my grades will automatically improve."

"What do you mean?" I eyed him suspiciously, thinking he was involved in some sort of computer hacking that enabled him to change his grades.

"What I mean is I don't have to study to get good grades. I have a photographic memory, and whatever we cover in class, I automatically remember. That's how I nail all my tests."

"Photographic memory. Wow, that's impressive. When I was in school, I had to cram hard for every test."

"I guess I didn't get that genetic gift from you, Malik." He shook his head as if only losers had to study for tests.

"No, apparently you didn't get that ability from me," I said with a chuckle.

His youthful appearance was misleading. Phoenix was at the maturity level of a sixteen- or seventeen-year-old—at least. He was confident and conversed with ease, and I liked the amiable personality he revealed when his mother wasn't around.

The atmosphere was less intense without Elle's anxious energy added to it. It was easier for us to break the ice and communicate when we weren't being observed by a third party.

Over the course of the next three hours that I spent with my son, I discovered numerous behavioral traits we had in common. Like me, he preferred Little Caesars to Domino's. His handwriting was as jagged and unattractive as mine. We shared the habit of chewing on our middle fingernail when we were in deep thought.

I learned that we were both Marvel super fans, and I told Phoenix that one of my secret wishes was to attend a thirty-hour Marvel marathon where twelve or so previous films in the Marvel Cinematic Universe were screened one after another, followed by the latest Marvel release.

"Yeah, only serious fans could endure a Marvel marathon. That's something we should do together one day."

"I'd like that, Phoenix." I wanted to call him "son." It was on the tip of my tongue, but realizing it was too soon to use a term that described a familial relationship, I restrained myself.

"What's your secret fear?" Phoenix asked, giggling in a playful sinister way as he raised his eyebrows up and down mysteriously.

"My fears?" I shrugged and shook my head.

"Yeah, everyone is afraid of something. Snakes, spiders, heights. You can be straight with me, Malik."

I thought about his question, and while I was considering my response, I noticed we were both nibbling on our middle finger-nail at the same time.

"I suppose I've periodically experienced glossophobia."

"Glossophobia? What's that?"

"The fear of public speaking. It's weird, but I can go on and on when I'm speaking to a small group, but put me in front of a large audience and I freeze up. How are you with public speaking?"

"It's a breeze for me; I love doing presentations at school. But lately, my greatest fear has been that I'll go bald. That's why I wear my hair cut low...for practice, you know," Phoenix said as he smoothed a hand over his buzz cut.

"Why do you fear going bald?"

"Well, the top of my dad's head is almost entirely bald, and up until the time I found out he wasn't my real dad, I thought it would happen to me, too." He eyed my full head of hair that was beginning to gray at the temples. "It's a relief to know that I'll keep all my hair when I get older. I'm sure I'll be able to deal with a little premature graying."

"Wait! Your dad is bald?" I couldn't keep the delight out of my voice. Although I had much respect for Everett for stepping up to the plate when I couldn't, I was only human and still harbored feelings of resentment toward him.

"By the way, I know you took swim classes when you were

much younger; did you become a world-class swimmer?" I asked, thinking back to those videos of Phoenix that I used to watch on Everett's Facebook page.

He furrowed his brows. "Did my mom mention that I used to take swimming classes?"

"No. I used to cyberstalk your parents' social media pages to watch your development."

"Used to? Meaning you stopped at some point?"

"Yeah, I forced myself to stop because not being in your life was painful, and watching you from afar only increased my sense of helplessness."

I thought about telling him that I'd been close to kidnapping him when he was three, but that was too much information. "Tell me about your fancy French school," I said, switching the topic.

He responded by showing off his fluent French, and I didn't understand a word he said.

"You'd think I'd be able to pick out a few words since my wife, Sasha, speaks French, but I never tried to learn. Our daughter..."

"You have another kid?" Phoenix blurted.

"I adopted her. Her name is Zoe. She's Sasha's biological daughter, but I love her like my own," I said, watching him closely and trying to get an idea of how he felt about having a stepsister. But his expression was unreadable.

"How old is she?" he asked, still maintaining a blank expression.

"She's nine, and the funny thing is Sasha has been speaking to her in French since Zoe was a baby, and although Zoe can understand the language, she can't speak it. Isn't that weird?"

"Not really. Zoe's immersed in American culture, and there's no reason for her to bother learning to speak a foreign language. I still haven't figured out how speaking French is going to enhance my life, here in the States."

"I suppose your parents wanted you to be well rounded. It's always beneficial to speak another language. It'll definitely look good on your college applications," I said.

"Yeah, I guess," he said with a shrug.

One of Phoenix's counselors came to the activity room to let us know that it was dinnertime, and I was welcome to join Phoenix for dinner. I wanted to join him, but I didn't want to wear out my welcome, and so I looked at him questioningly.

"Pizza's on the menu, Malik. It can't compare to Little Caesars, but it's palatable." He flashed me an inviting smile and it warmed my heart.

In that moment, I couldn't think of anything I'd rather do than share a slice of institutional pizza with my newfound son.

After dinner, Elle and Everett came to the hospital to participate in a family therapy session that included the four of us. As I shook hands with Everett, I noticed Phoenix making a face and furtively cutting his eyes toward Everett's shiny, bald dome. It was hard not to burst out laughing, but somehow I managed to keep a straight face.

My son and I were bonding quickly, and it felt amazing.

CHAPTER 12

At the end of the week, before leaving Philadelphia, I paid a visit to my parents.

Aside from them both being completely gray, they hadn't changed much since the last time I'd seen them during the Christmas holidays six years ago. The healthy diet they adhered to seemed to be working. They looked great. My father's olive complexion was smooth and unwrinkled, and my mother's coffee-colored skin contrasted well with her glistening silver hair. To keep fit, my father walked five miles a day and my mother practiced yoga at a senior center. In their mid-sixties, they both maintained full-time jobs, determined not to retire or collect social security until they reached age seventy.

Recalling my last visit home put a bad taste in my mouth. Zoe was three years old at the time and I wanted her to experience winter weather, particularly snow. I also wanted her to get to know her step-grandparents, but they were so lukewarm toward Zoe, Sasha felt offended. She vowed never to visit them again and I supported her decision and stayed away as well.

But here I was, standing in their living room, and telling them I had some important news to share.

"I think you both should sit down," I suggested.

"If this is bad news, I'd rather take it standing," my father grumbled, stubbornly folding his arms as he stood near the staircase, as if prepared to bolt up the stairs if I said something he didn't want to hear.

My mother took a seat on the sofa. "What's this about, Malik? Does it have something to do with Elle calling last week to get your number? And now you turn up…what a coincidence. Have you two decided to get back together?"

"It's a little late for that," my father chimed in. "She's married with a child and you're married with a stepchild."

"Believe me, Elle and I are not having an affair," I said.

My mother peered at me through the tortoise shell glasses that were perched on her nose. "When are you and Sasha going to have a child? Your father and I aren't getting any younger, and we'd like to experience being grandparents before we depart this Earth."

"That's exactly what I want to talk to you about."

"Is Sasha pregnant?" my dad asked hopefully.

"No, but I wanted to tell you that you're already grandparents. Elle's son, Phoenix, is also my son."

"What are you saying, Malik?" My father gazed at me confusedly.

My mother briskly patted the empty space next to her. "You'd better sit down, Winston."

Taking her advice, my father flopped down next to her. Sitting together, my parents held hands as they stared at me, waiting for me to provide an explanation for my earth-shattering news.

"Elle got pregnant around the time that I overdosed. When I was in prison…"

At the word, *prison*, my mother breathed out a loud sigh, one hand fretfully twisting a lock of her silvery hair.

"Elle came to see me when she was seven months pregnant and

told me she was getting married. I let her talk me into signing over my rights to our child."

My father reared back and gave me a look of disdain. "Why would you do something like that, son?"

"Under the circumstances, I felt like I was doing what was best for the baby."

My mother pulled off her eyeglasses, something she did when she was upset. "So, let me get this straight…we've been grandparents all these years, with a grandchild who lived nearby, and you didn't think we had a right to know?"

She pressed four fingers against her forehead and rubbed circularly. "This can't be true. All these years we've been yearning for a grandchild and we had one all along. Yet we weren't even allowed to meet him. How old is the child—about eleven or twelve?"

"He's thirteen."

She dropped her head in her hand briefly and when she looked back up, there was anger in her eyes. "You waited until the child was practically grown before you decided to tell us that he existed." She gawked at me and then turned her incredulous gaze toward my father. "Can you believe this, Winston?"

"No, Ruth Ann, I cannot believe that our son would deprive us the right to be grandparents for all these years." He leaned forward. "Let me make sure I have a clear understanding of all this. You let another man raise your son while you were off raising someone else's daughter. What kind of cockamamy nonsense is this, Malik?"

"Mom! Dad! I came to Philly to spend time with my son—to officially meet him for the first time. But he's not doing well right now, and I—"

"What do you mean he's not doing well? What's wrong? Is he sick?"

"It's a long story, but he only recently found out that Elle's husband is not his biological father, and he's having a tough time dealing with it. I'd like for you to establish a relationship with Phoenix, but not right now."

"Then, when? Don't you think thirteen years is a long enough wait?" my mother asked.

I had no intention of telling them about Phoenix's suicide attempt and thirty-day hospital stay. I didn't think they could handle it. "He's going to therapy and his doctor says he needs about a month to process everything. Phoenix thought that Everett's parents were his grandparents, so he's going to need about a month before he's ready to meet you two. Are you okay with that, Mom and Dad?"

My mother's expression softened. "Of course we are. Do you have a picture of our grandson?"

I took my phone out of my pocket and pulled up a picture of Phoenix that I'd taken the other day. He was holding a ping-pong paddle in the activity room and there were no telltale signs that he was in the mental unit of a hospital. The picture could have been taken at school, at a rec center, or anywhere.

"This is your grandson, Phoenix," I said, handing the phone over to my mother.

"Oh, my God, look at him. What a handsome boy. He's the spitting image of you, Malik."

"I know," I said proudly.

"And I see a little bit of Winston in the way he's standing," she added.

"Really?" My father took the phone from my mother and scrutinized the picture. "He sure is a handsome boy, and he has your mouth, Ruth Ann." He took on a sudden stern expression and said, "Did you get a DNA test done?"

"No."

He burst out laughing. "It doesn't matter; you don't need one.

If that boy isn't your own flesh and blood, then I don't who is. " He peered at the photo again. "Look at him! He's you all over again at that age, only you were a little taller."

"Yeah, he didn't get the growth spurt yet, but I told him that it's coming," I said gaily.

The tension in my parents' household had lifted. All of their pent-up resentment and disappointment seemed to dissipate with the glimpse of their grandson. Seeing them happy made me happy, and I was finally able to forgive them for treating Zoe so coldly. I couldn't force them to love her, and with the way Sasha and I poured our love on her, she wasn't missing anything.

"Let me send a copy of this pic to your phones," I said, retrieving my phone from my father's hand. "Elle is going to send you guys a ton of pictures of Phoenix over the years. I gave her your email address, Mom, so be on the lookout for an email from her."

I sent the picture to their phones. My father pulled his phone from his pocket, and my mother bustled to the dining room to get her phone that was plugged in and charging at an outlet.

The smiles on their faces put a smile in my heart. It was a shame that it took Phoenix's near-death experience to bring our family back together.

Now I had to get back to Arizona and make sure that my marriage was intact.

At the airport, Sasha and Zoe stood near the baggage claim area, waiting for me. I saw them before they noticed me and drank in the lovely sight of them. I'd never been away from my girls for longer than an overnight business trip and hopefully, I'd never have to leave them again.

As I grew closer, Sasha saw me and broke into a smile. "There he is," she said, nudging Zoe.

Thrilled to see me, Zoe ran toward me. "Daddy!" She leapt into my arms, her long legs wrapping around me as she hugged me tightly.

Sasha joined us in a family embrace, and I felt like the luckiest man in the world. I was completely at peace with everyone who was important to me: my parents, my son, and my wife and daughter.

During the ride home, Sasha quietly concentrated on driving while Zoe excitedly filled me in on all the adventures I'd missed at the Grand Canyon.

"We have to go back next year, Daddy."

"Absolutely," I agreed.

"Do you promise?" Zoe asked, aware that it took years to pull this trip together due to her mother and my hectic work schedules.

"I promise, Zo-Zo."

"Mom said you had an emergency in Philly, but she wouldn't say what it was."

"We'll talk about my trip later," I said, glancing at Sasha and trying to gauge her feelings, but her expression was imperceptible.

"I hate it when you guys treat me like a baby and keep secrets from me."

"We'll talk about it after your mother and I have a serious discussion."

Zoe frowned and held up her hands. "What could it be? Did Grandma and Grandpa Copeland die and leave us a fortune?"

"No, they didn't die. Don't be disrespectful, Zoe," Sasha chastised.

I understood Zoe's blasé attitude regarding my parents. She barely had a memory of her trip to Philly, but she remembered that they made her feel unwelcome. She was aware that my relationship with them was strained and she sensed that it had something to do with me adopting her. She therefore felt no loyalty or connection to them at all.

"I made your favorite meal, *Foza sy hena-kisoa*," Sasha said, trying to elevate the mood in the car.

I didn't speak or understand much French or Malagasy, but I knew that *Foza sy hena-kisoa* was an incredibly delicious dish that consisted of stir-fried pork, crab meat, lobster, fresh greens, and lime juice that was served with a pile of rice. I wasn't sure about the herbs and spices that gave it that Madagascar island flavor, but my stomach began to rumble at the thought of the meal.

At home, the three of us sat in the dining room, eating dinner. Sasha and I chatted, but Zoe didn't join in on the pleasant small talk. She picked at her food, deciding to pout until she got the information about my trip to Philadelphia.

I cleared my throat. "I went to Philly to meet your stepbrother."

Zoe frowned. "What stepbrother?"

I looked at Sasha and she placed her hand on top of mine and squeezed it.

"His name is Phoenix, and he's thirteen," I said before I launched into the sad story of my life before I'd met her mother. I told her about my drug usage and the time I'd spent in prison. I even told her how a change of heart about kidnapping Phoenix had led me to my new life in Phoenix, Arizona. Then I divulged that Phoenix was so unhappy not knowing the truth about his paternity that he'd tried to commit suicide.

"But he's doing fine, now," I quickly added.

"Wow!" Zoe said after taking it all in.

Despite the good food, the mood at the dinner table changed. We were all so somber and quiet, you could hear a pin drop.

"Let me get this straight," Zoe said, breaking the silence. "If your son had been named Memphis, you would have ended up in Tennessee?"

Sasha and I burst out laughing. The levity Zoe brought to the grim situation was exactly what was needed.

"So, when am I going to meet Phoenix?" Zoe inquired.

"If things go as planned, he's going to spend two weeks with us this summer," I replied. I spoke in a casual manner, but inside I was giddy—as happy as a kid at Christmastime.

Later that night, in bed, Sasha revealed that during my absence, she feared that old feelings would spark up between Elle and me.

I propped myself up on an elbow and stared down at her. "Why would you think that? I would never betray you, Sasha."

"I let my insecurities get the best of me."

"What insecurities? You're the most confident woman I know."

"I thought so, too, but this past week I've been terrified that the old flame between you and Elle had been rekindled."

"I don't understand why you would think that."

"Well, you were barely over her when we met. We were both rebounds," she admitted with a sad smile. "And you never said that you two had stopped loving each other. You said she moved on because your addiction left her no choice. I feared that seeing the wonderful man you've become would make her want to reclaim you. And I feared that now that Phoenix knew the truth, you'd be eager to begin a life with your real family."

"You, Zoe, and Phoenix are my real family—not Elle. Elle and I were like strangers, and our son was our only connection. Whatever we had in the past is long gone. It's dead! I love you, Sasha, so please, don't ever think that you can't trust me around Elle or any other woman."

That night Sasha initiated sex. She told me to lie back and enjoy myself, and I did. She made love to me with an intense passion and I wasn't sure if the passion was ignited by the fact that she missed me or if she felt like she had to compete with Elle.

CHAPTER 13

Sasha and I were a bundle of nerves during the days leading up to Phoenix's arrival. We wanted his two-week visit to be perfect, and we had put together an itinerary of activities we hoped he'd enjoy. From family outings to private male bonding time for Phoenix and me, we made sure that his vacation would be eventful and without a dull moment.

Together, Sasha and Zoe had worked hard to give the guest bedroom a makeover, transforming it from a nondescript space into a contemporary teenage boy's bedroom featuring sports-themed décor. We wanted Phoenix to be comfortable enough to view the room as his personal sanctuary.

"Remember, don't bombard your stepbrother with questions and don't feel slighted if he's not interested in interacting with you as much as you might like. He's a teenager and kids at that age can be moody. We're all going to have to respect that and be willing to give him his space," Sasha told Zoe as we drove to the airport.

"I'm practically a teen, too," Zoe said, sounding a little indignant.

"We're well aware that you're smart and mature for your age, but the fact is, you're only nine and you're going to have to stay in your lane with Phoenix," I reminded Zoe. Sasha and I allowed her to engage in our conversations, but I doubted if a teenage boy would be as tolerant as we were.

"I know how to conduct myself around older kids. If I get the impression that Phoenix isn't interested in my conversation, I'll back off. I'm not oblivious to the feelings of others," she added with a nonchalant shrug.

Impressed by Zoe's level of maturity, Sasha and I exchanged a look of pride.

At the airport, the three of us stood together, eagerly waiting for Phoenix to disembark his plane and join us at the baggage claim area. My pulse raced with excitement; I'd been waiting for this day for so long. My boy and I had bonded so well when I was in Philadelphia, and he was as eager as me to try to make up for those lost years by spending quality time together.

I was looking down at my phone reading a work-related email when Sasha suddenly made a gasping sound. I yanked my head up and she was pointing excitedly at Phoenix who was bounding toward us.

I dashed toward my son and wrapped my arms around him. When I released him, I couldn't stop grinning. "You're really here. You made it!"

"Yup. I made it. What's up, Pops?" he said with a huge grin.

Pops! It had a nice ring to it and sounded much more intimate than Bio Dad or Malik, which was how he interchangeably referred to me. Everett already had the title, Dad, and I was perfectly fine with being called Pops.

Wearing welcoming smiles, Sasha and Zoe approached us.

"Hi, I'm Zoe, AKA pesky little sister," Zoe blurted before I could begin making introductions. "I promise not to talk too much. I've been warned not to get on your nerves."

"Aw, you can talk all you want, Little Sis. You won't get on my nerves."

He turned his attention to Sasha. *"Bonjour maman, ravi de vous rencontrer,"* he said to her. *"On m'a tellement parle de vous."*

"En bien j'espere?" Sasha replied with a slight smile and an arched brow.

"Bien sur," said Phoenix.

"What did they say?" I asked Zoe, who'd assumed the role of my French interpreter at an early age.

"Phoenix said, 'Hello Mom, it's nice to meet you. I've heard so much about you.' And Mommy said, 'You've heard good things, right?' And then Phoenix said, 'Of course!'"

"What would I do without you, Zo-Zo? Having one French-speaking person in the household was bad enough, but with two, I feel double-teamed."

"Don't worry. I got your back, Daddy," Zoe assured me.

The four of us chatted easily as we waited to collect Phoenix's luggage from the carousel, and Phoenix didn't seem like a stranger at all. He fit right in.

On our way to the car, he and Zoe joked around while Sasha and I walked together. I had insisted on carrying Phoenix's bulging duffle bag, my small way of trying to make up for my absence in his life and all the weight I'd never carried.

When Zoe complained that the walk to the car was taking forever, Phoenix offered her a piggyback ride, which she gladly accepted. When the car was finally in sight, Zoe pointed to it and Phoenix took off running with her on his back.

I loved hearing the sound of their laughter, echoing in the distance.

Sasha squeezed my hand, letting me know that she was happy too.

With Phoenix here in Arizona, I felt as though my life had come full circle.

During the ride home, Zoe pointed out landmarks and other areas of interest along the way, providing long-winded historical information that I doubted Phoenix cared about. He could have tuned Zoe out or mumbled disinterestedly, but remarkably, he seemed interested, asking questions that she eagerly answered. Any concerns about the possibility of our blended family not getting along, quickly melted away. I appreciated that he was making an effort to interact with Zoe and had the patience to put up with a talkative nine-year-old.

We entered our affluent neighborhood in Springfield Hills, and I slowly drove along the twenty-mile-per-hour streets where the impressive dwellings were canopied by lush Palo Brea trees and framed by stately Aleppo pines. I made a right turn onto our equally attractive street. Thankfully, with Sasha's and my combined incomes, we were able to afford an expensive home with landscaped flower gardens and stone pathways and many other perks.

Although I doubted if Phoenix would have cared where we lived, the petty side of me was relieved that Sasha and I were as well-off as Everett and Elle.

As we neared our driveway, Phoenix gave a friendly wave to Baxter Westfield, a bespectacled kid who lived down the street from us. The kid was out in his yard diligently working on a bike. He pushed his thick-rimmed glasses up and gazed at us quizzically, but barely raised his hand to return Phoenix's greeting.

From the corner of my eye, I could see that the Westfields' garage door was up. Inside the garage, I detected about a dozen bikes in various states of disrepair. I rarely saw Baxter riding a bike, but he was always working on them. It was his hobby to upgrade them to look like flamboyant, pimped-out rides.

Baxter was quiet and reserved, yet his bikes were showy works of art.

"His name is Baxter Westfield," Zoe informed Phoenix as we rode past the Westfield home. "It's not that he's an unfriendly jerk; it's just that he's shy…and nervous from getting picked on at school," she explained. "I heard that he gets bullied all the time at his middle school, and that's probably why he keeps to himself. I talk to him sometimes, but he doesn't say much, and it's totally boring trying to hold a one-way conversation." She gave a one-shoulder shrug.

Phoenix's mouth grew taut and his eyes narrowed, signaling irritation. "The middle school should have a no-bullying policy like my school does. Kids shouldn't have to put up with mean-spirited crap in the classroom."

"You're right, son. I'm sure Zoe will make sure they change their policies by the time she starts middle school. She's already an advocate for environmental awareness," I said proudly, recalling how she had initiated a green project for her third-grade classroom. "It's only a matter of time before she takes on social injustice."

"Stop, Daddy. You're embarrassing me," she whined.

The four of us climbed from the car and walked past an array of flowers as we trekked along the winding stone path that led to the front door. I unlocked the door and disarmed our alarm system, and as we filed inside one-by-one, I noticed Phoenix lagging behind as he glanced over his shoulder, obviously concerned about Baxter, a kid he didn't know from a can of paint. Obviously, my son was a compassionate soul, yet another good trait that he possessed.

"Why don't you go introduce yourself to Baxter after you get settled in," I suggested, giving him a pat on the back.

"Yeah, I was thinking the same thing."

We gave him a tour of the house, saving his bedroom for last.

"Thanks for welcoming me into your home," he said, sounding like he was reading from a script. I was sure that his mother had fed him that line.

"It's your home too," I quickly replied, not wanting my son to feel like a guest in our home.

As Sasha and Zoe hovered in the doorway of his room, I stepped inside. "Do you need some help putting your things away?"

Phoenix gave me a patient smile. "Chill out, Pops. I got this."

"Okay, okay. Let's give Phoenix some space," I said, motioning for Sasha and Zoe to move along.

While Phoenix seemed to be completely at ease, the rest of us were a bundle of nerves as we tried to make him feel at home. Zoe was super-talkative, Sasha was uber-polite, and I couldn't stop checking on his comfort level.

"We'll be downstairs, son," I added and immediately felt foolish. Phoenix was a self-confident young man, and he didn't require any form of hand-holding or coddling.

I offered him a resigned smile and exited his room.

Downstairs, Sasha busied herself in the kitchen while Zoe and I played a game on her Xbox. Though Zoe usually played *Lego City*, she selected *Star Wars Battlefront II*, a more mature game that she figured Phoenix would enjoy playing.

When we heard him bounding down the stairs, Zoe held up her controller in offering. "You can play Dad if you'd like, Phoenix."

"No, I'm good. I'm going down the street to meet my first friend."

In two seconds flat, he was out the door, and Zoe and I lost interest in the video game.

Hearing the alarm system announce that the door had opened and closed, Sasha emerged from the kitchen. "Did Phoenix go out?" she asked with her brow creased.

"Yeah, he doesn't want to play with Daddy and me. He prefers the company of Baxter." She made a go-figure gesture, which brought out titters of laughter from both Sasha and me.

"Dinner will be ready in a half hour. Should we eat without him or should we text him and tell him what time to come home?" Sasha asked.

In a quandary about how to parent a teenage boy, I scratched my head in befuddlement. "Maybe we should give him a little bit of rope. He'll come home when he's hungry. Let's not make him feel like he has to sit for formal meals."

"You're right," Sasha said. "I'll make him a plate and leave it in the microwave."

"Or maybe we should let him make his own plate," Zoe suggested. "He seems like the independent type." She made an adorable face and I felt compelled to lift her up and playfully spin her around the room.

As she squealed delightedly, I felt relieved that I had one child who hadn't yet crossed over to mysterious-teen territory.

CHAPTER 14

I didn't expect an outgoing kid like Phoenix to find so much in common with an introvert like Baxter Westfield, but amazingly the two of them became thicker than thieves. Phoenix spent hours holed up in the garage with Baxter, working on bikes. Being that Phoenix considered himself to be the cerebral type, I was surprised that he enjoyed working with his hands, particularly when the work was being performed with a newfound friend who wasn't much of a conversationalist.

It was often said that opposites attract, and I supposed it was true since Phoenix was spending more time at the Westfields' home than ours.

He'd already reneged on two family outings that we'd planned, and it seemed that the only way to get him to spend family time with us was to invite Baxter along.

Sasha and I both took off from work on Friday to take the kids to a popular water park. We drove for an hour and when we finally arrived, I was astonished that Baxter didn't bring along any swimwear.

Zoe was eager to get wet, but I told her to hold on until I got Baxter squared away with a pair of swim shorts.

"I'm sure the gift shop has swimwear, Baxter. We'll pick up something for you," I said, trying to keep the annoyance out of my voice.

"That's okay, Mr. Copeland. I don't like water rides," Baxter said, scratching his left cheek that was marred by old acne scars.

I glanced at Sasha, making an expression that said, *'Who goes to a water park without a swimsuit?'*

Sasha returned my silent inquiry with an expression of puzzlement.

Baxter was weird. But it wasn't his fault. His dad was some kind of computer geek who was rarely home and spent most of his time at his job in Scottsdale, Arizona. His mom seemed to be overmedicated on antidepressants and she didn't seem to interact much with the kid, either. It was no wonder that his social skills were sorely lacking.

Seemingly unconcerned about Baxter's comfort, Phoenix and Zoe were already in line to get on the Aqua Loop, a water ride that resembled a roller coaster and was a little too lively for Sasha and me. We opted to try out the Lazy River ride, something that was much more sedate.

"Hey, Baxter," Phoenix called out from the long line he and Zoe was standing in. "Go get Zoe and me some nachos. We're gonna be starving by the time we get off the ride."

Mechanically, Baxter turned and headed toward the refreshment area.

I could tell by Sasha's expression that she didn't approve of the way Phoenix had ordered Baxter to go fetch him something to eat. It was bossy and insensitive, not at all the kind of behavior I expected from my son.

"I'm going to speak to him," I said and then meandered over to Phoenix.

"Hey, Phoenix," I said with my voice dipped low enough to prevent the other people in line from hearing what I had to say. "Baxter's your guest, not your servant. You should be more considerate of his feelings."

"It's cool, Pops. Baxter doesn't mind."

"It's not the way you should treat a friend," I insisted.

"It's an equal friendship, Pops. I'd do the same for him if he asked me," Phoenix replied, sounding a little hurt that I'd accused him of being unkind to his friend.

I suddenly felt like I was making a big deal out of nothing. I turned my attention to Zoe. "Your mother and I are going to get on the Lazy River. Do you want us to wait for you?"

She scrunched up her nose. "No! That ride is boring."

Phoenix laughed. "Don't worry, I'll take good care of her."

"Okay, we'll catch up with you kids later."

"All right," Zoe said distractedly as she and Phoenix moved forward in the line.

After the Lazy River ride, Sasha and I spent some time browsing around the park and then we rented a cabana and relaxed while being served umbrella cocktails, like we were on an island vacation. I drank virgin Pina Coladas while Sasha had the real thing.

Having a stationary spot made it easy for the kids to periodically check in with us. It was a fun day, and the only thing that disturbed me was the uncaring manner in which Phoenix treated Baxter.

At one point, when the kids stopped by our cabana, I noticed that Baxter was carrying Phoenix's and Zoe's wet towels.

"Zoe, why is Baxter schlepping your towels around?" Sasha inquired, speaking directly to Zoe and no doubt expecting me to follow her lead and query Phoenix.

"Oh, he's taking those to the towel deposit and then he's gonna pick up dry ones for us."

Sasha shot a look of disapproval at Zoe.

My sweet Zoe, a future crusader for social injustice, was picking up Phoenix's conduct and was seemingly oblivious to the way they were treating Baxter, and I didn't like it. I made a mental note to have a long, stern conversation with both Zoe and Phoenix. Their entitled behavior was unacceptable and I intended to nip it in the bud before it got out of hand.

Later that evening, after dropping Baxter off at his house, we sat Phoenix and Zoe down and began the discussion.

"Zoe..." Sasha began in a soft, calm voice that meant she was dead serious.

"Yes, Mom?"

"In my business I have employees who perform various duties for me. Now, what I'd like to know is when did you put Baxter on your payroll?"

Zoe frowned uncomprehendingly. "I don't have a payroll."

"Of course you don't, which is why you have no business giving Baxter any duties to perform. I'm very ashamed that I have to have such a discussion with you. I raised you to be kind and thoughtful and considerate of the feelings of others."

"I'm sorry, Mom," Zoe responded with her eyes downcast.

"I'm sorry, too," Phoenix volunteered before I'd even started in on him. "I didn't realize I was being inconsiderate, but I see it now."

There was nothing more to say on the subject and I was spared from having to give Phoenix a long lecture. We were so new in our roles of father and son that I wasn't comfortable at all with the idea of reprimanding him.

Tired from all the water rides and stuffed from devouring nachos, hot dogs, burgers, and all sorts of junk food, we all turned in earlier than usual. In the morning, Sasha and I both slept in, figuring the kids could fend for themselves and have cereal for breakfast.

Early Saturday morning the persistent ringing of the doorbell pulled me out of a leisurely sleep. I stumbled out of bed and made my way down the hallway. I noticed that Zoe was sitting up in bed wearing headphones, unaware that someone was at the door. I glanced at the closed door of Phoenix's bedroom, and assumed that being a sound sleeper, he hadn't been the least bit disturbed by the noise.

"Hold your horses," I muttered as I trotted down the stairs. I disarmed the alarm and swung the door open and was startled to find Baxter standing on the porch.

"Hi, um, Mr. Copeland. Uh, is Phoenix home?" Baxter's voice was hesitant, on the verge of stuttering.

"Yeah, but he's not out of bed yet," I replied, scowling.

I wondered what was with this kid, coming over early in the morning. "Why don't you come back in a couple of hours? He should be up by then."

"Okay." Baxter stuffed his hands in his pockets and turned to leave. There was something so forlorn and pitiful in his demeanor that my heart ached for him.

Baxter left and I headed for the stairs and then halted. There was no point in trying to get back to sleep, so I made my way to the kitchen to make coffee. While waiting for it to brew, Zoe wandered in.

"Can you make me some blueberry waffles, Daddy?" she asked, flashing an irresistible smile.

"Well, it's not only about you, Zo-Zo. Phoenix may not like blueberry waffles." I pointed toward the staircase. "Go upstairs and ask him what he'd like for breakfast. Maybe you guys can come to a compromise."

"Phoenix isn't home."

"Where is he?"

"He went bike riding with a group of boys."

I scowled. "What boys?"

"They're from around here, but I don't know their names."

"How does Phoenix know them?"

Zoe shrugged.

"He should have let me know before taking off like that," I muttered in irritation.

"He didn't want to disturb you and he asked me to let you know."

"Oh, okay," I said tentatively, trying to process the fact that he hadn't asked permission to leave the house.

At thirteen I didn't ask permission every time I hung out with friends, so I supposed it was okay. But on second thought, this was a different time period, and the world wasn't as kind as it had been when I was a kid. For my own peace of mind, I'd have to set up some ground rules and Phoenix would have to follow them.

I poured coffee while Zoe poured herself a glass of orange juice.

"How'd he get a bike?" I asked as I lightened my coffee with nondairy creamer. "Did one of the kids loan him one?"

"No, he borrowed one from Baxter. Baxter has, like, two dozen bikes that he never rides."

"Why didn't he invite Baxter to go along?"

"I have no idea," Zoe replied and took a big gulp of juice.

I felt immense disappointment in Phoenix for neglecting his friend, and I wondered what had happened to the thoughtfulness and compassion that I thought my son possessed.

It was the height of disrespect for him to borrow a bike from Baxter and not invite him along to go riding with him and his newfound friends. I didn't know how I was going to get through to Phoenix about treating others with respect. Was that something you could teach someone or was it an innate trait? I didn't know, but as a parent it was my responsibility to guide him as best I could and keep pushing the issue about compassion and respect until it finally sunk in.

"So, can I have blueberry waffles?" Zoe asked.

"You sure can. Blueberry waffles coming up," I said in a cheerful tone that didn't betray the concern I felt inside. I couldn't shake the ominous feeling that trouble was brewing on the horizon.

I texted Phoenix and asked whom he was with, where he was, and what time he planned to return home.

It took a full fifteen minutes for him to respond. He said he was bike riding on the trails with Ryan, Matthew, and Dustin and he'd be back around two.

The boys' names didn't ring a bell. Aside from Baxter, the only kids I was familiar with were Zoe's friends and classmates.

Having communicated with Phoenix made me feel less on edge, and I launched into preparing breakfast. I whipped up waffles, scrambled eggs and bacon for Zoe and me and popped a few slices of bread into the toaster oven for Sasha, who rarely ate a big meal at the start of the day.

As the three of us sat at the breakfast nook, Zoe filled Sasha in on Phoenix's early morning activities.

"How'd he meet the kids he's bike riding with?" Sasha inquired.

I lifted up a palm. "I have no clue. But their names are Ryan, Matthew, and Dustin."

Sasha's brow creased. "Shouldn't we know more than the first names of the boys he's associating with? Suppose something happened…we don't know their parents or where they live. We don't anything about them. For all we know he could have gotten involved with a rough crowd…the kind of kids that could lead him astray."

Sasha was right, but for some inexplicable reason, I felt the need to downplay my own concern.

"He's a thirteen-year-old boy, Sasha. Boys are adventurous. We can't monitor his every move…and we can't pick his friends, either."

Sasha's eyes bore into me. "*Boys* are adventurous! That's a sexist remark."

"I didn't mean it that way. I meant to say that teenagers are adventurous. But as soon as Phoenix gets home, I'm going to lay down some ground rules."

"Good! I don't know what we would tell his parents if they called at this moment," she added.

"I am his parent, and while he's here in Arizona, I don't intend to answer to Elle and Everett as if I'm a glorified babysitter." My words came out with much more bite than I'd intended, and I should have apologized but I didn't.

"I'm not suggesting that you're a babysitter; I only meant…" Sasha's voice trailed off. She looked at her watch. "Zoe, your hair-braiding appointment is in an hour. We better get going."

It was rare for there to be any degree of discord in our household. Sensing the unusual tension between her mother and me and not wanting to add to it, Zoe jumped to her feet without delay and raced up the stairs to grab her backpack. She was back downstairs in record time, wearing a glittery backpack that was no doubt stuffed with books and numerous electronic devices that would help her endure the four-hour hair-braiding session.

When Sasha and Zoe left, I was glad to have the house to myself. I needed to figure out how to deal with the Phoenix situation without any input from Sasha. We were always in agreement when it came to parenting Zoe, but I found myself on the defensive when it came to Phoenix. Until I became comfortable assuming the role of his parent, I didn't need the added pressure of Sasha's concerns regarding his behavior.

Parenting a teenage boy wasn't as easy as I'd thought it would be. I cherished our friendly relationship and I didn't want to say anything that might alienate him. But I couldn't simply be his buddy; I also had to guide him and take some sort of disciplinary action when necessary.

Disciplining him was something I didn't look forward to, and hopefully after I laid down the household rules, he wouldn't break any of them.

CHAPTER 15

I was watering the front lawn when Phoenix rode up on Baxter's mountain bike. It was a beauty with snazzy gold chains replacing the typical silver ones that adorned the average bike. The pedals were neon green, the fancy handlebars were a matching green color, and the rims of the tires were custom-painted orange and green and embellished with beautiful Aztec designs.

Baxter had obviously put a lot of time and love into accessorizing his bike, and it bothered me that Phoenix hopped off the bike and let it fall to the ground with a clatter.

"Hey! That's not your property. Treat it with respect and use the kickstand."

"My bad." Phoenix picked up the bike and stood it up properly.

"Why'd you leave Baxter behind? He's been a loyal friend to you, and he was nice enough to loan you a bike. It's inconsiderate to abandon him for new friends, don't you think?" I didn't want to sound like a nagging parent and I was careful to keep my voice in as neutral a tone as possible.

"Baxter has asthma, Pops, and he's scared of having an attack. He says that not being able to breathe is terrifying. He told me that every attack lands him in the hospital, and he really hates the spectacle of an ambulance ride and the entire hospital scene. That's why he wouldn't get on any of the water rides yesterday. So, that's the reason I didn't invite him to go biking with me and the guys. He wouldn't have accepted, anyway," Phoenix explained.

I felt bad that Baxter had health issues, but I was relieved to know that Phoenix wasn't insensitive.

"Son, I'd appreciate it if in the future, you let me know where you're going before you leave the house. If something were to happen to you, I wouldn't have any idea where you were or who you were with. We have house rules, Phoenix, and neither Sasha nor I am comfortable with you coming and going as you please."

"I get it, Pops. It won't happen again."

"Good, good," I said, nodding my head. "So, where'd you meet the guys you hung out with today?"

"Around the neighborhood," he said vaguely.

I didn't want to press him for more information, but I knew Sasha, a much more responsible parent than me, would want to know more than the first names of his new associates.

"Are the boys your age or older?" I asked, trying to sound casual.

"I can invite them over if you want to inspect them," he said with a chuckle.

Before I could respond, he pulled his phone out of his pocket and started texting. A few moments later, his phone pinged with a response.

"I asked Dustin to round up Matthew and Ryan, so that you can interrogate the three of them and make sure that I'm not being influenced by thugs," he said with a smirk.

"I don't want to interrogate them, Phoenix. I only—"

"I'm kidding. I invited them over to play video games. That way you can look them over and form an opinion about their character without actually interrogating them." Phoenix winked, and I nodded dumbly.

My kid was quick on his feet—quicker than I was.

The three polite boys that came over didn't have a thuggish bone in their scrawny, little bodies. Even though they seemed completely harmless, I made sure to get their last names. I didn't want to embarrass Phoenix by asking for their exact addresses, but I managed to find out the general vicinity of where they lived.

I was in my office behind the kitchen, going over the work assignments for the upcoming week, when Phoenix popped his head in.

"Is it okay if I go swimming at Ryan's house?" he asked, adhering to the house rules I'd put into place.

"Sure. But...for my own peace of mind, I need you to text me Ryan's address," I said with an apologetic smile.

"Okay." He gave me a wink, like we were in on a secret. In a way, I supposed we were in cahoots because Phoenix was aware that I wasn't personally concerned about Ryan's exact address; I was only asking to appease Sasha.

He and his friends left and I went back to setting up the weekly work schedule for my five employees. The doorbell suddenly rang, and I assumed that Phoenix had left something behind, including his keys. It was a big surprise to find Baxter on the front porch.

"Sorry to disturb you, Mr. Copeland. Is Phoenix around?"

"No, Baxter. He, uh, went out."

Baxter scratched his left cheek, where the skin had erupted in red, angry pimples. The kid couldn't catch a break. It was bad enough that he suffered with asthma, but he had also developed a bad case of acne overnight.

"Do you know when he'll be back?" he asked, awkwardly shifting his feet.

I felt a pang of guilt, as if Phoenix were cheating on Baxter with his new friends. "He'll probably be back around dinnertime."

"Okay. Would you tell him to give me a call or stop by my house? It's really important." There was a desperate tone in his voice, and I wondered if he was concerned about the bike he had loaned Phoenix.

"Yeah, I'll be sure to give him your message," I said, making a mental note to take Phoenix shopping for a bike tomorrow.

After swimming at Ryan's, Phoenix returned home with Dustin and Matthew trailing behind him. I'd forgotten how inseparable teenage friends could be. Sasha and I would have to get accustomed to having teenage boys underfoot for the duration of Phoenix's visit.

Zoe seemed delighted to have boys around, and she joined them in the living room, hoping to be included in playing their video game. After a while, the boys put down the controllers, and all three trotted to the rear patio. When Zoe got up to follow them, Sasha held up her hand, stopping her in her tracks.

"They're here to visit Phoenix, young lady, so leave them be," Sasha said sternly.

"But—"

"But, nothing," I interjected. "You're supposed to stay in your lane, Zo-Zo. Remember?"

"Aw, it's not fair that Phoenix gets to have all the fun while I'm bored to death." Swinging her long, freshly braided hair, Zoe flopped back down on the sofa and picked up a controller and began playing a game by herself.

While Sasha puttered around the kitchen, I went back to my office. From the window behind my desk, I could hear the boys horsing around and seemingly enjoying typical adolescent fun. As I smiled at their youthful exuberance, I suddenly recalled that I hadn't given Phoenix Baxter's urgent message.

I scooted my rolling chair back, stood up and raised the blinds, prepared to rap on the window and beckon Phoenix to come inside for a moment. But when I peered through the windowpane, I could see the boys hovering around Phoenix, gazing at something on his phone. Simultaneously, Matthew and Ryan pulled out their phones, and with mischievous grins, they stared at their screens.

"Oh, man, I gotta send this to Dustin. He's not gonna believe it," Ryan said, giggling and elbowing Matthew.

They were obviously all viewing the same thing, and there was something about the tone of their laughter—it had a jeering ring to it—that led me to suspect they were looking at something forbidden. Something X-rated. Most likely, they were looking at porn.

Once again I was in a quandary as to how I should react. Would a responsible parent go outside and demand to see his son's phone to find out if he was on an adult site? Shaking my head, I decided against that idea. Demanding to know what Phoenix and his friends were looking at on their phones was taking my parenting role to an extreme.

Boys will be boys, I told myself. Sexual curiosity was a normal part of growing up, and in this instance it was best to mind my business and get back to work.

Fully immersed in creating a staff schedule, I had no idea how much time had passed when I was startled by the shrill sound of a siren—something rare in our neighborhood.

Sasha, Zoe, and I rushed to the front lawn to find out what was happening. The boys came running from the patio with excitement glinting in their eyes.

"I bet it's a fire," Matthew exclaimed gleefully.

"I bet some old lady's cat got stuck in a tree," Ryan added glumly.

When the ambulance stopped in front of Baxter's house, Sasha shot a worried look at me. "Oh, my God! I knew that Mrs. Westfield wasn't feeling well, but I had no idea that it was serious."

The EMTs brought out a stretcher and Mrs. Westfield emerged from the house, crying and motioning for the men to hurry inside.

"Something must be wrong with Baxter," Zoe murmured.

"Probably an asthma attack," Phoenix offered grimly.

"Shouldn't we go offer Mrs. Westfield some emotional support?" Sasha asked.

"We'd only be in the way," I said, protectively wrapping my arm around both Sasha and Zoe, grateful that my family was safe from harm.

Moments later the EMTs dashed out with Baxter on the stretcher. They loaded him into the ambulance and Mrs. Westfield tried to climb inside. One of the men blocked her from getting in and closed the ambulance door.

I wondered what had brought on Baxter's asthma attack, and hoped it wasn't an emotional response to feeling rejected by Phoenix. As I pondered the situation, I noticed Mrs. Westfield standing at the curb, her face buried in her hands as she wept.

"I'm gonna give her a ride to the hospital," I said to Sasha as I pulled my car keys from my pocket. I raced to our two-car garage and swiftly backed out, swerving as I peeled out of the long driveway in reverse.

Split-seconds later I was parked in front of the Westfield home.

"Mrs. Westfield! Do you want me to call Mr. Westfield for you? Can I give you a lift to the hospital?"

Crying bitterly, she said, "I already called him. He's on his way home. But I need to be with my son."

"Absolutely," I said as I got out of the car, so that I could assist her.

"You need to lock your house up and grab your keys and handbag," I said slowly and clearly, as if speaking to someone who was hard of hearing or learning disabled.

I guided her to her front door. Inside her home, she shuffled to the kitchen area, walking with the unsteady gait of someone twice her age. She emerged from the kitchen with a set of keys.

"We need to hurry," she said.

I nodded and relieved her of the keys and locked the door myself.

Apparently she wasn't concerned about carrying a handbag to the hospital and under the circumstances, I couldn't blame her.

While escorting her to my car, I was keenly aware of Sasha, Zoe, and the boys watching our every move. I helped Mrs. Westfield into the passenger's side, and on the way to the hospital, I broke all sorts of traffic laws, trying to get there as quickly as possible.

"I don't understand why he would do something like this," she cried. "It doesn't make sense. Why? Why? Why?" she cried.

"What doesn't make sense? Baxter had an asthma attack, didn't he?"

"No, he tried to kill himself," she sobbed. "He slit both his wrists, and I never saw so much blood in my life," she said, gasping and crying hysterically.

Jesus! A wave of guilt washed over me as I drove on. I couldn't help thinking that if I had remembered to deliver Baxter's message to Phoenix, Baxter wouldn't be lying in the back of an ambulance.

I'd never been much of a religious person, not as far as attending church, but I prayed hard for the duration of the drive, asking God to help Baxter pull through.

I also prayed that whatever had caused Baxter to attempt suicide had nothing to do with my son. Perhaps Phoenix had been an inconsiderate friend, but he was only a kid and had no way of knowing that neglecting Baxter would result in such dire consequences.

CHAPTER 16

Baxter survived his self-inflicted wounds.

After he was out of the woods, I called Sasha and filled her in.

"What's the next step for him?" she asked.

"A mental health evaluation. I know from dealing with Phoenix's suicide attempt that Baxter's facing at least a seventy-two-hour hold, and possibly a thirty-day stay in a psychiatric facility. After he's discharged, he'll receive outpatient treatment with a therapist and possibly medication."

"Thank God he's all right," Sasha said.

"Yeah, it was a close call. What is with these teens today? Why do so many of them think that ending their life is the answer to escaping the normal pressures of adolescent life?"

"I wish I knew the answer."

"It's becoming an epidemic, and I don't get it."

"Are you worried that Phoenix might try it again?"

"No, not at all. In Phoenix's case, he wasn't trying to escape anything, and intense therapy wasn't recommended for him. His doctor recognized his experimentation with drugs was a cry for attention. He didn't want to die. Messing around with heroin was a childish way to force his mother to reveal my identity. Baxter, on the other hand, apparently has serious issues that are so severe he doesn't want to be here anymore."

"I feel so bad for him," Sasha murmured.

"Yeah, me too. Meanwhile, I might be home pretty late. I'm going to sit with Mrs. Westfield until her husband gets here."

"Okay. Love you, honey," Sasha whispered.

"Love you, too."

I hung up and rejoined Mrs. Westfield in Baxter's room.

I took a seat next to her. "What time is your husband arriving?"

She stood up and motioned for me to follow her into the hallway.

"I didn't want to risk Baxter overhearing," she said in a confidential tone. "His father can't leave Scottsdale right now. He's in the middle of an important project, but he'll be here in the morning."

I was shocked. It was a life-and-death matter, but despite the severity of the situation, Mr. Westfield preferred to hang back at work and not check on his son until it was convenient for him. I couldn't sit in the hospital room with Mrs. Westfield until morning, so I told her that I had to go. I told her not to hesitate to call me if she wanted to talk or needed anything.

Driving home my mind wandered back to Mr. Westfield. His less than caring attitude toward his son was most likely the root of Baxter's problem. The man was never around. He never put in any quality time with Baxter, and the boy was basically left on his own to navigate the road toward manhood.

Baxter's brush with death gave me a sense of urgency in making sure that my connection with Phoenix was secure. I decided that it would be a good time for some father-and-son bonding while we were looking at bikes tomorrow. I never wanted him to feel that I was emotionally unavailable. It was time to start telling him how much I loved him instead of assuming that he already knew.

And it was time to start doling out more hugs instead of holding back for fear of making him uncomfortable.

Eager to get home to my family, I pressed on the accelerator.

As I hastily parked in the driveway, I frowned at the sight of Baxter's flamboyant orange and green bike tossed carelessly on our front lawn. Hurrying inside the house, I made a mental note to speak to Phoenix about returning Baxter's bicycle first thing tomorrow.

I bounded up the stairs and found Sasha sitting up in bed reading. Zoe was stretched out on the bed beside her, sound asleep.

"Zoe was so upset about Baxter, she stuck to me like glue all evening."

I glanced at Zoe who was wearing a pajama set that was adorned with pink dinosaurs. She looked so sweet and innocent, and it was my hope that her life would never seem so painful and hopeless that she would want to die.

"Is Phoenix in his room?"

"Yes, he was listening to music when I told him goodnight."

"How was his mood?"

"He seemed okay. He was pensive, but didn't seem overly sad."

I nodded as I gingerly lifted Zoe from our bed. "I'm going to put her to bed and then check on Phoenix. Be back in a few."

"Sure, babe," Sasha said, sending a warm smile in my direction.

After tucking Zoe in, I went to Phoenix's room. As a courtesy, I didn't barge in; I tapped softly on his door. When he didn't answer, I cracked the door open and peeked in.

In a teenage world, music was a dependable companion during good times and bad, and I expected to find him bobbing his head to music that poured through his headphones. But he was knocked out. Sleeping as hard as ever, his mouth hung open and he snored loudly. Rap music blasted from the headphones that covered his ears. It was so loud I could hear it from the doorway. It was a mystery how someone could fall asleep with that kind of racket blaring in their ears.

I entered the room and moved softly across the floor, intending to remove the headphones. As I drew close to his bed, I noticed that he'd set his phone on the nightstand.

Curious about what he and his friends had found so entertaining earlier in the day, I made a snap decision to snoop through his phone. As a parent, I had a right to know, even if my discovery was done in secret. Stealthily, I lifted his hand and used his thumb to unlock his phone. I tapped on the photo app and scrolled through his pictures and videos, but didn't see anything unusual.

Next I went through his text messages. There were about twenty texts between Phoenix and Baxter, stamped with today's date. A feeling of apprehension settled over me as I wondered why there so many messages between them in the course of one day. As suspicion corkscrewed its way into my consciousness, my eyes began to zoom over their texts and I was deeply disturbed by what I read.

Baxter: I thought we were best friends.

Phoenix: I'm my own best friend.

Baxter: If you want to be that way, then return my bike.

Phoenix: Make me. I'll return it when I'm finished riding with my friends. Get a life and stop bugging me.

Baxter: I don't understand why you're being so mean. What did I do to you?

Phoenix: Your existence bugs me. Besides, I don't associate with pervs.

Baxter: Don't call me that. I'm not a pervert.

Phoenix: Whatever, man. Just stop calling and texting me. If you don't, you'll be sorry. You won't be able to show your ugly mug at school or anywhere else if I reveal your dirty secret.

Baxter: I trusted you, Phoenix. Please don't show the video.

Phoenix: I'll think about it, but I'm not making any promises.

Baxter: Please, I'm begging you.

Phoenix: Okay, let's make a deal. Let me have your bike and I won't show the entire neighborhood your X-rated performance.

Baxter: But I worked so hard on that bike. I can let you have another one.

Phoenix: Nope, I want the one I chose.

Baxter: Okay, it's all yours. You can keep it.

Phoenix: Cool. Now fuck off, loser, and leave me alone.

After that exchange, there weren't any more messages from Baxter.

A great sense of sorrow and shame fell over me. I was absolutely horrified by Phoenix's heartlessness. I thought about the way he and his two friends had laughed contemptuously while looking at their phones.

It was now apparent that Phoenix hadn't kept his promise to Baxter.

Infuriated, I gripped his shoulder and shook it. "Phoenix! Phoenix!" I spoke in a harsh whisper, trying to quietly awaken him without alerting Sasha.

His eyelids fluttered open, but he was in such a deep state of sleep, his eyes were bleary and unfocused.

"I need to talk to you," I said gruffly as I snatched his headphones off.

He mumbled something incoherent, and I gave up trying to get him to respond in a lucid manner.

Certain that whatever he'd sent to Matthew's and Ryan's phone was of a provocative nature and undoubtedly involved Baxter, I quickly scrolled to Matthew's name and opened up his and Phoenix's texts.

My mouth fell open and my legs nearly gave out when I found myself staring at a still shot of a video that featured a bare-chested Baxter wearing a helpless expression.

I wondered if the contents of the video were the reason he'd tried to kill himself.

Deeply troubled, I took a deep breath and ran a shaky palm over my jawline. Before tapping on the arrow and bringing the video to life, I took a seat on Phoenix's bed. Split-seconds later, I was viewing Baxter walking to the other side of what appeared to be his bedroom. I winced when he lowered himself to his knees.

It was painfully clear that I was viewing a sexually explicit video of Baxter and another boy…or possibly an adult man, whose face wasn't revealed. In fact, the only part of the unidentified person's anatomy that was visible was his genital region.

It had never entered my mind that Baxter was gay, not that it mattered. Someone had taken advantage of him, probably some immoral child predator he'd met online.

Apparently, he had trusted Phoenix enough to share his secret with him, and Phoenix had cruelly used it against him. He'd even gone as far as blackmailing him into giving him one of his prized possessions.

And even after he gave Phoenix his bike, Phoenix still betrayed him.

He shared the video with his new friends, and together they had laughed derisively at Baxter. There was no telling how many other kids had viewed the video, but I would bet that most of Baxter's schoolmates had seen it by now.

I slumped forward with my elbows digging into my thighs, my hands cupping my face as I tried to figure out how to handle the dilemma. I needed to share the video with Baxter's parents. Hell, I needed to alert the police, but before doing so, I had to figure out a way to keep Phoenix out of the equation.

Desperate to protect Phoenix, I refused to provide anyone with information that would label my son as a bully, responsible for destroying another kid's life.

I concluded that it was best not to tell anyone about my discovery of the video. In protective parent mode, I deleted the texts between Baxter and Phoenix, and I also deleted the texts Phoenix had sent to Matthew and Ryan, containing the damning video. Then, with my middle finger poised to delete anything that contained sexual subject matter, I searched through his pictures and videos once again but found nothing.

Satisfied that I'd gotten rid of any material that could possibly point to Phoenix having any involvement in Baxter's suicide attempt, I walked stiffly back to my bedroom.

"What's the matter, Malik?" Sasha asked, putting her book down as she gazed at me.

"Nothing's wrong; I'm just tired."

"I bet you are. Take off your clothes and get in bed, honey. I'll give you a relaxing massage to help you sleep." She patted my side of the bed.

I could tell by the sensual tone of her voice that she intended to give me much more than a massage, and for the first time in our marriage, I wasn't in the mood for sex.

I simply wanted to slip into a deep sleep and forget that Baxter's innocence had been stolen.

And I also wanted to forget that there was something terribly wrong with my son.

He lacked empathy. He was a bully. And he was mean-spirited and unkind.

But I still loved him with all my heart and soul, and I would do everything to protect him…even from himself.

I couldn't talk to Sasha about what I'd discovered because I didn't want her to look at Phoenix differently. I didn't want her to fear that he might be a bad influence on Zoe.

My son was my problem, and I intended to get the problem

fixed. First of all, I had to get him professional help. If I had to drag him kicking and screaming to a therapist's office, then so be it. But the nature of his therapy sessions wouldn't be anyone's business except his and mine.

Of course, I'd have to tell Elle to ensure that he continued with therapy when he returned to Philadelphia. Whether or not she shared the information with Everett was up to her. But if she felt remotely close to the way I felt, she'd keep the distasteful information about our son's lack of character to herself.

CHAPTER 17

I woke up Sunday morning with a feeling of dread that I couldn't identify. As the cobwebs cleared from my head, I remembered that Baxter was lying in the hospital with his wrists sutured and bandaged.

I could hear the distant sounds of clanging pots and pans coming from the kitchen and the muffled voices of the family I loved. Yet those sounds gave me no joy. I was a troubled man and I felt utterly alone.

And I felt scared.

I rolled out of bed, threw on a robe, and then trotted downstairs.

"Good morning, Daddy," Zoe said when I entered the kitchen.

"Good morning, sweetheart," I replied in as cheerful a voice as I could muster.

"Mommy told us that Baxter's going to be okay."

"Yeah, he's going to be fine," I said, cutting an eye at Phoenix, who was wolfing down milk and Cheerios.

I made eye contact with Phoenix and said, "Let's go look at bikes at the mall. You won't have to borrow Baxter's bike if you have one of your own."

"I wanna go, too," Zoe squealed.

"You can come along, Zoe," Phoenix said good-naturedly.

"No!" I quickly interjected. "Not today, Zoe. Some other time."

"Why not?" she asked, looking hurt.

Sasha gazed at me questioningly, but I wouldn't meet her gaze.

With my eyes fixed on Zoe, I searched my mind for an explanation that would soften the blow of leaving her behind. "You know how you and your mother have girl-time, where you do girly things like getting your hair and nails done? Well, I want to spend some guy-time with Phoenix. Okay, Zo-Zo?"

She nodded, but I could tell that she didn't like being left out.

I turned my attention back to Phoenix. "By the way, I want you to return Baxter's bike while I'm upstairs getting dressed. If his parents aren't home, then leave it outside their garage."

"Okay," he answered nonchalantly. He turned the cereal bowl up to his lips and slurped down the remaining milk and then pushed away from the table.

Seemingly without a care in the world, he sauntered to the living room. Whistling cheerfully, he went outside to retrieve the flashy bike that he'd blackmailed Baxter into giving him.

I slowly climbed the stairs, confounded by his obvious lack of remorse regarding Baxter. Very much concerned about the moral character of the child who shared my DNA, I let out a sigh as I wondered if it was best to shorten the length of Phoenix's visit and ship him back to Philadelphia before he caused any more trouble.

In the car on the way to the mall, Phoenix fiddled with the radio, searching for a hip-hop station. When he found a song he liked, he reclined his seat and relaxed.

"I saw that video with Baxter," I said solemnly.

"I figured that," he said tonelessly. "It was obvious that you went through my phone and deleted a lot of messages."

"Why, son? Why would you take advantage of such an easy-going and nonthreatening kid like Baxter? He practically worshipped you, yet you treated him horribly. Those texts you sent him were absolutely vicious, and resulted in him doing something unthinkable."

"I was only playing around with him. Honest."

"Playing around?" I scoffed.

"Yeah."

"You exposed his sexuality to your friends and turned him into a laughingstock."

"He was already a laughingstock," Phoenix said, defiantly justifying his actions.

"Where's your compassion? You taunted your friend about being gay and threatened to expose him. That's wrong, Phoenix! And who's the guy in the video with him?"

"I don't know. Some dude he met online."

"An adult?" I asked fearfully.

"No, it was a boy his age...maybe a year or two older."

I was instantly relieved that Baxter wasn't involved with an online predator. I reasoned that since his sex partner was a kid his own age, I didn't have to concern myself with alerting the police. I definitely wanted to avoid saying anything that would result in Phoenix's name being dragged through the mud.

"Baxter thinks he's in love with the video dude," Phoenix confided with a chuckle.

"There's nothing funny about any of this. Your friend came close to bleeding out. Don't you feel any sense of responsibility?"

"Not really. It's not my fault that he can't take a joke."

"Yes, it is your fault. You taunted and bullied him and shared a sensitive video that he asked you to keep secret."

"Can we please change the subject? I don't like thinking about that disgusting video."

"Oh, no? You didn't mind looking at it with your friends."

"The video doesn't exist anymore. I told Matt and Ryan to delete it."

"Do you think they did?" I asked hopefully.

"Yeah, I *know* they did. So, can we please move on?"

"Why? Does it make you feel uncomfortable to discuss how you betrayed your friend?"

"He's not my friend. Not anymore."

"Oh, so you're admitting to being homophobic? I hope you're proud of your narrow-minded world view," I said sarcastically.

"I'm not proud of it, but it's the way I was raised. My dad always taught me that homosexuality was wrong."

I swallowed down a knot of guilt. I'd allowed a homophobe to raise my son and pass on his misguided ideas. With a sigh, I accepted that I had no choice but to step up to the plate and work with Phoenix and try to undo the damage that Everett had caused.

"Phoenix," I said in a gentle tone. "I feel that you should have gotten outpatient therapy after your suicide attempt."

"I didn't try to kill myself. It was an accident. How many times do I have to tell you that?" Clearly upset, the veins at his temples visibly throbbed.

"Something's not right with you, son. And you need therapy." I spoke in a low, placating tone.

"So, in other words, you think I'm crazy," he said, rolling his eyes and sulking.

"I didn't say you were crazy, but your behavior is destructive and your words matter. It's troubling for me to discover that you lack empathy for what you did to Baxter."

He let out a long sigh. "I don't lack empathy; I just don't like homos. You can send me to a million shrinks and none of them will be able to change my beliefs on the subject."

"Maybe not, but a skilled therapist can possibly teach you that lashing out at people who are different than you is not honorable," I explained as I pulled into the parking lot of a medical center. I'd already called and made an emergency appointment for Phoenix. Now, all I had to do was get him to walk through the door.

Phoenix did a double-take as he looked at the signage in front of the building and then gawked at me. "I thought you said we were going to the mall to get me a bike."

"I said that for Sasha's benefit. Do you honestly believe that I would reward your antisocial behavior? I made an appointment with a psychologist and if you refuse to talk with him, then I don't know what else to do except send you back to Philadelphia."

Phoenix flinched and gave me a look of shock, like I was the worst traitor in the world. Then he smiled wryly. "You abandoned me once, so why am I surprised that you're doing it again?"

"I'm not abandoning you, but I can't ignore your frightening and insensitive conduct."

He sucked his teeth. "You're acting like I'm the one who took a knife and slashed Baxter's stupid wrists."

"You just don't get it, do you?" I said, shaking my head.

"Whatever, Pops. Use any excuse to get rid of me again. Take me to the airport—I'm ready to get out of this boring town, anyway."

"I'm changing Phoenix's flight. He's decided to shorten his visit," I said to Elle over the phone.

"Why? Did something happen?"

"No, but he's kind of homesick," I said, unable to bring myself to reveal the sordid details of why his visit was really being cut short.

"All right. Everett and I will pick him up."

"I really want to continue building a relationship with Phoenix, and hopefully we can reconnect around Christmastime. My wife, daughter, and I were considering coming to Philadelphia to visit my parents during the holidays. If Phoenix wants to, we can spend some time together then."

"You're not being straight with me, Malik. I sense that something is wrong. Did Phoenix do something wrong?"

I went quiet. I wanted to gently convey to Elle that I suspected that our son had serious mental health issues. He was missing vital components of the human experience: morality, compassion, human decency. But how do you tell a mother something like that? Besides, I could be wrong. He was only thirteen and was still maturing. Still forming his opinions of how he viewed the world.

"Elle," I said softly. "I think he needs therapy."

"But his psychiatrist at the hospital didn't recommend outpatient therapy."

"He's a smart boy and he fooled the doctor. I'm serious, Elle. Phoenix needs help."

"Can you be more specific," she said with an edge to her voice.

"For one thing, he's homophobic and incapable of tolerance toward gay people. And he told me his opinion was influenced by Everett."

"That's not true! Everett isn't biased toward gays or anyone else."

"Well, that's what Phoenix told me."

"Then he's lying."

"Maybe so. But if he made up that story, then that's proof that he needs help."

"Kids at that age lie, Malik. You're making a big deal out of nothing."

"If you choose to keep your head buried in the sand, then there's nothing I can do about it. Like I said, I'll be in town during the holiday season, and I'll see Phoenix then."

"You don't have to do him any favors," Elle spat bitterly and then abruptly ended the call.

CHAPTER 18

After a two-week stay in a psych hospital, Baxter came home and once again spent most of his time holed up in the family's garage customizing bikes. One day as I drove past, I felt obligated to stop and say hello.

"How are you doing, Baxter?"

"I'm okay," he said, squinting at me like I was from another planet. I supposed it was weird to see me standing outside his garage slash workshop.

"You're good with customizing bikes. You ever think about going into business?"

He blushed and scratched a fresh batch of pimples on his cheek. "No, it's just a hobby. Something I like to do."

"Listen, Baxter, I'm really sorry... Uh, I know that Phoenix wasn't very nice to you and I want to apologize for him."

"What did he tell you?" Baxter's voice rose in panic.

"I know about you and that boy...in the video, and uh, I want to talk to you about it. There's nothing wrong with being gay, but you're much too young to be sexually active."

His eyes darted wildly, like a trapped animal, and I was sorry that I'd brought up the subject. My intention was to be supportive, not to embarrass him.

"But I'm not gay," he protested.

"Maybe not. You're, um…probably too young to know what your sexual orientation is."

"I know that I like girls," he blurted, sounding tearful.

"Well, how do you explain the video that Phoenix had on his phone?"

"I didn't want to do it; he forced me."

"Who forced you?" My voice rose in pitch as I imagined beating the hell out of the child molester who'd taken advantage of a thirteen-year-old kid.

"Phoenix did. And he filmed it."

"What?" I shook my head briskly, thinking I'd heard wrong.

"He said it was a friendship pact—a way of proving that I was his best friend. After I did it, he threatened to tell all the kids in the neighborhood that I was a freak." Right before tears began streaming down his face, Baxter made an anguished sound that seemed to come from deep within his soul.

I kept my own anguished cry bottled up inside of me with a hand covering my mouth.

"Please don't tell my mom," Baxter pleaded.

I nodded and began to slowly walk backward out of the garage. In a state of disbelief, I mumbled that I'd talk to him later.

Back in my car, I drove in circles wondering what kind of monster-child I had created with Elle.

Phoenix was devious. A liar. Cruel. And sexually deviant.

Not because of any homosexual tendencies, but he had basically molested Baxter and then blackmailed his victim.

There was no point in telling Elle; she wouldn't allow herself to believe it.

And I couldn't bring myself to tell Sasha, either. The subject matter was unusually awful and too painful to discuss.

In my confused mindset, I held the irrational belief that I was somehow responsible for my son's immorality. My absence in his life. My drug usage before he was conceived. The wanton orgies I'd engaged in when I was getting high had something to do with his lack of character.

Or maybe I was simply being punished for all the pain I'd caused my loved ones in the past. I thought that serving a jail sentence was sufficient payment for my previous transgressions. I thought that becoming an upstanding citizen would absolve me of my sins, but I was wrong.

Phoenix, my terribly flawed child, was living proof that the past had a way of catching up with you, no matter how fast and how far you tried to run.

I drove for another half hour before pulling into the lot of a random, dive-type bar. Although I hadn't touched alcohol in over ten years, I had never needed a drink as badly as I needed one right now.

And a shot of heroin would be even better.

In a rundown place like the bar I was about to enter, I was sure that the bartender or one of the patrons could point me in the direction of a dealer.

Don't do it! I told myself.

No matter how much pain you're in and no matter how much self-blame you heap on yourself, you still have to hold on. Don't allow a moment of weakness to cause you to throw your life away.

I'd hoped that the pep talk I'd given myself would make me feel better. Make me feel stronger. But it didn't; I felt worse. Without warning, the floodgates opened and I surrendered to my emotions, dropping my head into my hands and weeping bitterly.

In a moment of complete despair, I reached for my phone and called my old friend, Ahiga.

"I need to talk," I rasped when he picked up.

"Did you use, Malik?"

"No. But I want to."

"Hold on, friend. You don't want to go back to that life—not after all you've accomplished. Give me your location and I'll be there ASAP."

I told him where I was parked and then began reciting the serenity prayer as I waited for him to arrive.

In record time, Ahiga's silver Toyota Tundra came careening into the parking lot. He beckoned me and I got out of my vehicle and slid into the passenger's seat of his. He drove to a nearby Dunkin' Donuts. We went inside and he ordered two large cups of black coffee.

Ahiga tented his fingers and focused his dark brown eyes on me. "What's troubling you, Malik? Marital problems?"

"No, Sasha and I are fine. It's my son, Phoenix."

"Ah!" he said with a knowing twinkle in his eyes. "I'm glad my two children are grown. Teen years are rough. It's a stage in life that I wouldn't want to revisit with my kids. But looking back, I realize that teenagers are hardwired to butt heads with their parents."

"I wish my trouble with Phoenix was something as simple as our butting heads, but it's a much bigger issue. Very serious."

Ahiga narrowed his eyes. "Tell me what's going on."

I took a deep breath and began to unburden myself, confiding to Ahiga all of the ugly and scandalous behavior that Phoenix had exhibited in his short stay in Arizona. I even admitted to my own feelings of guilt, and it felt good to finally talk to someone and get it out of my system.

At the conclusion of the awful tale, I said, "What Phoenix did to his friend, Baxter, borders on criminal activity. If he were a little older, he'd be tossed in prison for sexual misconduct." I groaned at the thought of Phoenix making the National Sex Offender Registry at such a young age.

I searched Ahiga's face. "If he's this heartless, sexually deviant, and deceitful at his young age, what kind of sociopathic behavior can I expect out of him when he's older?"

Ahiga grunted and took a big gulp of coffee. As he pondered my question, we sat in silence. He busied himself, folding a Dunkin' Donuts napkin into various places until it took on the appearance of an interesting geometric design.

Satisfied with his paper creation, he set it in the middle of the table and then gave me his full attention. "Your son is not likely to change for the better without hands-on guidance from his parent, but it sounds to me like you've already given up on him."

"Why do you say that?"

"You sent him back to Philadelphia knowing full well that his people there aren't equipped to deal with his issues."

"I'm not equipped, either!"

"But at least you're able to acknowledge that he has serious problems and needs help. From what you've told me, it doesn't sound like his Philadelphia family, particularly his mother, is willing to face any unfavorable truths about him. In my opinion, you threw in the towel too quickly, Malik."

"I gave him an ultimatum…get therapy or get to packing. What was I supposed to do, handcuff him and march him into a therapy session at gunpoint?"

"First of all, before you label him as sexually deviant, take into consideration that confusion about sexual orientation is perfectly natural."

"But he deliberately targeted someone he perceived as weak. And after he coerced the boy into doing something he didn't want to do, he bullied, shamed, and blackmailed him. And then he had the sheer gall to invite others to join him in taunting a nice kid who had only wanted to be his friend." I shook my head regretfully. "You can't convince me that any of that is typical teenage behavior."

Ahiga smiled gently. "I'm not a shrink, but indulge me and let me play armchair psychologist for a moment."

"Be my guest."

"It seems to me that in order to cope with his conflicted emotions, Phoenix projected his own feelings of shame and self-loathing onto the other boy. It wasn't a wise thing to do, nor was it kind, but I want you to take into consideration that most teenagers are completely self-absorbed; seldom are they wise or kind.

"You have to heal your relationship with your son because he needs you now more than ever. I realize you envisioned stereotypical male-bonding experiences with your kid: fishing, camping, or whatever. Unfortunately, your situation is not that simple. In fact, it's extremely urgent. You have to step up to the plate, Malik, and figure out how to help your son. No more self-pity sessions; there's no time for that. You have to roll up your sleeves and do the work."

"I don't know where to begin," I admitted.

"Begin with a phone call. Assure him that your love is unconditional and you need to apologize for kicking him out of the home."

"I didn't kick him out."

"You know what I mean. You gave him an ultimatum, and that wasn't right. Telling him, *'My way or the highway'* is not how a loving parent responds to a teenager in crisis."

Ahiga was right. When the going got rough, I quickly bailed out. Despite the realization that Phoenix had significant problems, I was willing to let naïve Everett shoulder the responsibility of raising my deeply troubled child.

Knowing what I had to do, I slurped down the rest of my coffee and stood up. "Thanks, buddy. You gave me a lot to think about and I'm going to reach out to Phoenix with a phone call."

"I expect to see you at the next recovery meeting," Ahiga said as we headed for the door. "There's no cure for addiction, Malik. Once an addict, always an addict, and believe me, every major life crisis will make you keenly aware of that fact," he said with a sage expression on his face.

"I'll be at the next meeting. I promise."

CHAPTER 19

A higa drove me back to my car. After he left, I sat in my car thinking about our conversation.

I started the motor, but before pulling off, I gave Phoenix a call. I expected that after seeing my name on the screen, he would decide not to pick up.

Surprisingly, he answered on the second ring.

"Hey, Phoenix. How are you?"

"I'm good."

I couldn't read his tone; he sounded noncommittal. Without a clue as to how he felt about hearing from me, I pressed onward, trying to draw him into a conversation.

"I, uh, wanted to apologize for the way I handled the situation. I made a mistake. I shouldn't have given you an ultimatum. I let you down, and I'm really sorry, Phoenix."

"It's okay, Pops. You didn't let me down," he said with a bit of warmth in his tone that let me know that we were making progress.

As much as I would have liked to skip right over the pain Phoenix had caused Baxter and simply focus on rebuilding our relationship, I couldn't dismiss what Baxter had told me.

"Phoenix," I said and then cleared my throat. "Uh, regarding what you told me about that video with Baxter, I now know that there's more to the story than you admitted."

"I don't know what you're talking about." On the defensive, his voice hardened.

I released a long breath. "Baxter told me that the other male in the video is you."

"He's lying!" Phoenix's voice cracked and went up several pitches. The fear and panic in his tone was painful to hear.

It was unbelievable that in this day and age the stigma surrounding homosexuality still existed, and that stigma was causing my son an incredible amount of anguish.

I chose my next words carefully and spoke them lovingly. "You don't have to pretend to be something you're not. If you're attracted to boys, it's nothing to be ashamed of."

"But I'm not gay," he insisted.

"Then why did you coerce Baxter into giving you…" It was difficult for me to put a name to the sex act. I couldn't bring myself to utter the word *oral*. By no means was I prudish or strait-laced, but talking about adult subject matter with my son was terribly uncomfortable.

I heard a strange noise coming from Phoenix's end of the phone.

"What's going on, Phoenix?"

He didn't answer, but the noise persisted, and I recognized the sound of sniffling.

"Are you crying?"

"No. I'm just upset that you're accusing me of being gay," he said in a trembling voice.

"I'm not accusing you of anything. I want you to know that I love you whether you're straight or gay. Your sexual orientation doesn't matter to me. What matters is your character. The kind of man you turn out to be. Life is confusing for you right now, but I promise you that over time, it's going to get easier. But you've got to be true to who you are and you have to be kinder to others."

The sniffling escalated to full-fledged tears, and I wished that I could have physically given him a hug.

"Hey, hey, hey," I soothed. "It's gonna be all right, Phoenix."

"But I don't like boys, Pops, I swear I don't! I just wanted to know what it felt like to get a BJ. I didn't think Baxter would really do it, but he did. And after it was over, I was so freaked out and disgusted with him and myself that I sort of took it out on him."

"Tell me this…why did you film it if you were so freaked out and disgusted?"

"I don't know. I thought I might want to look at it later."

"Phoenix, you're too young to handle the emotional responsibility of sexual activity, whether it's with a girl or a guy. Do you understand?"

"Yeah, I think so."

"What's upsetting to me is the way you turned on Baxter and vilified him."

"I just wanted to cover myself…protect my reputation in case he decided to blab about it."

"I understand. But I want you to know that the way you handled it was less than honorable. If a man doesn't have personal integrity, he doesn't have anything at all. Believe me, I know what I'm talking about. When I was in my addiction, I started every day trying to figure out how I was going to get high. Manipulating, lying, and stealing were at the top of my list of important personal attributes, while honor, decency, and self-respect were at the very bottom.

"I didn't like myself very much back then, and it took a long time for me to be able to look in the mirror and not cringe." Feeling myself getting choked up, I took a deep breath and swallowed. "Son, you know right from wrong, don't you?"

"Yes," he said quietly.

"Then live in truth. Starting rumors about another person simply to keep the spotlight off of yourself is wrong."

"You're right, and I'm sorry."

"I still think that you need to talk to a professional. Not because I think you're crazy or think something is wrong with you. I feel that therapy sessions would be beneficial in the long run. Your mom wouldn't hesitate to get you counseling if you requested it."

"But…I can't tell her the reason that I want therapy. It's too embarrassing."

"You don't have to tell her about any of this. And you only need to tell the therapist as much as you're comfortable talking about. Over time, as you develop a rapport with him or her, I'm sure you'll start sharing more. A therapist's job is to listen and help you gain insight regarding the things you want to change in your life."

"Okay. I'll do it."

A big smile blossomed on my face. Phoenix wasn't the monstrous individual that I'd made him out to be. He was merely a scared kid who made stupid choices.

"Good choice, and I'm proud of you. By the way, I hope I'll get an opportunity to see you during the Christmas holidays when Sasha, Zoe, and I visit Philly."

"Yeah, you'll see me. Grandma Copeland already told me you were coming."

"Oh, yeah? She told me how thrilled she was that she and my dad finally got to meet you. She couldn't stop raving about how handsome and smart you are. She's real proud that you're fluent in French. Nowadays, you don't find many kids that can speak a second language."

"Did you tell her that attending an all-French-speaking school wasn't my decision? My parents thought it would help me get into Harvard one day."

"No, I didn't tell her that because I didn't realize that you felt forced to attend your school."

"Yeah, I pretty much hate it."

Hearing the joy drain from Phoenix's voice, I switched topics. "So…tell me, is it weird to suddenly acquire an additional set of grandparents?"

"It's not weird at all. I feel like I've always known them. And it's kind of cool seeing myself in them. I never had a close connection with my dad's parents, and now I know why."

"Listen, son. I take the full responsibility for all the lies you've been told. If I'd had my life together, things would have gone in a completely different way. Both your mother and Everett thought they were doing the right thing for you."

"By lying about who I really am?"

I sighed. "Anyway, I'm glad you're developing a relationship with my parents. They have a lot of love in their hearts for you. And so do I. I really love you, Phoenix."

"I know you do, Pops."

I didn't expect a thirteen-year-old to be comfortable throwing the word *love* around, and I was okay with him not saying that he loved me, too. Instinctually, I knew that he did.

We ended the call with the promise to check in with each other at least once a week.

Ever since the incident between Phoenix and Baxter, I'd been depressed and felt disconnected from everyone I loved. I hadn't been the best husband to Sasha or the best father to Zoe. I'd been moody and distant, and the only reason Sasha put up with it was because she knew how badly I was suffering over the estrangement between Phoenix and me. I never told her the details of our riff; I merely told her that Phoenix had a sudden and severe bout of homesickness and wanted to go home.

I could tell that she sensed there was more to the story, but she never pressured me to open up to her.

But now that Phoenix and I had mended the relationship, my brooding was over and I felt like my old self. In fact, I felt better than I had in a long time.

Driving home, there was a huge smile plastered on my face, and my sense of euphoria persisted when I entered the house.

"What are you grinning about?" Sasha inquired, looking amused.

I didn't answer. I simply took her in my arms and hugged her tightly as I lifted her off the floor and swung her around.

"What's going on, Malik?" she asked as she squirmed out of the tight clutch I had around her waist.

"I spoke to Phoenix over the phone, and we're good again."

"You never mentioned that there was anything wrong between you two. You said that his sudden departure was due to being homesick."

"I wasn't totally honest with you, Sasha. We had a disagreement over the bike he wanted me to buy him, and it escalated into a yelling match in the middle of the mall."

The lie rolled off my tongue with surprising ease.

"Why couldn't you tell me that when I asked why he left so abruptly?"

"I was embarrassed."

"Why were you embarrassed?"

"I wanted so desperately to have a great relationship with my son, and I felt like a failure, Sasha," I said. It was a little white lie, but at least my statement was partially true.

However, I was aware that my relationship with the truth had suffered greatly ever since Phoenix had entered our lives, and I promised myself that tonight would be the last time that I was dishonest with Sasha.

With Phoenix back in Philadelphia, I couldn't imagine any circumstances that would motivate me to hide the truth from her, ever again.

Two weeks later, while jogging through our neighborhood, I noticed a gigantic U-Haul in front of the Westfields' house.

"Are you guys moving?" I asked Baxter when he came outside carrying a box to the truck.

"Yeah, my dad thinks it's best for us to make a permanent move to Scottsdale…uh, since he's there most of the time," Baxter said without meeting my gaze.

"Wow! This is pretty sudden. I'm gonna miss you, buddy." I made an exaggerated sad face that was meant to make him laugh, but he didn't crack a smile.

"He thinks that a fresh start will be good for me. You know… after everything that happened."

My heart did a sudden nosedive. "Did you tell your dad about you and Phoenix?" The idea of anyone being aware of the role that Phoenix had played in Baxter's suicide attempt sent me into a panic.

Baxter turned beet red. "No! Of course not. I try not to even think about that anymore. He thinks I slit my wrists because he's hardly ever around."

Immense relief flooded through my system, and my erratic heartbeat calmed down.

"I'm sure your dad knows what's best for you." Awkwardly, I stuck my hands inside the pockets of my running shorts. "Well, I wish you the best, Baxter. Keep your head up, all right?" I patted him on the back, an unspoken apology for the pain and suffering my son had caused him.

Baxter nodded. Clutching the cardboard box, he lumbered over to the truck.

I resumed running.

As my feet pounded against concrete, I wondered if I'd done the right thing by withholding important information from the Westfields.

It bothered me that I had become such a hypocrite. In one breath, I told Phoenix to live in his truth. Yet I had carefully protected him and hid his actions in fear of what people would think of him.

CHAPTER 20

The summer passed quickly and before I knew it, it was the middle of August and the temperature had spiked to 114 degrees, a scorching heat that was unheard of in my hometown. But after so many years of living in the desert, I'd learned to work with the heat. When it was hot like this, my daily run took place right before dawn, and any physical tasks, such as mowing the lawn, had to be accomplished before mid-morning or after the sun went down.

Installing a swimming pool in the back was something that Sasha and I had planned but had never gotten around to it. When I acquired a pool company as a client, I began to think seriously about investing in a pool.

Zoe couldn't swim, and it would be great for her to be able to take lessons in the convenience of our own backyard.

August was a busy time at Sasha's dental practices, and she left the design of the pool and the other particulars up to me. It was an especially stifling-hot afternoon when I paid a visit to the showroom of Diamond Pools and Landscaping. I had a vision of how I wanted the pool and the surrounding area to look, and I hoped that construction, including excavation, wouldn't take more than six weeks.

The climate would still be in the eighties in early October, and we'd be able to enjoy our pool for another month or so before we were hit with winter weather when temperatures plummeted to fifty degrees and sometimes lower.

As I explored the showroom with the sales manager named Arturo, I found myself growing more and more excited, especially after he promised a huge discount due to my business connection with the pool company.

"What about pool cleaning…do you guys handle that?" I asked, finding myself growing more enthused about the idea of jumping in the pool every evening after a hard day's work.

"Sure, we handle pool cleaning, and you'll be happy to know that if you sign the contract today, we'll throw in three months of free pool cleaning service," he informed with a gleaming smile.

I had no idea why it had taken so long to make the decision to get a pool built since we were doing great financially, but now that we had committed to the idea, I was impatient to get the process underway.

Off the bat I knew that I wanted a Pebble Sheen pool, but I had some concerns. Glancing at the Notes app on my phone, I began firing off the questions that I had jotted down. In the middle of listening to Arturo's response, my phone buzzed in my hand, and I was surprised to see that the call was from Elle.

As far as I knew, she wasn't speaking to me. My mood quickly went from surprised to worry as it dawned on me that the only reason she'd call me was if something had happened to Phoenix.

I held up a finger, excusing myself as I took the call, and Arturo politely moved to the other side of the showroom, giving me privacy.

"Hey, Elle. Is everything okay with Phoenix?" I asked anxiously.

"No, it isn't."

"What's wrong?"

"He had a big blowup with Everett. They've been arguing a lot lately, but last night it escalated into a shoving match. I don't know what's wrong with him, Malik, but lately I feel like I don't know him anymore. When he's not brooding and acting sullen, he speaks to us sarcastically and makes spiteful comments."

"It's a phase, Elle. He'll get past it, eventually."

"Eventually sounds like a long time, and I don't know how much longer I can exist in such a hostile environment."

I didn't respond and she let out a breathy sigh of exasperation.

"Making matters worse," she continued, "we received a letter from his school today. They're not inviting Phoenix back for high school."

"Why not?"

"Those thirty days he spent in the hospital really hurt his grades, and he didn't try to improve them when he returned. He lost interest in all of his extracurricular activities, and was basically only taking up space in the classroom. He barely made it out of the eighth grade."

"He told me that he hates that ritzy, prep school. Maybe a more down-to-earth learning environment is exactly what he needs at this stage of his life."

"Well, he says that he wants to attend high school in Arizona, which is the reason for this call."

"What?" I was stunned.

"He says you're the only person who understands him. At this point, Malik, I need a break. That boy is giving me gray hairs. He acts as if he hates me—"

"I'm sure he doesn't hate you, Elle."

"Well, it sure feels like it. For once, I'd like an opportunity to be the parent that he has fun with during holidays and for two weeks during the summer instead of being on the receiving end of his scorn and disgust."

Elle had gone from not wanting me to be involved in our son's life to wanting to turn him over to me permanently. I was both flattered and nervous. I wasn't sure if I was equipped to deal with Phoenix on a daily basis. Facetime and phone calls was a lot easier than helping him figure out his teenage angst as a full-time parent.

But I didn't have a choice. My son needed me, and despite how challenging it might be to raise a complicated teenager, I owed him my full support, and I intended to be there for him.

"I'll have to talk to Sasha before I can give you a definitive answer, but I'm sure she'll be delighted to have him back in Arizona with us. I'll give you a call tomorrow."

After I hung up from Elle, a foreboding feeling hung over me, and I lost interest in selecting a pool design. I went along with everything Arturo suggested, without paying attention to cost, nor was I particular about the materials. We shook on the deal that I half-heartedly agreed to, and afterward I hastily signed on the dotted line.

At home, sitting at the dinner table with Sasha and Zoe, I brought up the topic of Phoenix moving in with us and attending school in our area.

"Yay!" Zoe clapped her hands delightedly. "With my big brother walking with me to the school bus stop, I won't have to worry about big-headed Myron and his sidekick, Aubrey, teasing me and playing stupid pranks on me all the time."

"Why didn't you tell me you were having trouble with those two boys?" Sasha asked with her brows scrunched in displeasure. "Had I known, I would have spoken with their parents months ago."

"It's not that big of a deal, Mom. I was handling those two jerks. If kids don't try to work through their conflicts, they'll never be prepared for the real world," Zoe said, showing a burst of wisdom that defied her nine years.

Sasha and I exchanged glances, both of us impressed by Zoe's insight.

"Since Phoenix is a kid, too, it's okay for him to intervene on my behalf."

"Hmm, I see. In other words, it would be embarrassing if your mother or I made a fuss about those two knuckleheads picking on you, but it's okay if Phoenix sets them straight?"

"Exactly," Zoe agreed. "But mostly I'm looking forward to Phoenix coming back. He left so suddenly, and I wasn't emotionally prepared for him to go. I've really missed him," she said, sounding choked up.

"Aw, Zo-Zo. I've missed him, too," Sasha said, reaching across the table and patting Zoe on the hand.

Later on in bed, Sasha and I discussed the pros and cons of raising a teenage boy.

"His entire identity abruptly changed when he discovered that Everett wasn't his father. I'm not surprised that he's acting out at home and portraying Elle and Everett as the bad guys. They lied to him, and he doesn't understand that they had good intentions and believed they were looking out for his best interests," Sasha said.

"Right. And with so many changes in his life, he needs to continue his therapy sessions when he moves here. It may not fix all of his problems, but certainly couldn't hurt," I added.

"I agree." Sasha softly ran a hand over my shoulder. "It's a big change for all of us, Malik. Maybe we should think about family therapy."

The thought of Phoenix confessing to his involvement in Baxter's suicide attempt in the midst of a family therapy session sent me into a wild panic, but I kept my cool.

"I don't agree, Sasha. I think the focus should be on Phoenix getting help. With the major life changes he's been dealing with,

I feel that he should have a safe and private place to share his innermost feelings without monitoring his words for fear of what we might think of him."

"Again, you're right, honey. But I also think we should revisit the subject of family therapy in about six months, okay?"

"Sure, that's fine."

I pulled Sasha close to me, nuzzling her neck while clinging to her. Sasha had always been an anchor for me. The security of her love was what grounded me and kept me from drifting into the unforgiving and crashing waves that life sometimes brought my way.

Phoenix's flight arrived in early afternoon. This time I went alone to pick him up from the airport. We gave each other a loose embrace that symbolized the distance that had grown between us.

We'd talked easily over the phone these past few months, but there was no denying that we were uncomfortable with each other in person.

"I suppose we're going to have to start all over again," I said, acknowledging the awkwardness we both felt.

"Yeah," he muttered in agreement.

"Your mother is going to ship the rest of your belongings," I said, nodding toward the single duffle bag that he was carrying.

"Yep."

"Oh! By the way, we're having a pool built. It should be completed in about six weeks."

"Cool," he replied without much interest. He inserted the earbuds that dangled around his neck, putting a stop to my attempts to strike up a conversation.

Obviously he no longer perceived me as a buddy that he could talk to. I was officially the un-fun parent, and I realized that I'd have to get used to his disinterested, one-word responses.

CHAPTER 21

Phoenix liked his new school and was doing well both academically and socially. He joined the French club, the cycling team, the debate club, and signed up to volunteer once a month at a local nursing home. I couldn't have been prouder of the way he dove in and became an active member of his school and community. Although he maintained his friendship with Dustin, Matthew, and Ryan, he also made lots of new friends at school.

I was happy to report to Elle that our son was flourishing in Springfield Hills and was always respectful and polite toward Sasha and me.

But I didn't mention that he had become much closer to Sasha and Zoe than he was with me. He had essentially put up a wall between us. I had hoped that his going to therapy would help bridge the gap, but he continued to politely keep me at arm's length.

Although I was hurt, I understood that Phoenix was embarrassed that I knew about his deepest secret.

For his fourteenth birthday, a week before Halloween, I tried to buy his affection by purchasing him a high-priced, high-performance dirt bike that he absolutely loved. But when I suggested getting one for myself and mentioned that it would be nice if the two of us could ride together on Saturday mornings, he frowned so excessively that I instantly walked back the idea.

That was my final attempt at trying to win Phoenix over. I gave up and accepted the annoying-father role that he had assigned me. Zoe still adored me and thought I was cool enough to converse with, so I focused my attention on her.

"When is the pool going to be finished?" Zoe asked as I helped her with some last-minute alterations to her Halloween costume.

I shrugged in disgust. The mere thought of all the things that had gone wrong with building the pool put me in a foul mood. I had hoped that our pool would be finished by now, but the project was stalled due to a misunderstanding between the pool company and an outside contractor who was in charge of installing the plumbing.

Unfortunately, remedying the problem was an excruciatingly slow process, and we were left with a huge hole in the backyard and a network of twisting pipes that snaked into the ground. The pile of dirt that should have covered the pipes had turned into a heap of mud at this point.

Zoe handed me the hot-glue gun and a handful of silver stars. She turned around so that I could affix the stars to the back of her ankle-length, black dress. She was originally supposed to dress as a witch, but changed her mind and decided to be a wizard. We had to hastily glue glow-in-the-dark silver stars to her black witch's hat and dress to give her more of a wizardly appearance.

Working on costumes was usually Sasha's forte, but she was out of town for the next few days, attending a dental conference in Portland, Oregon.

Phoenix peeked into Zoe's room and gave her a thumbs-up.

"You like it?" she asked, twirling around, showing off her glittery face makeup and her blue, synthetic hair.

"You look bomb," he complimented.

"Thank you. It's so fun dressing up; I don't know why you only want to wear a stupid mask," she said with a little frown.

"I'm too old for the full regalia. This is sufficient," he replied, waving a rubber clown mask.

"But you're not too old to accept free candy," she retorted with a smirk.

Phoenix laughed as he turned from the doorway.

Before he galloped down the stairs, Zoe dashed into the hallway. "I saw those egg cartons you hid in the backyard," she said in a whisper that was loud enough for me to hear.

"Sssh!" Phoenix warned, holding a finger up to his lips as he cut his eyes at me.

Pretending not to hear what Zoe said, I became busy, picking up the excess silver stars that had scattered on the floor.

The tradition of egging houses and cars on Halloween was older than me. I'd done it in my day and back then I considered it harmless fun. As an adult I realized that broken eggs could be extremely corrosive to paint surfaces. Glad that I'd gotten a heads-up, I reminded myself to move my vehicle from the driveway and make sure it was safe inside the garage.

Applying a little more pink glitter to Zoe's face was the final touch, and I took lots of pictures before we left the house and joined the swarms of noisy ghosts and goblins that had infiltrated our typically quiet neighborhood.

I walked with Zoe from one house to the next. While she and her two best friends went up to the front doors to collect candy, I stayed behind on the pavement, conversing with other parents who were tasked with trick-or-treat duty.

Most of the younger children were accompanied by a parent, but I did notice that quite a few kids in Zoe's age group were on their own. No matter how safe our neighborhood was, Sasha and I would never allow Zoe to wander freely at night.

As we progressed on our journey, I recognized Phoenix's mask and bike as he and three other masked bike riders rode through the streets, popping wheelies and exhibiting other bike tricks. I didn't see them getting off their bikes and actually trick-or-treating, and I hoped they weren't considering snatching bags filled with candy from any of the younger children.

Bag snatching was a lot easier than walking around and yelling, "Trick-or-treat!" Stealing Halloween candy from smaller kids was yet another mischievous activity that I had participated in during my youth. Knowing that Phoenix and his friends might be up to no good, I kept an eye on the masked trio whenever we were in the same vicinity.

I felt worn out after an hour of walking up and down one street after another. But Zoe and her exuberant friends were just getting started. The group of girls agreed that they wouldn't call it a night until their bags overflowed with goodies.

Indulging my Zo-Zo, I trudged along, wearing a patient smile.

Finally, after two-and-a-half hours of nonstop trick-or-treating, the girls admitted to being tired and were ready to go home.

Under a starry October sky, Zoe and I headed for home. With one hand, I carried her bag that was loaded with treats and with the other, I protectively clasped her hand.

"My science project is due in two days," Zoe mentioned as we walked along.

"So soon? Why'd you wait until the last minute? That's not like you, Zoe."

"Well, I decided to keep it simple this year. I'm making a Cyclone in a Bottle, and it's easy. But the imagery is powerful."

I had no idea what the construction of a Cyclone in a Bottle entailed, but I was certain that tomorrow Zoe would hand me a long list of items that she needed for the project.

"Do me a favor and write your list of the materials you need before you go to bed. I'd rather pick them up in the morning rather than rushing around after work."

"It's a simple experiment, Daddy. We have all of the materials I need around the house."

"Perfect!" I said, smiling down at her fondly, and I didn't balk when she began to swing my arm to and fro as we approached our home.

Zoe suddenly released my hand and pointed upward. "Look! A shooting star, Daddy. Make a wish!"

I closed my eyes and wished that the remainder of Zoe's childhood would be filled with rainbows and unicorns. I vowed to shield her from the ugliness in life for as best I could.

Awakened by a loud and shocking noise, I bolted upright and glanced around the bedroom. My attention was drawn to my phone that I'd placed on the nightstand before falling asleep. The phone was vibrating wildly while emitting a dreadful blaring sound.

I grabbed the phone. It was an Amber Alert, which was unheard of in our upscale and otherwise peaceful neighborhood! I couldn't continue reading the alert without checking on the kids. I dashed to Zoe's bedroom, clicked on the light switch, and let out a breath of relief when I saw her lanky form sleeping peacefully beneath a colorful polka dot comforter.

Next I checked on Phoenix. Sleeping with his headphones on, it was satisfying to see that he was safe and sound in his bed as well.

With both my children accounted for, I returned to my bedroom and continued reading the grim news. The child, seven-year-old Taylor Flanagan, was wearing a Wonder Woman costume and red boots when she was last seen outside her home on Birchwood

Circle. She weighed forty-nine pounds and had brown hair and hazel eyes.

As the reality of the news set in, I dragged my fingers down my face. A child who lived only a few blocks from our home had been abducted while hordes of people had drifted along the streets, unsuspecting that danger lurked. Nothing like this had ever happened in our city and I couldn't begin to imagine what the little girl's parents were going through.

I called Sasha and woke her up. She let out a frightened shriek when I told her the news.

"Is Zoe okay?"

"Yes, she's fine."

"And Phoenix?"

"They're both fine. Neither knows about this yet. I'll tell them in the morning."

"I don't understand how something like this could have happened. Where were the child's parents? Why'd they let her out of their sight?"

"I don't have any information, but I'm sure we'll find out a lot more tomorrow."

"This is horrible, Malik. There's no way I'm going to be able to get back to sleep after hearing this news. And I can't stay in Oregon knowing that a child predator might be on the loose in our community. I'm going to cut this conference short and take the first flight out of here in the morning. I think we should keep the kids home from school tomorrow. Can you ask Weston to handle your workload, so you can stay with the kids?"

"Yeah, that's not a problem."

"Okay, honey, I'll see you soon."

When we ended our call, I knew that I wouldn't be able to get back to sleep, either. I padded down the stairs and turned on the kitchen light. After tapping the touch screen of the Keurig coffee maker, I stared out the kitchen window with a thousand thoughts flitting through my mind.

How could anyone harm an innocent child? Did Taylor know her abductor? Would she be found alive?

CHAPTER 22

We'd never been considered a tightknit community since most of the residents kept to themselves. But today the entire community had come together to help search for Taylor Flanagan. Some were merely gawkers, drawn to the scene by the flashing lights of police cars, but most people earnestly wanted to do what they could to help.

Many parents had thought like Sasha and had kept their children home from school. Along with their parents, the children pitched in, helping to hand out fliers and put up posters.

Not only were the police swarming in full force, but there was also a private search and rescue team that the missing child's family had hired.

Noisy helicopters hovered above as newspaper journalists mingled with the crowd, asking questions. Local TV news personalities, with microphones in hand, were eager to interview anyone who was willing to talk.

The entire scene was surreal, and I looked around in wonderment at the yellow tape that blocked off the lawn of the missing girl's home, preventing citizens from wandering onto an active crime scene. It was something that I normally observed on TV crime shows, and the yellow tape looked out of place and foreign in our cozy neighborhood.

"Do the police have any leads?" I asked as I sidled up to Tessa Jordan, a middle-aged woman who had lived in the community for most of her life and who made it her business to know something about every member of the community.

"No, they don't have any leads, at least not yet. I heard they used tracker dogs in the wee hours of the morning, but the dogs lost the child's scent right outside her home."

"Do you know who escorted Taylor around the neighborhood last night?" I asked.

"Not her lazy mother, that's for sure," Tessa spat. "I heard that a fourteen-year-old babysitter accompanied Taylor while she was out trick-or-treating. The babysitter and one of her girlfriends insisted that they walked Taylor to her door, but they got distracted and didn't witness her enter the home. According to them, she waved goodbye and that was the last they saw of her."

"It only takes a second for a child to be abducted," I said gravely.

"The mother, Heather Flanagan, is single. She's a widow. She was married to an older man, and he died of cancer. He left her that lovely home, and rumor has it that he left all of his money to his only child, Taylor. Believe me, it wasn't Heather who paid for the private search team."

"No? I heard on the local news early this morning that the Flanagans paid for the private search party."

"Right! Heather's not a Flanagan by blood. The child's family on her father's side put up the money for that service."

"I see."

"By the way, Heather has a boyfriend." Tessa gave me a significant look.

I showed no emotion.

"He has long hair, tattoos, and rides a motorcycle," she added with a twist to her lips.

"Hmm," I murmured. The noncommittal utterance was my way of showing interest without passing judgment.

"As we speak, the police have the boyfriend down at the station for questioning. They have Heather down there, too." Speaking confidentially, Tessa lowered her voice. "They're both persons of interest at this point, and I wouldn't be the least bit surprised if those two did something awful to that child in order to get their hands on her inheritance."

Tessa hadn't wasted any time in coming up with a scandalous theory. Not wanting to be associated with someone who was eager to spread vicious rumors, I inched away from her.

The entire time she'd been talking, I kept my eyes glued on Zoe as she handed out fliers. I motioned for Zoe to join me as I meandered over to a woman holding a clipboard and giving out assignments to members of the search party. There had to be something that I could do that was more interesting than handing out fliers.

As a family we planned to volunteer our time and effort for as long as our help was needed. Unfortunately, Sasha hadn't been able to get an early flight from Portland, and she wasn't expected to arrive home until early evening.

I would have preferred that Phoenix worked alongside Zoe and me, so that I could keep an eye on him and know for certain that he was safe. But he chose to join a few other high-schoolers, who were using their dirt bikes to traverse the hilly area of the woods, searching for the little girl.

While waiting in a long line to find out how I could help the search party, my phone jangled in my pocket. It was a number that wasn't in my contact list, and I answered with a question mark in my voice.

The caller turned out to be a new contractor that said he'd like to get started running the plumbing system and building the pool's frame. He assured me that if he could get started today, he'd be ready to pour the concrete in less than a week.

The excitement about building a swimming pool had diminished with the long delay, and now with a missing child so close to home, I felt more aggravated than delighted about the prospect of strange men traipsing through my backyard on a daily basis.

The entire neighborhood was on high alert regarding strangers, and I was inviting them in. With all the money I'd already sunk into the pool project, I had no choice but to move forward and allow the contractor and his workers to get the job finished.

Sasha and I would have to sit down and have a long talk with Phoenix and Zoe and reiterate the rules of stranger danger.

Zoe and I hopped in my car and I slowly drove past the unified crowd of people who stood outside a tent, which was the temporary headquarters for the "Find Taylor" committee. As we cruised through the streets, we noticed how our neighborhood had changed overnight. Yellow ribbons encircled telephone poles and trees, as well as posters that bore Taylor's photographic image.

"What do the yellow ribbons represent?" Zoe asked.

"They symbolize the community's belief that Taylor will come home soon."

"Suppose she doesn't."

"She will," I said, patting Zoe's hand. "We have an excellent police force, and they won't leave a stone unturned until they bring her back, safe and sound."

The words sounded hollow as they emerged from my mouth. I was well aware that every minute that Taylor Flanagan was missing diminished her chances for survival.

Designed to be a cheerful display of community solidarity, the yellow ribbons were actually heartachingly sad. Picking up speed,

I whizzed past the sorrowful reminders that one of our children was missing, and most likely wouldn't be found alive.

At home I shook hands with the contractor named Raymond, a chubby guy with a thick head of yellowish hair and a weather-beaten face, no doubt from years of working in the sun. Raymond introduced his two-man crew, Fred and Timothy.

Timothy didn't waste any time bringing up the topic of last night's child abduction.

"We heard about it on the news, and saw the posters and yellow ribbons on our way here. Do the police have any leads?" Fred inquired, his eyes twinkling in his eagerness to receive firsthand information from a member of the very community where Taylor Flanagan lived.

"As far as I know, the police don't have any leads yet. I didn't know the child, but that doesn't make it any less tragic. For an innocent kid to go missing here in Springfield Hills is unheard of." As I spoke, I noticed the three men leaning in, not wanting to miss a single word of the salacious story.

I instantly clammed up.

I wasn't comfortable sharing information with virtual strangers. For all I knew, one of them could very well have been involved. Everyone was a suspect until the police announced that they had taken someone into custody.

I steered the conversation back to the issue of pool plumbing, and looks of disappointment were evident on their faces.

"Daddy! I can't find any duct tape, and I need it for my science project," Zoe yelled from the patio.

"Okay, I'll find it. Give me a second."

I returned my attention to Raymond. "How much longer is this project going to take?"

"I can't give you a definitive answer because a lot goes into building a pool, but I can tell you I checked and it looks like the previous contractor completed most of the plumbing. All we have to do is haul out the mud pile that was left behind. Bring in some fresh dirt and cover up those pipes. You'll be ready for the concrete pour by the end of today or no later than tomorrow."

"So, maybe I'll be able to get a swim in before it gets too cold?" I asked hopefully.

"Anything is possible," he said, deliberately not committing to a time frame. I supposed his evasive reply was payback for me not indulging his curiosity about the Taylor Flanagan case.

Raymond checked his watch. "Ready for lunch, fellas?"

I couldn't believe it. They'd only been here for about thirty minutes and were already taking a break. Shaking my head, I headed for the backyard shed to look for duct tape for Zoe.

The moment I stepped inside, I noticed that some of my yard tools had been disturbed. The rake was propped against the wall at a slant, and I always kept it in a perfect upright position. The lawn mower had been moved about two feet from its normal location.

Scratching my head, I looked around wondering if a thief had gotten inside and stolen anything. A cursory glance didn't reveal any missing items, but something wasn't right.

The stepladder was marked with muddy footprints that were too small to be mine. Besides, I was a neat person, and being very particular about my tools and other possessions, I would have never left mud tracks inside the shed.

Looking for duct tape, I climbed the ladder and searched inside a cabinet that contained neatly stacked boxes of assorted nails and screws. I found the tape, but noticed that above the boxes was an alcove that was hard to reach. In that darkened area, something red caught my eye. I stretched my arm and fingers to the point of discomfort as I attempted to get a grip on the strange red object. Using my fingertips, I grabbed ahold of it and yanked.

In a state of disbelief, I gawked at the child-sized red boot that I held in my hand. It was such an unexpected and disturbing sight, I flung it from my hand and winced at the sound of it crashing against a shovel, causing it to hit the floor with a metallic clatter.

A combination of shock and fear caused a sharp spike in my adrenaline levels. Feeling lightheaded, I teetered on the ladder. I pressed a palm to my chest and took in a deep, cleansing breath, but it didn't help. Perspiration trickled down my face, and I gripped the sides of the ladder before carefully descending the steps.

When I reached the bottom rung, I collapsed against a wall. Panting, I cut an eye toward the red boot. It was such an innocent object, yet it possessed the same amount of threat as a gun pressed to my head.

I felt cornered. Trapped. Terrified.

Motivated solely by instinct, I gathered my wits and rushed to the spot where the boot had landed. I picked it up and wondered if the mate was also hidden somewhere inside the shed.

Frantic, I searched every nook and cranny of the shed, but I didn't find the other red boot.

Panting and sweating as if running a marathon, I encased the boot in a piece of dark fabric that had been wrapped around a collection of wrenches and pliers. I secured the cloth with the black duct tape that Zoe needed for her science project.

Lugging a bag of soil, I exited the shed and threw the cloth-covered red boot inside the deep hole. I poured in enough soil to conceal the damning evidence, and then I returned to the shed and stuck the open bag of soil next to a five-gallon container of paint.

I dusted off dirt from my hands as I left the shed, and I

wondered if a three-hundred-dollar tip would persuade Raymond and his crew to finish the job today.

When Sasha arrived home that evening, I greeted her with a quick kiss. Not wanting Zoe to overhear our conversation, I motioned for her to follow me upstairs to the privacy of our bedroom.

Although I was devastated by my discovery in the shed, I tried my best to hide my anxiety. With a steady voice and a calm demeanor, I brought Sasha up to speed regarding the abduction, and shared with her the information that Tessa Jordan had shared.

"Do you mean to tell me that the child was snatched right outside of her own front door?" Sasha said with horror in her tone as she shook her head incredulously.

I nodded distractedly. With my thoughts focused on the child's red boot that I'd discovered, it was difficult to keep up my end of the conversation.

"You're awfully quiet, Malik. How can you be so calm at a time like this?" she asked. "What happened to Taylor Flanagan is every parent's worst nightmare, and until they catch the guy who's responsible, I'm not going to have a moment's peace."

"I'm upset, too, Sasha. In fact, after being out there in the heart of the search with tracker dogs and helicopters whirring, the reality that there's a real-life monster on the loose has me on edge, but I don't want the kids to know how shaken up I actually am."

"They should know," she snapped. "And they should be equally upset. We can't sugarcoat a situation like this. The first few hours after a child is abducted are the most critical, and little Taylor has been missing for almost twenty-four hours. I hate to say it, but Taylor is probably already dead," Sasha said, her voice cracking.

"We don't know that," I soothed. "She could very well be one of the kids who beat the odds. She could be hidden away in some remote place…but still very much alive. I prefer to be optimistic, Sasha."

"Optimism is not helpful at a time like this. I think we should be up-front with Phoenix and Zoe and present them with the worst-case scenario, so that they know it's imperative to follow safety tips. We have to ratchet up our own supervision of them and set boundaries about the places they can go."

"I don't know if scaring the hell out of them is the right thing. Sure, we want them to be cautious, but we don't want them to be overly fearful and anxious."

Sasha eyed me curiously. "What's gotten into you, Malik? If there was ever a time to be overly cautious, that time is now. We can't watch over them every second of the day, and for their own protection, they need to be on high-alert. We have to sit them down and go over the basics on how to avoid and—if necessary— how to escape potentially dangerous situations."

"You're right. My mind is all over the place. I have this thing— this desire to preserve Zoe's innocence, but I'm obviously being ridiculous." I made an apologetic face.

"You're not being ridiculous," Sasha said in a softened tone. "You've always been a doting parent to Zoe, but I need you to get tough and support me in laying down the law to her—and Phoenix, too."

"Yeah," I muttered disinterestedly as my mind wandered back to the red boot I'd found. "Uh, about that talk with Phoenix and Zoe. It might not be a good idea to lecture them together. Phoenix is at that age where he's a know-it-all, and he'll probably try to blow us off when we speak to him about taking extra safety precautions. To get through to him, I may have to pepper my words with profanity and possibly grab him by the collar and scare some sense into him. That said, I prefer to speak to him privately."

Sasha nodded. "I get it, Malik. Teenagers think they're invincible, and they think their parents' concerns are baseless and unreasonable." Sasha looked down at her watch. "Where is Phoenix, by the way? Shouldn't he be home by now?"

"I texted him about twenty minutes ago. He's still out with his friends, searching the woods. He wanted to stick around for the candlelight vigil that's being held tonight, but I told him to wrap things up and start heading for home."

Sasha joined Zoe in the dining room where she was practicing her science experiment.

I paced in the living room as I waited for Phoenix, periodically peeking through the curtains, and then continuing to pace. At last I saw his bike lights and reflectors, and I hurried outside.

The moment he hopped off his bike, I nodded toward the car and gruffly said, "Get in."

"Wait. Can I lock up my bike, first?" There was irritation in his tone.

"Funny how you were never concerned about securing Baxter's bike whenever you borrowed it. You simply tossed it on the ground like it had no value."

Phoenix flinched at the mention of Baxter's name. We had an unspoken agreement not to talk about Baxter because it made Phoenix uncomfortable. But tonight I relished the opportunity to break our pact, and I took pleasure in seeing Phoenix's wounded expression.

"Where are we going?" he asked snappishly.

I backed out of the driveway without bothering to answer him.

"Where are we going?" he repeated.

"To the convenience store."

"For what?"

"We're out of dish detergent."

He grimaced like there was a bad taste in his mouth. "And you need me to go with you because…?"

"Because we need to talk."

"Oh, God! What did I do now?" His voice was testy and filled with theatrical persecution. "Seriously, what are you accusing me of this time?" he asked while smirking at me.

"I found Taylor Flanagan's red boot," I said with a calm demeanor. However, my words had power, and they knocked the pompous smirk right off his face.

CHAPTER 23

Phoenix's eyes widened in shock. "I didn't do anything! It's not what you think, Pops."

"Tell me why a child's fuckin' boot was hidden in the goddamn shed?" Uncharacteristically, I hurled profanities and bellowed in a voice so loud, Phoenix nearly jumped out of his skin.

His lips began to tremble, but I didn't feel a shred of compassion. He had lied repeatedly and used my unconditional love for him to play me. No more! I was through being Mr. Nice Guy.

I balled my fist up and shook it in his face. "I'm two seconds from busting you in your mouth, so start talking, you little bastard."

Having never seen the side of me that was coarse and street-hardened from my junkie years, Phoenix recoiled in shock and fear.

"I...I...found the boot in the woods, underneath a log. I was going to turn it over to the police, but I figured, why get involved and possibly become a suspect when it might not even belong to the missing girl? I hid it because I didn't know what else to do—I was scared."

"Stop it!" I shouted. "It's crystal-clear that you're lying. If you can't convince me that you're telling the truth, how the hell are you going to convince the police?"

"I'm not lying. What reason would I have to hurt a little girl?"

I had no idea why he'd hurt a small child, and a part of me believed that he'd happened upon the boot like he'd said and decided to keep it. But for what reason would he bring it home and hide it? An innocent person wouldn't want any part of a victim's belongings. But then again, teenagers sometimes harbored morbid thoughts. Maybe he thought it would be fun to show it off to his friends—a way to freak them out, just for laughs.

Phoenix sat next to me, nervously zipping and unzipping the front of his hoodie. "Are you going to turn me in?"

"I'm confused and angry that you'd do something so stupid as bringing home evidence in something as serious as a missing child case. But I'm still your parent, and I love you no matter what." I sucked in a deep breath. "I got rid of the boot."

There was a flicker of something in Phoenix's eyes. It could have been relief. It also could have been disappointment. The flicker happened too quickly for me to identify the emotion he was feeling.

"If you have any other articles of the child's clothing, you need to tell me now. I won't be able to help you if you continue to lie to me."

"I only had the boot. That's it. That's all I found."

Feeling calmer, I drove to the store and left Phoenix in the car while I went inside and picked up dish detergent. We rode back home in silence, but after I pulled into the driveway, I reached over and squeezed his shoulder. It was my way of letting him know that I intended to stand by him no matter what.

If he was indeed, the monster that I was afraid he might be, then I had to protect him. He was my flesh and blood, and he was my responsibility.

In our effort to supervise the children more closely, Sasha and I decided to take turns driving them to and from the bus stop every day. We also coordinated our work schedules, so that we could donate a few hours a day to the search party.

On our way to the bus stop, Phoenix carried Zoe's science project to the car. After Zoe was strapped in the backseat, he carefully handed her the Cyclone in a Bottle experiment. From the rearview mirror, I watched how Phoenix and Zoe interacted. He was a patient and protective big brother, and his gentle treatment of her assured me that he couldn't have possibly done anything to endanger an innocent seven-year-old.

"Wow, look at Myron's eye," Zoe said enthusiastically as she pointed to one of the boys who taunted her regularly. "It looks like the bully got a taste of his own medicine."

"Yep, I'm sure he got what he deserved," Phoenix replied stoically.

I gazed out my window and saw that Myron was sporting a black eye. I shot an accusing look at Phoenix, and he shrugged like he had no idea what had happened to the boy.

But I knew better. I knew instinctively that Phoenix was responsible. Hell, I would have gladly beaten the crap out of those two kids if there wasn't the risk of facing criminal charges.

Phoenix reached for the door handle and I clutched his arm. I wanted to congratulate him for sticking up for Zoe, but that would have sent the wrong message and given him the impression that I approved of physical violence.

"You made your point, so make sure you don't touch the other boy," I said in a lowered tone.

He scowled. "I didn't hit that boy. I wouldn't lay a hand on either of those stupid little kids."

I released his arm and sighed.

If he would lie about something that I wasn't concerned about, then he'd certainly lie about any involvement in the disappearance of a child.

Not knowing the truth had placed me on an emotional roller coaster. My heart ached for the little girl and her family, and I desperately wanted the child to be okay. But at the same token, I was terrified for Phoenix's well-being.

If my son turned out to be responsible in any way, the residents of the town would be out for bloodshed and who could blame them? Over and over, I asked myself if Phoenix was a sicko and a killer or was it truly a lapse in judgment that prompted him to hang on to evidence as if it were a trophy?

If I wanted to get to the truth badly enough, I could have beaten a confession out of him, but knowing the truth came with consequences. If my conscience compelled me to turn him in, Phoenix's life would essentially be over, and our family's reputation would be tarnished forever.

Sitting behind the steering wheel, I kept a watchful eye on Zoe as she climbed aboard the elementary school bus. I continued sitting with the motor idling when the middle school bus arrived, and I didn't drive away until I saw Phoenix take a seat on the bus that was headed to the city's high school.

Before rejoining the search party, I stopped at home and watched as concrete was poured inside the gaping hole in our backyard. Feeling immensely relieved that Phoenix's secret was safe, I left the house.

There was an undercurrent of tension when I reached Birchwood Circle and I wondered if there'd been any new developments since yesterday. I scanned the crowd and spotted Tessa Jordan and made my way in her direction. From Tessa I found out that Heather Flanagan was scheduled to give a statement in ten minutes.

"See that fellow with the suit on?" Tessa asked, pointing to a balding man with a bushy mustache. "That's Heather's lawyer, and he set up this little press event, allegedly to keep Taylor's name and face in the news, but I think he's trying to soften Heather's image. People are noticing that she doesn't seem to be grieving like a normal mother. If it were my child, I'd have to be put on medication and hospitalized until somebody brought her back home. Heather, on the other hand, has been acting like she doesn't have a care in the world."

"What makes you say that?"

"One of the photographers that's been roaming around here used a long-lens camera and was able to get a video of Heather and the boyfriend relaxing on the patio, laughing and drinking Tequila. Some grieving mother." Tessa rolled her eyes, conveying her disgust.

I found a bit of comfort in Tessa's comments. It was becoming more and more clear that Heather Flanagan was not the least bit distraught over the disappearance of her daughter.

And she had a motive—money.

Phoenix, however, had absolutely no reason to want Taylor dead.

Tessa elbowed me, bringing me out of my reverie. "Here she comes," she hissed.

A microphone and stand had been set up on the pavement in front of the Flanagan home. As Heather approached it, I instantly noticed that she'd lightened her hair and changed it to a more glamorous style. She was being depicted as an uncaring mother, and her ripped jeans and off-the-shoulder top didn't help her image.

"Can you believe that tramp? She obviously loves being in the limelight," Tessa said, pursing her lips in disapproval.

"I want to thank everyone for pitching in and helping in the effort to bring my baby home safely," Heather began. "I am heart-broken over this tragedy. And I want to appeal to whoever is responsible for snatching my child. Let her go. I can only imagine how terrified she is. If you're watching, Taylor, I want you to know that Mommy loves you, and I'll never find peace until I'm holding you in my arms again."

She covered her face and made sobbing sounds, and when she removed her hands, it was apparent that her eye makeup was not tear-streaked or smudged.

"Taylor was my best friend," she continued. "We did everything together...played with her dolls, baked cookies; we even dressed in mother and daughter outfits on many occasions." Heather smiled wistfully, as if recalling fond memories that she'd shared with her daughter.

"If you did everything together, why didn't you personally take her out for Halloween?" someone yelled from the crowd.

"I bet you can't wait to collect Taylor's money," someone else jeered.

Heather swiveled her head from one side to the other, trying to determine who had hurled insults at her.

"For those of you who are spreading vicious rumors and insinuating that my boyfriend, Cory, and I are responsible for Taylor's disappearance, I can only say that there's a special place in hell for you," she barked, her face twisted in anger.

From the crowd, more people spoke up, demanding to know what Heather had done with Taylor's body.

"I don't have to take this shit!" Heather spat, practically snarling at the crowd. Her long-haired and tattooed boyfriend escorted her back to the house, and her lawyer took over the press conference.

From my perspective, Heather Flanagan did not appear to be a grieving parent, and I found myself wholeheartedly agreeing with the consensus that she was guilty as sin.

I helped with the search for two hours and then went to work. When I returned home at nightfall, I learned that there were no new developments.

Sitting up in bed, Sasha and I watched the local news channel, and we both peered at the TV intently when images of Heather's press conference from earlier in the day flashed across the screen.

Sasha's mouth was gaped open as she listened to Heather speak. "I can't believe she mimicked crying sounds, trying to get the public's sympathy. It's painfully obvious that she doesn't care."

"I got the same impression while I was out there today. I'm starting to feel foolish for participating in a search for a child we'll probably never find. Cory, her boyfriend, has a sinister look. He seems to be the type that wouldn't hesitate to choke the life out of a child and then toss her body in the river."

Sasha visibly shivered. "That poor little girl didn't stand a chance with that mother of hers." She turned toward me and touched my hand. "But we can't allow our suspicions to stop us from searching for her, Malik."

"I know."

I clicked off the TV and snuggled close to my wife, comforted by her sweet smell and her warm, soft body. While waiting for sleep to overtake me, I wrestled with the idea of pulling Phoenix from the search party. God forbid if he ran across another item of clothing and once again did something stupid.

Then again, his absence from the search might cause people to look at him suspiciously, and I doubted if I'd be able to conduct myself in a calm manner if the police came snooping around here and asking questions.

Even though the red boot would never be found, I wasn't a hundred percent certain that the mate wasn't hidden somewhere on our property.

The thought of it turning up at a most inappropriate time gave me the shivers.

CHAPTER 24

A month elapsed without any sign of Taylor.

Despite all the accusations made against Heather and her boyfriend, there was no proof that they were involved. With no arrests and no viable suspects, the case was swiftly going cold, and many members of the community no longer expected to see the child alive again.

Wanting closure and determined to make someone pay for the crime, an infuriated neighbor spray-painted the words, "Child Killer," on Heather's garage door. People shouted epithets at her whenever she had the audacity to show her face in public, and demanded to know where she'd hidden her daughter's body.

Rumor had it that Heather was trying to pressure the state into providing her with a death certificate for Taylor, so that she could collect the child's inheritance. But without a body, there wasn't any proof that a death had actually occurred.

Residents insinuated that if Heather wanted the money badly enough, sooner or later, she'd figure out a way to lead the police to Taylor's remains without implicating herself.

By the time the Christmas season rolled around, the search parties grew smaller, the posters began to wither and curl at the edges, and the bright yellow ribbons had turned a dull beige color. Other than a balloon-release ceremony to remember Taylor on her birthday in early December, there weren't very many gatherings in her name anymore.

Our family had planned to spend the holiday vacationing in Philadelphia. Although each of us could have benefited from spending some time away from Springfield Hills, my parents were so obvious in their show of favoritism toward Phoenix that Sasha and I concluded that a visit to their home wouldn't be healthy for Zoe's self-esteem.

Phoenix, however, planned to make a solo trip. He wanted to spend some time with Elle and Everett, and I was secretly delighted to get a break from him. I'd been watching him like a hawk since the day I'd discovered the red boot, and had grown weary of keeping tabs on him and putting up with his sighs and eye rolls whenever I questioned him about his whereabouts.

I'd also begun to develop sleuthing skills, and often spied on Phoenix, checking his phone and other electronic devices for clues that would reveal if he was unbalanced and criminal minded. I was so convinced that he was leading a double life that I sometimes tailed him in my car. I needed to see with my own eyes that he was actually hanging out with his friends as he claimed and wasn't at a clandestine location chopping up a body or secretly admiring the Wonder Woman costume that belonged to a dead little girl.

Suspecting that my son had killed Taylor Flanagan kept me on edge, and I was constantly on the verge of pleading with him to tell me where he'd hidden her body. The main reason I wanted to know was so that I could get rid of any incriminating evidence that he may have foolishly left behind.

Despite my fatherly intuition that pointed to Phoenix as the killer, he appeared to be as innocent as a lamb. He engaged in normal teenage activities, and I never caught him doing anything that was even remotely sinister. He continued to keep up with his therapy sessions, he helped around the house, and was excelling at school.

From all appearances, Phoenix was a well-adjusted adolescent boy.

But I still needed a break from him. I needed cessation from chronic worry. Not a day went by that I didn't wonder if I was raising a psychopathic serial killer.

A week before Christmas, I happily drove Phoenix to the airport. He was much more animated and talkative than usual, and I attributed it to him being excited about seeing Elle and Everett.

"Guess what, Pops?"

"What?"

"Matt's grandfather lives on a ranch—about five miles from our house. He offered to give me horseback riding lessons if it's okay with you."

"It's fine with me as long as you don't try to convince me to buy you a horse," I said, trying to make a joke.

"I wouldn't ask for a horse. I don't actually need to own one. Matt's grandfather has two large stables filled with horses, and he said I can ride whichever one I like whenever I visit. Matt's been riding horses since he was a little kid, and he can't believe that I've never ridden one."

"You catch on quickly to anything you put your mind to. You'll be an excellent rider in no time."

"Thanks for the vote of confidence," he said with a smile. In that moment, I saw a light in his eyes that glimmered with child-like joy, and I felt ashamed of myself for mistrusting him and for even thinking that there was a possibility that he was a murderer.

I was sure that Heather Flanagan was the real killer, and it was only a matter of time before the truth came out.

It was time for me to stop expecting the worst out of Phoenix and to stop allowing the secret we shared to destroy our relationship before it had time to blossom. It was also time for me to start giving Phoenix the benefit of the doubt regarding his innocence, instead of waiting for the other red boot to turn up.

Exhaling audibly, I returned his smile.

This was a new beginning for us, and I could feel a positive shift occurring.

"I'm gonna miss you, kid," I said sincerely.

"Don't get mushy, Pops. I'll only be gone for ten days."

"I know, but I'm still gonna miss you."

Springtime in Arizona began in early March. Despite the fickle heat that sometimes shot up to a hundred, it was a time of the year that I'd come to appreciate and love.

There was no comparing March in Philly, with its cold, biting wind known as "The Hawk," with spring in Arizona when the lemon, orange, and grapefruit trees bloomed, filling the air with a wonderful, citrusy perfume.

Due to unseasonably warm days, our family was able to get an early start in enjoying our lovely, new pool. Zoe's swimming lessons weren't scheduled to begin until May, but in the meantime, we all pitched in, trying to teach her how to float.

But our efforts weren't very successful. She admitted to a fear of drowning and said she was too terrified to even attempt to hold her breath and submerge her head in water.

"But you love the rides at water parks," Sasha reminded her.

"That's different. You only get splashed at the water park, and you don't have to try to swim underwater."

I suspected that Zoe's fear of drowning was merely a phase. In no hurry to learn how to swim, she seemed content to splash around in the pool with an inflatable ring encircling her body for the rest of her life. Sasha and I didn't think we should force her to do something that terrified her, and there was a strong possibility that we would cancel her upcoming swim classes in May.

From my home office, I enjoyed hearing the gleeful sounds of Phoenix and Zoe playing around in the pool. Often Phoenix would pretend to be a shark, swimming underwater, playfully nipping at Zoe's ankles and legs. Her squeals of delight verified that the high cost of building a pool had been worth every dollar.

One day while the two of them were in the pool and while I stared at my computer monitor, reading up on tax tips for small business owners, I noticed that the kids were unusually quiet. Assuming they'd tired of the pool and were stretched out on towels, sunbathing, I ventured to the window to check on them.

My eyes nearly popped out of my head when I viewed Phoenix with his palm placed on top of Zoe's head, forcibly holding her underwater.

Hyperventilating with fear for Zoe, I knocked over a wastebasket as I raced to the backyard. Running at full speed, I zoomed down the hallway and out the kitchen door. By the time I reached the backyard, Phoenix had allowed her to come up for air. Looking tortured, the poor child was wild-eyed and gasping for breath by the time I made it to the edge of the pool.

"What the hell is wrong with you, Phoenix? Are you out of your mind?" I was dangerously close to hauling off and clocking him in the face, but I somehow managed to restrain myself.

"I'm okay, Daddy. Really, I'm okay," Zoe sputtered as she simultaneously tried to assure me of her well-being while also trying to recover from being forced to endure her worst fear.

"Chill, Pops. I was only trying to help her," Phoenix said with a stunned expression as if I was behaving like an irrational, crazy man.

"If you ever do anything like that to her again, I'll break your fuckin' neck...do you hear me?" Spittle flew from my lips, and I was practically foaming at the mouth as I took angry steps toward him.

"Daddy, your language," Zoe shouted, covering her ears.

Ignoring her protestations, I pointed a finger at Phoenix as I revved myself up, ready to continue my tirade.

"Stop it, Daddy. Please. Phoenix didn't do anything wrong. I asked him to help me learn how to hold my breath under water. I wanted to surprise you and Mommy by overcoming my fear."

My anger was replaced with shame, and I couldn't meet Phoenix's eyes. I wanted to tell him I was sorry for jumping to conclusions, but instead of expressing regret for my violent reaction, I inexplicably continued to chastise him.

"I don't care if she asked for your assistance. You should have used better judgment before you held her head under water."

"Man!" he uttered in frustration. "I can't win with you. You blame me for everything...whether I'm right or wrong, and it's never gonna change." He jumped out of the pool and wrapped a towel around his waist. "If you don't mind, I'd like to go to the ranch and spend some time with the horses. Is that okay with you?" he asked snidely.

"Go ahead," I mumbled in a tone that suggested that I didn't care where the hell he went.

"And this time, don't bother following me because you're a lousy detective."

I was surprised that Phoenix had known all along that I followed him, and the realization scorched my cheeks with red-hot embarrassment.

"What's Phoenix talking about?" Zoe asked.

"Nothing that concerns you, honey," I mumbled. "Hey, you're starting to shrivel up like a prune," I said, changing my tone from furious to cheerful. "It's time to get out of the water. Okay, Zo-Zo?"

She nodded hesitantly as she watched Phoenix stomp toward the house. She turned her head in my direction and gazed at me questioningly.

I shrugged as if Phoenix was being overly dramatic for no reason.

I should have run behind him and expressed a sincere apology. I also should have brought to his attention the fact that I had stopped following him way back in December.

But I didn't.

After the pool incident, the gap between Phoenix and me widened even more. Due to my ego and my pride, I did nothing to repair our badly damaged relationship.

CHAPTER 25

After a week of avoiding each other and barely speaking, the tension between Phoenix and me did not dissipate.

"How long is this thing with you and Phoenix going to last?" Sasha asked one morning as we were having coffee and preparing for the day.

"What thing?"

"The rift."

"What rift?"

She sucked her teeth in exasperation. "Zoe told me that you jumped all over Phoenix for no reason while they were playing in the pool last week."

"I had good reason. He was dunking her head under water, knowing full well that she has a fear of drowning."

"But you were told that it was Zoe's idea."

"Zoe's only nine years old, and—"

"She'll be ten next week," Sasha reminded me.

"My point is she's too young to know the proper ways to overcome her fear. You should have seen her face when he finally let her up. A swim instructor would never use such a cruel method on a student."

"But he's not a swim instructor; he's just a kid. Don't you think you're being a little hard on him?"

"Not really."

"Zoe told me that she asked him not to let her up until thirty seconds had elapsed."

"I don't care what Zoe told him. He should have known better than to go along with it."

"You're being unusually stubborn."

"If Zoe told him to count to thirty while she jumped off a cliff, would he have agreed to do that? I think not."

Sasha cracked a smile. "Now, you're being silly. Honestly, Malik, you need to fix this. You are creating such a bad vibe in the household, I'm tempted to call Ahiga and ask if he would come over and perform a Native American ritual to bring peace back into our home."

"Are you making fun of the traditions of the Mojave people?"

"Of course not. My own people at home in Madagascar are indigenous, and we have many rituals and traditions that westerners would frown upon. But I can't get a Malagasy elder to travel all the way to America on the fly. Ahiga, on the other hand, is conveniently only twenty minutes away."

"I realize you're being playful, but do me a favor…"

"Yes?"

"If you should happen to speak with Ahiga in the near future, please don't mention my beef with Phoenix."

Sasha lifted an eyebrow questioningly. "Why not?"

"Ahiga tends to act like he's my father, and he would actually drive over here with a ceremonial peace pipe. And then he'd take us out in the backyard and make us smoke it."

Sasha gave a full belly laugh.

"I'm not being funny. I'm serious," I said, shaking my head.

"Thanks for giving me some leverage. And now I'm definitely going to call Ahiga and tell on you."

"You wouldn't sell your own husband out, would you?"

"I most certainly would. I'm tired of the friction in our home. You're the adult, Malik, and it's up to you to make things right with your son."

I held up my hands in surrender. "You win, Sasha. I'll patch things up with Phoenix. I promise."

Over the course of the next few days, I tried to strike up conversations with Phoenix, but he continuously gave me the cold shoulder. He was spending more and more time riding horses at the ranch, and when he wasn't physically there, he visited horse-related websites. He seemed obsessed with horses, and as a way to bury the hatchet, I offered to buy him his own horse. I'd done my homework and discovered that we had more than enough land to build a stable and provide open space for the horse to get some exercise.

But when I mentioned it to Phoenix, he wrinkled his nose and shook his head. "No point in going through all that trouble. I'm still learning the ropes from Gramps, and I'm too inexperienced to try to maintain a horse on my own."

Inwardly I flinched when he referred to Matthew's grandfather, Leonard Fawcett, as Gramps. He had bonded with a stranger instead of bonding with me. I supposed I should have stopped trying to win him over with material things rather than spending quality time with him.

I stood in his doorway trying to think of something that we could do together, and it dawned on me that he'd probably be thrilled if I taught him how to drive.

"What do you think about getting a jumpstart on driving?"

"It's a little early for that. I can't get a permit until I'm sixteen."

"No one needs to know except you and me. We can sneak

out at night and get a few lessons in once a week. How does that sound?"

I expected him to smile broadly at the prospect of driving lessons. But once again, he wrinkled his nose as if I'd invited him to join me at an old school rap concert featuring Big Daddy Kane, MC Lyte, Kool Moe Dee, and Salt-N-Pepa.

Feeling defeated and foolish for even trying to mend our broken relationship, I eased out of his doorway and trudged down the stairs.

The days leading up to Zoe's tenth birthday party were hectic. Never in my life had I spent so much time at Party City, Walmart, and Michaels crafts store. Wanting the party to be perfect, Sasha constantly added to the long list of mandatory items for Zoe's mermaid-themed slumber party.

We'd originally planned to give her a pool party, but we'd have to hire a lifeguard to ensure the guests' safety. Despite that extra precaution, we feared that something still could go wrong. Consequently, we decided that a sleepover was the safest option.

The scene was set for girlie night with an abundance of turquoise, teal, and aqua-green decorations. The entire downstairs was transformed, giving the area a whimsical "under the sea" appearance. Adding to the tropical concept, we scattered plastic seashells, sand dollars, starfish, faux coral, and silk seaweed throughout the living room floor.

Sasha took the entire oceanic motif to the next level with starfish-shaped pizza, blue punch, seashell pasta salad, and turquoise and white cupcakes.

Upon arrival with their sleeping bags in tow, the ten invited guests were greeted with bubbles and balloons. Thankfully, we rented a bubble blower and I didn't have to stand around blowing them through a plastic wand as I'd imagined when I'd heard about the floating soap idea.

After they ate food and cake, they sang karaoke. Sasha had prepared an itinerary for them to follow that included manicures and games and ended with the girls watching *The Little Mermaid*, and then going to bed. But the girls had other ideas, such as playing in makeup, swapping clothes, taking pictures for Instagram, and texting boys.

"We've done our part and I think we should leave them alone," I suggested, tugging on Sasha's arm and leading her upstairs.

After an hour or so, Sasha went back downstairs to do a head count, set the alarm, and make sure that each child was comfortable.

Not wanting any parts of girlie night, Phoenix asked in advance if he could stay overnight at Ryan's. Although we were still attempting to keep close tabs on our children, we had become acquainted with Ryan's parents and knew they would keep an eye on him and not allow him and Ryan to wander the streets after their ten o'clock curfew.

The girlish shrieks and squeals prevented Sasha and me from falling asleep, and we were both awake at midnight.

"Do you think they'll ever be quiet and go to sleep?" she asked.

"I don't have any experience with slumber parties, so you tell me," I said jokingly.

"I never had a slumber party or any other kind of party while growing up. My mother worked hard and was too tired to put up with a bunch of noisy girls. Besides, we didn't have the room in our three-room cottage."

I brushed a lock of hair from her face. "You work hard, too. Yet you took the time to put together a party that Zoe will fondly recall for years to come."

"I'm hoping she'll refer to her tenth birthday as the *best day ever*," Sasha said, mimicking a term that Zoe and her friends often used.

According to Zoe, this past Christmas was the "best day ever" and a month ago, a school trip to the Arizona Bird Observatory had been the "best day ever." For the most part, she was a happy child, and her mother and I could always be counted on to make sure that her happiness continued.

The girls quieted down at around twelve-thirty, and I was finally able to drift off to sleep. I was dog-tired from running around in the heat and preparing for the party. I should have fallen into a deep sleep, but I slept fitfully and kept waking up with a start. Each time that happened, I would hurry downstairs to check on the girls and obsessively recheck the alarm system, making sure that it was armed.

After the third trip downstairs, I returned to bed satisfied that the house was locked properly and everyone was safe and sound.

In a deep sleep, I dreamed that I was visiting Phoenix at the same hospital in Philadelphia where he had been admitted after he'd overdosed. In the dream, after inputting the numbers to unlock the door of his secured unit, there was a loud beeping sound, indicating that I'd put in the wrong code.

I could see Phoenix through a large, plate-glass window, and I yelled his name, but he didn't hear me. I punched in numerous passcodes, one four-digit sequence after another, and the beep grew louder and louder. Overtaken by a sense of desperation, I began yelling for someone to give me the correct code. Suddenly, there was the sound of alarms going off on every floor of the hospital causing me to crumble into a heap on the floor, yelling and covering my ears.

This time I awakened with the undeniable knowledge that something was wrong. I shot a look at Sasha and not wanting to worry her, I was relieved that she was in a deep sleep.

I took the stairs two at a time and rushed to the living room. My hand flew to my mouth as I stood in the middle of the room gawking in disbelief.

It took a few moments to process what I was looking at. Unable to accept the obvious, my brain frantically searched for an explanation, but there was none.

There were eleven sleeping bags. Little girls curled in various sleeping positions filled ten of them. But the blue sleeping bag, bedecked with fluffy white clouds and rainbows, was empty. The occupant, a freckle-faced girl named Paisley, was gone.

I struggled to comprehend the awful reality that a child who should have been safe while under Sasha's and my care was simply gone.

CHAPTER 26

Holding on to hope, I raced to the powder room. The door was wide open, but no one was inside.

I examined the keypad of the security system and discovered that it was set in "Away" mode instead of "Stay." And making matters worse, the motion detector had been disarmed.

With overwhelming fear, I punched in the alarm code. The beeping sound reminded me of my dream, and I realized that while I slept, I'd heard an intruder, disarming the system as he'd entered and then arming it when he'd exited with Paisley in his clutches.

But no random intruder had access to the passcode of our security system. No one except Phoenix could have stealthily gotten inside our home. Paisley knew Phoenix well and she may have trusted him enough to leave without putting up a fuss.

I had to find her before he harmed her, and I didn't have time to throw on some clothes. Barefoot and wearing pajamas, I grabbed my key ring from a kitchen drawer, disarmed the system and hurried outside to my car.

Where would he take her? Is he walking or riding his bike? Does he have a secret hiding place in the woods? I asked myself a dozen or more questions as I backed the car out of the driveway and slowly cruised down the street. There was no point in breaking speed limits since I had no idea where I was going. Turning left and then right, I drove around our neighborhood trying to get inside Phoenix's head.

There were hundreds of miles of wilderness in our area, and he could have been anywhere. I gnawed on my middle fingernail as I pictured him luring the child into the woods. But then, I was comforted by the thought that no matter how much Paisley trusted Phoenix and no matter what kind of a story he'd concocted, she'd never willingly enter the woods at night without yelling and putting up a fight.

Needing her to be quiet, he undoubtedly took her somewhere she wouldn't feel threatened. But where? Back to Ryan's house? No, not there. He needed to be somewhere with complete privacy. A place where he could commit a heinous crime without being interrupted.

Time was of the essence and I implored my sluggish mind to cooperate.

Then, it hit me. *Phoenix was at Matt's grandfather, Leonard Fawcett's, ranch.* The place was in the middle of nowhere, surrounded by mountainous backwoods and over fifty acres of land. Phoenix and old man Fawcett had taken me on a tour of the place back when Phoenix had first shown an interest in horseback riding. While there, the old man confided to me that he was going blind and was headed for a nursing home if his children had their way.

The ranch had seen better days, and judging by the lack of upkeep, it appeared that Mr. Fawcett's vision problems and advanced age were making it difficult for him to handle the responsibility of running such a large place. I noticed that quite a few isolated structures were scattered throughout the grounds. There were horse facilities that included two twelve-stall stables, a hay barn, several old sheds, an office building that was no longer in use, and a desolate-looking storehouse with a rusted lock dangling on the outside. And the diverse terrain included enormous rock formations as well as smooth riding trails.

As secluded and as rundown as Mr. Fawcett's ranch had become, it would be viewed as a haven to someone who had something to hide.

I hit the brakes and was about to turn the car around and head out to the ranch when it occurred to me that Phoenix wouldn't attempt a five-mile trip on a dark, rugged road with a little girl in tow.

He took her somewhere closer.

Where are you, Phoenix? Where the fuck are you?

Struck by a flash of clarity, I knew with certainty where he'd taken her.

I parked my car a couple houses away from the Westfields' former residence. Not wanting to be noticed by neighbors, I crept to the back of the empty property, pajama-clad and barefoot. I jimmied the basement window open and slithered in.

In the pitch darkness of the empty home, I could feel my heart slamming against my chest as I felt along the walls, finding my way to the main level of the home.

Don't let me find Paisley bloody and battered. Please, let her be all right.

The Westfields' home was designed similar to our house and I made my way through the darkened kitchen and dining room with ease. In the vast family room, I could hear the soft murmur of a voice coming from upstairs. I crept closer to the stairwell and was able to hear the voice more clearly. It was undoubtedly Phoenix's voice, but I didn't detect anger and he wasn't ranting like a lunatic. There was a rhythmic quality to his vocals, like he was reciting or reading something. A killer's manifesto? Some sort of satanic chant?

I didn't know what to think. Desperate to find Paisley unharmed, I raced up the stairs. The thick carpet muffled the sound of my pounding footsteps, and when I made it to the top of the landing, both Phoenix and Paisley released utterances of surprise.

But neither of them was more surprised than I when my eyes landed on a camping tent that Phoenix had set up in the middle of the empty bedroom. He and Paisley were seated inside the tent, their silhouettes illuminated by the glow of a flashlight.

"Phoenix! What the hell is going on?" The words came out breathless and in a rapid-fire staccato.

Phoenix popped his head out of the opening, and a look of astonishment appeared on his face. "What are you doing here, Pops?"

Paisley peeked out next and offered me an awkward smile.

Although I felt immense relief at finding her alive and apparently unharmed, I couldn't contain my rage.

"This is crazy. What is your problem?" I yelled as he crawled out of the tent.

Wearing a mermaid pajama set and a pair of flip-flops, Paisley emerged and stood next to him.

"Are you okay?" I asked her as my eyes swept over her tiny frame, making sure there were no injuries on her body and no signs of foul play. Thankfully, she looked perfectly fine.

"Why would you lure Paisley away from the slumber party and bring her here?"

"I didn't *lure* her anywhere. She was awake when I got home and she wanted me to play a video game with her. I told her I couldn't because we'd wake everyone up. She looked like she was about to cry, and I was reminded of how scared I used to feel when I was wide awake and my parents were sound asleep. I felt sorry for her, and I offered to bring her here."

"For what reason?"

"To read her a story and help her fall asleep. See…" He opened the tent's flap and shined the flashlight inside, revealing a Harry Potter book that was cushioned by a blanket that he'd taken from our linen closet.

My heart still didn't soften toward him. What he'd done was irresponsible and thoughtless, especially since there still weren't any answers regarding Taylor Flanagan's disappearance. No rational-thinking person would have behaved so recklessly during these sensitive times. But Phoenix was only fourteen and despite his intelligence, he occasionally did stupid things.

"How long have you been coming to the Westfields' place? Do you realize that trespassing is a crime? You could go to jail for this, Phoenix," I yelled.

"Calm down, Pops." He pressed both palms downward, gesturing for me to bring down the volume.

"Don't tell me to calm down. With everything that's going on in the neighborhood, why would you do something so incredibly stupid?" I folded my arms, waiting for an explanation.

"I couldn't get to sleep at Ryan's, and so I came home and…"

"You're lying and we both know it."

"No, I'm not."

"Please, stop it!" My hand shot up like a crossing guard bringing the flow of traffic to a sudden halt. I narrowed an eye. "You were never at Ryan's house, were you?"

"I was there for a while, but then I left and came over here."

"Why, for God's sake?" I asked with my arms outstretched, shaking my head in disgust.

"I don't know. I come here whenever I have a lot on my mind. It's quiet and I can figure things out."

I wanted to ask what kind of things did a fourteen-year-old need to figure out, but I was too exasperated to continue listening to his explanations. He always had a handy response to any question I asked him. I was getting to the point where I was questioning my own behavior. It couldn't be normal for a father to secretly suspect that his son could possibly be a killer. Maybe I was the one who needed to be in therapy.

"You had no business bringing Paisley here."

"Are we in trouble, Mr. Copeland?" Paisley asked in a timid voice.

I raised a hand, indicating that I didn't want to hear from her right now. Guiltily, her eyes shot downward.

And she wasn't exactly blameless. At ten years old, she should have known better than to leave the house in the middle of the night, no matter what Phoenix suggested.

I returned my seething gaze on Phoenix, waiting for him to make me understand his thought processes, but he didn't offer anything more.

I let out a weary sigh. "It's late and I'm tired. Let's get out of here." I waved an impatient hand, beckoning him and Paisley to follow me downstairs.

"What about my tent?" he asked, looking over his shoulder.

"Leave it!"

"But…"

"Leave the damned thing. You had no business carting it over here in the first place."

"Man!" he uttered in annoyance, as if he'd been unfairly wronged and was fed up with being mistreated.

I yanked the flashlight from his hand and led the way.

The three of us walked in silence to my car.

Two minutes later, we arrived home, and Phoenix went straight upstairs to his room.

Yawning and stretching her arms, Paisley meandered over to her empty sleeping bag. It was on the tip of my tongue to warn her against mentioning her adventure with Phoenix to her parents. But something told me I didn't have to worry about her volunteering information. Kids were great at keeping secrets from their parents, particularly secrets that had the potential of getting them in trouble.

Like a tired old man, I grabbed the railing for support as I slowly climbed the stairs. The only thing that could make this night any worse would be if Sasha was awake and sitting up in bed, waiting for an explanation as to why I'd gone out in the middle of the night.

I lacked Phoenix's expertise in quickly concocting a believable story, and I had no idea what kind of lies would emerge from my mouth. When I crept inside our room, my tension lifted. Sasha was curled on her side and was sleeping like a baby.

I eased into the master bathroom and sat on the edge of the tub and carefully washed the soles of my feet. As I watched the dirt run down the drain, I wondered once again if I was nuts to think that Phoenix wasn't as innocent as he pretended to be.

Until someone was officially charged with Taylor Flanagan's disappearance, I would continue struggling to believe that my son was totally innocent.

CHAPTER 27

Inoticed that there weren't as many parents dropping off and picking up kids at the bus stop. The beauty of the spring season seemed to have created a false sense of security, convincing many of the residents that if Taylor's mother and her boyfriend weren't responsible for her disappearance, then it must have been a drifter or vagrant—someone passing through. There was a general feeling that no one from Springfield Hills could possibly be responsible. The residents were upstanding citizens that were family-oriented and had Christian values, and were also far too image-conscious to get involved in something as repulsive as abducting a child.

While other parents gradually relaxed the rules they'd put into place after Taylor went missing, I ratcheted up the supervision of my children, especially Phoenix. After that stunt he'd pulled with Paisley, I was more suspicious of him than ever. He wanted me to believe that he had no other motives than to help a little girl in distress, but I wasn't buying it. Unfortunately, I couldn't prove that he wasn't being truthful.

Even though it appeared that his only crime was being a stupid teenager, I couldn't quiet the nagging voice in my head. After the

Paisley incident, I made him account for every hour that he was away from home, and I often double-checked to make sure he wasn't lying.

"What are your plans for after school today?" I asked Phoenix as he gobbled down his breakfast that consisted of a scrambled egg and cheese on a bagel.

"Nothing much," he responded with his mouth stuffed.

"Could you be more specific?"

"I might stop over Dustin's house and do some homework."

"You might stop over Dustin's?" I asked with the emphasis on the word *might*. "I need to know exactly where you're going to be. Don't forget to text me after you get out of school."

He rolled his eyes toward the ceiling and then made a big show of tossing the remainder of his sandwich into the trash bin before storming out of the kitchen.

"It's time to go. You guys are going to miss your bus if we don't speed it up," I said grumpily.

"I have to get my backpack from my room," he said snappishly.

Sensing the tension and not wanting to make waves, Zoe sprang up from her seat. "I have to get my backpack, too."

"Make it snappy," I said in a much softer tone than I'd used with Phoenix.

Sasha's eyes bore into me as she observed my behavior. "You're being awfully hard on Phoenix, and for no reason. He doesn't have any behavioral issues at school or at home. He doesn't hang out with a bad crowd and he's not struggling with his grades. I don't get why you're tightening the reins on him instead of loosening them."

"That's the problem with the parents in this town. Everyone is slacking up instead of remaining vigilant. That monster that kidnapped Taylor is still out there, roaming free. Unlike everyone else, I don't think that the person responsible is an outsider. It's just a theory, but I think it's someone we know and trust. And until the police finally bring that animal to justice, I'm going to keep tightening the reins on our children. Having them a little peeved with me for being an overbearing parent is preferable to losing them altogether."

For an uncomfortable interval, Sasha gave me a long look, as if she realized there was something I wasn't telling her.

I wanted to confide in her. I wished that I could share my fears and concerns about Phoenix, but I couldn't risk the possibility of her regarding him as a menace to our community and a danger to our very household, especially if he turned out to be as innocent as he professed to be.

I drove Phoenix and Zoe to the bus stop, and once again, I reminded Phoenix to text me after school. He didn't bother to respond, but I noticed his expression hardening.

He and Zoe bolted out of the car, both seemingly eager to get away from me. I watched as they boarded their respective buses and didn't drive away until both buses had merged into traffic.

Sasha would pick them up after school. She didn't openly complain, but I could tell that she was growing weary of the rigid daily routine and was particularly fed up with my authoritarian parenting style. If I didn't want to cause a family mutiny, I would have to let up on everyone very soon.

On my way to work, while stopped at a red light, I noticed a Hertz car rental location on my right, and I was struck by the idea that I could successfully tail Phoenix if I drove a vehicle that he didn't recognize. A minor disguise wouldn't hurt my efforts, either.

For the remainder of the morning commute, I was less bothered than usual by bumper-to-bumper traffic. I felt optimistic about finally getting some answers to the troubling questions that kept me up late most nights.

I put in a short workday, finishing up a typical six-hour job in only four hours. I left my car in the parking lot of the work site and walked three blocks to Hertz. After signing the paper work for a tan Mazda, I left the place feeling pretty certain that I wouldn't be easily detected. Such a nondescript car would blend into the scenery and wouldn't stick out in Phoenix's or anyone's mind.

A pair of clear eyeglasses and a wide-brimmed Western-style hat that I picked up from a thrift store didn't drastically alter my appearance, but it was enough of a disguise to prevent anyone from immediately recognizing me.

At three o'clock, my phone pinged with a text from Phoenix, letting me know that he was working on a school paper at Dustin's house. If that text and all the other texts he had sent in the past were true, Phoenix and his friends would have to be leading the dullest lives of any of the kids in our town.

But I knew better. They'd start out at Dustin's, playing Fortnite or some other popular video game, but when boredom set in, they'd ride their bikes to the next spot, which was frequently the local skate park.

My instinct told me that at some point, Phoenix would separate from the group, but he wouldn't go home. He'd isolate himself at another location. In the past, Baxter's old house had been his refuge from family and friends, the place where he conducted his secret life.

I was sure that by now he had located another private hangout, and I wanted to know where it was and what he kept hidden there.

On a narrow road behind the skate park, I sat in the rental car, which was concealed by the lush sweeping branches of tall Palo Verde trees. I watched through binoculars as talented skateboarders, bike riders, and kids on scooters put on flashy exhibitions that featured complicated tricks.

I was surprised to see how much Matthew had built up his skills, becoming proficient in backflips and tail-whips on his BMX dirt bike. Dustin and Ryan appeared to be engrossed in filming Matthew jumping the half pipe, while Phoenix was on the sidelines preoccupied with tightening his handlebars.

Once Phoenix was done, he didn't rejoin his friends. He put his tools inside his backpack and began slowly walking his bike away from the crowd. Looking over his shoulder and making sure that he wasn't being watched, he quickened his steps and then hopped on the seat of the bike.

Without bothering to tell his friends goodbye, he made a quick getaway, pedaling swiftly toward the entrance of the park.

There was no need for me to rush to catch up with him. The road I was on was a loop that would take me back to the main street, and if I didn't give him a healthy head start, there was the possibility of us running into each other.

After waiting a full five minutes, I exited the park and spotted Phoenix in the distance, pedaling along Sun Valley Avenue. Instead of traveling behind him, I cruised down Daisy Grove Street, which ran parallel to Sun Valley Avenue.

Every few minutes I would turn at the cross street and make my way back to Sun Valley Avenue, keeping a safe distance from Phoenix while also watching to see if he'd make a detour. After following him for a half-mile, it was clear to me that he wasn't headed for home. If that's where he was headed, he would have turned left at Old Mill Street, but he didn't.

A seasoned sleuth surely would have been amused by my amateurish tracking method, but it was working for me. As I continued to follow him, undetected, I began to feel a prick of excitement over the possibility of finally learning what my son was up to.

He was a skilled liar, but I wouldn't accept any more untruths or excuses.

Four cars separated us and when he made a sudden sharp turn from Sun Valley Avenue to Tijera Springs Road, I knew without a doubt that he was going in the direction of Mr. Fawcett's ranch. But I couldn't follow him down that desolate road without being spotted by him.

Determining that it would take him about thirty or forty minutes of riding on the rough, unpaved road before he reached the ranch, I pulled over and parked.

And waited.

Fifteen minutes later, I eased into the flow of traffic on Sun Valley Avenue and then made the same tricky left turn that Phoenix had made onto Tijera Springs Road, an unpaved road where a sign warned: "Primitive road, no maintenance, proceed at your own risk."

A quarter of a mile into the journey, the dirt road's perils began to reveal themselves as I encountered sharp-tipped rocks thrust from the ground like shrapnel. Trying to avoid a succession of potholes was like navigating a minefield. I slowed down to a crawl, and luckily I wasn't in a hurry.

Riding a dirt bike, Phoenix was much better prepared for the unforgiving terrain than I was. Had I thought about the possibility of him visiting the ranch, I would have selected an SUV instead of a sedan. Clearly, the Mazda I'd rented was no match for the twists and jerks along the rocky road, but I gripped the steering wheel and persevered.

Driving at a snail's pace allowed me to take in the majestic desert landscape that was studded with tall saguaro cactus, grassy pastures dotted with colorful wildflowers, and unobstructed mountain views in all directions.

Upon reaching my destination, I left the oversized Western hat inside the car and left the car on the side of the road, and began walking to the ranch. Wanting to avoid Mr. Fawcett and any workers that might be around, I took a back trail. On the trail I noticed narrow tire tracks made from a bicycle and I assumed that Phoenix, not wanting to encounter Mr. Fawcett, either, had taken the same route.

At the end of the short trail, I found myself behind the stable. I could hear the horses, but the windows were too high to take a peek to see if Phoenix was inside. With my back flush against the outer walls of the stable, I moved stealthily to the front and slipped inside. Only the horses were inside, and Phoenix was nowhere to be found.

There were so many ideal hiding places on the property, I didn't know where to begin, and my biggest worry was that someone would find me roaming around on private property. I didn't have a prepared excuse, and as I stopped for a moment, attempting to come up with one, my attention was drawn to a shiny object on the ground, sparkling in the sunlight. It was about fifteen feet from me and when I approached it to investigate, I realized that it was only a green piece of glass, jutting from the ground. It was possibly a piece of an old beer bottle that had been tossed aside long ago.

Amazingly, the partially buried green glass was adjacent to a grassy path that cut through the wooded area on the property. On that path were bicycle tire tracks, leading me to Phoenix like a trail of breadcrumbs.

The path started out on even ground but quickly turned into a gravel and dirt incline that was so steep I found myself taking heaving breaths and breaking out in a sweat. The uphill hike was a killer quad and hamstring workout that only an adventure junkie would enjoy. I was certain that my aching muscles would require cold compresses in the morning. As I struggled to continue on the incline, I suddenly skidded downhill, and I was moving fast— so fast, that I lost my balance and rolled the rest of the way, and landed on something hard and metallic.

Feeling vulnerable on the ground, I reflexively jumped to my feet. Looking downward, I was surprised to see Phoenix's bike lying on its side, partially hidden by tree branches and brush.

Had Phoenix fallen also? Was he lying somewhere injured with a broken bone or a concussion? Concerned, I walked a few paces and looked around, but didn't see any sign of him. Nor did I see any man-made structures that he could hide out in. All I saw was miles and miles of wilderness.

Scratching my head, I scanned the area where he'd laid his bike down and was completely baffled as to where he could have run off to. Other than the trail that had deposited me at the bottom of a gravelly hill, there were no other discernible trails, no foot-prints on the ground, and no bike tracks to indicate he had ridden any farther than where I'd landed.

I was tempted to use his bike for transportation while I searched for him, but I didn't want to risk going deep into the woods without a compass or a map. I stared down at the ground, and out of the blue, my eyes landed on a small opening in the Earth. And next to the opening was a rock.

The pieces of the puzzle quickly came together in my mind, and I moved swiftly toward the opening, lay down on my side, and peeked inside. I couldn't see a thing; there was only darkness. Yet, sparks of exhilaration raced through my system as I realized that I was looking into the mouth of a cave.

The jagged rock that was set next to it had served as a makeshift door and had also been used to camouflage the opening. I could have walked past the cave opening a thousand times without noticing it, and I wondered if Mr. Fawcett or any of his family members were aware of the existence of the cave on the property.

Undoubtedly, there was one person who knew about it and had gained access...and that person was Phoenix.

Although I didn't have a flashlight or even a lighter in my pocket, I squeezed into the circular opening, which was approximately four feet in diameter. I dropped down into a vast open area, and when my eyesight adjusted to the darkness, I could see that I was in a large chamber with a ceiling that appeared to be about twenty feet high. I thought it would be chilly inside the cave, but the air was thick and dry.

Taking in the sights as best I could in the darkness, I felt a creepy sensation that was followed by fear of encountering a bat, a snake, or some other deadly creature.

But those feelings of dread were replaced with awe and wonder as my eyes roved the rocky interior of the natural wonder that was potentially millions of years old. I could feel the sacredness of the environment, and I wished I was there under different circumstances.

I walked a little deeper into the cave and became aware of a dim light in the distance. Of course, Phoenix would be prepared with a flashlight or even a lantern. I crept along in the direction of the light and as the cave brightened, I was amazed by its vibrant colors and the spectrum of red, purple, yellow, and orange.

Following along a tight corridor, I was suddenly outside a smaller room. A large flashlight with a handle was set on a shelf-life ridge that protruded from the wall. Below the light, Phoenix sat on a rock formation. He appeared to be in a calm, blissful state. Unaware of my presence, he didn't look up.

I noticed something on his lap, and his hand moved over it in a stroking movement. But in the semidarkness, I couldn't figure out what I was actually looking at. At first I thought that an animal was in his lap, and that he was petting it comfortingly.

Sensing me standing in the crude doorway of the chamber, his head jerked around. Upon seeing me standing there, he covered his face with both hands and groaned as if in anguish.

"It's time to talk, Phoenix."

"I don't want to talk! Why're you stalking me? You shouldn't have followed me here." He bent over, using his torso in a desperate attempt to conceal whatever was resting on his lap.

I took steps toward him.

"Get out of here, Pops. I'm serious, you should leave!" he said pleadingly.

I jutted out my chin determinedly and slowly approached him, and then stood over him in the gloom of the cave. Racked by tears, his body shook, and I placed a hand on his shoulder and gently tugged, lifting his torso, so that I could see what he was trying to conceal.

My eyes traveled down to his lap and I clapped a hand over my mouth. He was right. The thing on his lap wasn't something I wanted to see. In fact, it was the worst sight that I'd ever seen.

My fourteen-year-old son, who many perceived to be a normal adolescent boy, was holding the mummified corpse of Taylor Flanagan, which he had been in the act of caressing when I arrived at the rear chamber of the cave.

CHAPTER 28

Taylor's facial features were no longer identifiable, but I recognized the Wonder Woman costume. The costume was once a vibrantly colored representation of a little girl's desire to be a super hero, but now it was faded and shabby.

My heart clenched at the wretched sight. My stomach heaved mightily, yet I managed not to throw up. Pulling myself together, I sighed deeply, pinching the bridge of my nose as I tried to come up with a plan. There had to be a way for me to help Phoenix get out of this horrible mess.

"How many others are there?"

He looked up at me, bleary-eyed, wiping away tears. "There aren't any others."

"Why, son? Why did you hurt an innocent little girl?" I nodded toward the dead child that was draped over his lap.

"I don't know. It just happened," he said as his fingers unconsciously brushed against the tufts of hair that remained on the child's head. What he was doing, stroking her hair with his fingertips, was a barely perceptible micro-movement. But I noticed it and it triggered a feeling of rage inside of me.

"Stop touching her like that! Put her down," I snapped, feeling as if Phoenix had drawn me into a scene of a horror movie.

He carefully laid the body on the floor of the cave and then gave me his undivided attention.

Not wanting to look at the dead body on the ground, I kept my eyes focused on his face. "What happened on Halloween? How did it happen?"

"It was an accident."

"From the moment you made contact with Taylor, what happened? Walk me through it and don't leave out anything."

"I was riding my bike on Halloween night, fooling around with my friends, and I saw these two girls from school—Nikki and Sloan. They were walking with Taylor…" He paused and nodded his head toward the corpse on the cave's floor and I winced in revulsion.

"They were taking her door-to-door…and we followed them for a while, making smart-ass comments and joking with the girls. And then we just rode around, messing with people."

"So, when did you bump into Taylor again?"

"About an hour later, Nikki and Sloan walked her up to the house on Birchwood Circle. Matt and Dustin were fooling around with the girls and telling them they were having a get-together in the woods."

I gave him a perplexed look.

"Some of the kids go there to drink and chill out. The girls followed them to the woods, and since I don't drink, I didn't go. I told them I'd see them later. They were so shocked that Nikki and Sloan agreed to go with them, they never looked back. Taylor stood there on her porch, and I could tell that her bag wasn't even halfway filled. I got the impression that Nikki and Sloan had rushed her back home before she was ready to go in. So, I asked if she wanted to collect some more candy, and she said, 'yes.'"

"Someone might have noticed you, Phoenix," I blurted, feeling fearful as I imagined police dressed in SWAT gear, breaking down the door of our home and dragging Phoenix out.

"No one noticed me. That street was quiet; no one was around."

"And what happened next?"

"I asked her if she wanted to ride my bike. She smiled and nodded. So, I sat her on the seat and let her hold on to the handlebars, but since her feet couldn't reach the pedals, I had to guide her through the breezeway that I always used as a shortcut."

"A shortcut to where? Where'd you take her?"

"I took her to Baxter's old house. I told her there was lots of candy there, enough to fill her bag up."

"Oh, God!" I groaned. In an effort to get Phoenix to confide in me, I'd been stoic up until now, but hearing him admit that he used the promise of more Halloween candy to lure a helpless little girl to her death was difficult to hear.

I glanced down at the hardened corpse that used to be Taylor Flanagan, and quickly looked away.

"As soon as she realized that the house was empty and didn't have any electricity, she started crying. Not whimpering and whining like most little kids....she was loud! Ear-splitting loud! And I didn't have a choice; I had to shut her up."

"What did you do to her?" I braced myself for the worst.

"I told her to be quiet, but she wouldn't. I took my shirt off and used it to cover her mouth. But she kept on screaming and struggling with me. It was an accident, Pops. I didn't realize that I had smothered her until she went limp. I tried to give her mouth-to-mouth, but it didn't work."

"Why did you try to resuscitate her if your plan was to kill her all along?"

He shrugged. "I didn't want to kill her that way."

"How did you want to kill her?"

"I wanted to hang her," he said quietly.

I flinched and emitted an involuntary sound of horror. "Why did you have a desire to hang her?"

"I like watching public executions online. They're uploaded and posted from different places in the Middle East and Asia. When a person gets hung, their body convulses and jerks in a way that's fascinating, and I wanted to see it in person."

Hearing my son admit that he sought out online videos that featured public executions was so nauseating I could feel the muscles around my mouth straining to twist into an expression of extreme displeasure. My face felt hot and my stomach lurched. In fact, every part of my being reacted negatively to Phoenix's admission.

"Did you plan to hang Paisley? Is that why you took her to Baxter's?" I asked, powering through the vile questions while striving to keep my vocal quality even-toned and without an inkling of judgment.

"Yeah, I planned to hang Paisley. I was going to do it after I finished reading to her. She seemed like a sweet kid and I didn't want to kill her without making her happy, first. But...as you know, my plan didn't succeed," he said with a rueful smile.

"I don't understand why you target young children? Do you have sexual fantasies that involve little kids?"

"Ew, no! I pick them because they're easy to manipulate, and they're such lightweights, it's easy to physically overpower them."

"How'd you get Taylor's body all the way from Baxter's house to here?"

"I wrapped her in trash bags and tied her onto my bike and then I pushed it here. It was hell pushing a bike on rugged Tijera Springs Road, but I didn't have a choice. I couldn't leave her at Baxter's and let some nosey real estate agent find her body."

"No, I suppose you couldn't," I said resignedly. Although I'd had a gut feeling that he wasn't mentally all there, he was much sicker and more dangerous than I could have ever imagined.

I doubted if there was anything I could do to help a psychopath that had no intention of ending his killing spree.

"Does Mr. Fawcett know that there's a cave on his land?" I continued.

"Yeah, he knows. He's the one who told me about it. He says he's only been down here…maybe three or four times in the forty-plus years that he's owned the ranch. He never told anyone about it because he didn't want the place crawling with tourists, and he didn't want the government butting in and making claims on the cave."

"Hmm," I muttered.

"As you know, he can barely see, Pops, so you don't have to worry about him coming down here."

"How long do you plan on leaving Taylor in this cave?" I asked with heartfelt compassion. It hurt me to my core to realize the extent of his psychosis. He was so screwed up in the head, it was clear to me that he was going to end up being confined to a mental institution for the rest of his natural life.

Of course a good lawyer could make sure that he was charged as a juvenile and set free at age eighteen.

I wondered if Elle realized that our child was a lost cause. Was his deteriorating mental state the reason that she so easily turned him over to my care after years of keeping him away from me?

And what about the therapist that Phoenix saw once a week? Did he know that Phoenix yearned to kill people and wanted to watch their bodies twitch and writhe? I imagined the therapist's records being subpoenaed and his notes being reported in newspapers across the land. And I shuddered as I envisioned the trial being televised.

Sasha and I as well as Elle and Everett would become pariahs in our communities. The businesses that Sasha and I worked so hard to build would surely fold. And it wouldn't stop there. Sweet little Zoe would also be ostracized. Her mermaid slumber party would be the last event that she would ever host. No parent would allow their child to socialize at our house, and who could blame them?

"We've got to move the body out of this cave," I said, thinking out loud.

"Why? She's safe here. No one will ever find her."

"She deserves a proper burial, Phoenix. Her family should be allowed to say goodbye."

"But she doesn't even look like herself anymore. Why would they want to tell a corpse goodbye?"

"It doesn't matter what she looks like. Her family still loves her and they need closure."

My thoughts went to Tessa Jordan, my busybody neighbor, and I could only imagine the tales she would tell after word got out that my son was the perpetrator of the most heinous crime to ever take place in peaceful Springfield Hills.

I imagined her saying, *Malik Copeland stood right next to me, asking questions and acting concerned when all the time, it was his own monstrous son that snatched that sweet little girl. I think Malik knew all along, and he did everything he could to cover for his son.*

"What do you plan to do with her?" Phoenix asked, looking down at Taylor's corpse with a warm look in his eyes, as if the mummified remains were a beloved pet that he couldn't bear to part with.

"We have to put her in a location where someone will find her," I said logically, as if having a discussion about moving a dead body was a normal conversation between a father and son.

"What about me? Are you going to tell the police?"

"Of course not."

"I'm not stupid, Pops. You're too much of a goody-goody and too moralistic to let me get away with this."

"You're not going to get away with it, Phoenix. Although I'm not going to turn you over to an angry mob, I'm definitely going to make sure you get intensive therapy. Perhaps another thirty-day stay in a mental hospital… But not any time soon. We need to allow some time to pass. It might draw unwelcome attention to you if you were hospitalized in the midst of the media circus that's going to ensue when the body turns up."

He nodded, relieved that he wouldn't be locked up in a mental institution.

"Can I tell you something, Pops?"

Not sure if I could withstand another bombshell revelation, I nodded hesitantly.

"I was going to hang Baxter, too. But his family moved before I could get around to it."

Fighting against a violent reaction, I swallowed hard and bit down on my bottom lip. "Baxter's not a little kid; how'd you plan to overpower him?" I asked reasonably.

Phoenix gave me a sly grin. "I would have overpowered him with logic. I'm a skilled debater, you know."

Uncomprehendingly, I gazed at the face of madness that belonged to my son. "What does being on the debate team have to do with overpowering Baxter with logic?"

"There wouldn't have been a need to struggle to get a noose around his neck; I could have used the powers of persuasion to get him to willingly do it."

"That's ridiculous!" I was so sickened by Phoenix, I wanted to flee the cave and put miles and miles of distance between us, but I stood there and continued to endure the madness.

"Baxter was suicidal, Pops," Phoenix explained. "Slitting his wrists wasn't his first attempt to kill himself. He had lots of issues with his parents, kids at school…and he just didn't want to be here anymore. But he was too scared to go through with it. If I were there with him, I would have given him the rope and instructions on how to do it right. Most importantly, I wouldn't have allowed him to punk-out of it like he'd done many times before.

"It would have been more like a mercy killing than murder," Phoenix rationalized. "But he moved, and that pissed me off. It really pissed me off," he repeated in a louder tone.

He glanced down at Taylor's corpse on the floor. "This stupid little kid died so fast, I didn't get a chance to enjoy it."

He stood up and began to savagely kick the corpse. The sound of his sneaker connecting with the child's hardened dead body was so repulsive, my lips curled into a grimace as I recoiled.

"That's enough, Phoenix!"

"It's true, though. And it's messed up the way nobody will cooperate with me," he said, frowning disdainfully. "It's not my fault that I have this urge, but if I could do it one more time— without being rushed—I wouldn't have to kill again."

In so many words, he was asking me to endorse and possibly participate in his final murderous escapade, and I was stunned.

"It's getting late," I said. "We have to get the body out of here, and go home. We'll talk more about your situation tomorrow."

"Do you promise that we'll talk about it?"

"Yeah, I promise," I mumbled.

CHAPTER 29

P hoenix was experienced in getting in and out of the cave. Getting a footing on the stones that jutted out of the wall, he scampered upward without any difficulty. Once he was outside the cave, I hoisted the body up to him.

Although Phoenix had wrapped the body in the same plastic trash bags that he'd wrapped it in when he'd brought it there, and despite that it felt more like a statue than a person, it was difficult for me to handle the child's remains without losing my mind.

I wanted to put this nightmare behind me so badly, I amazed myself with my agility and swiftness in climbing out of the cave.

Once outside the cave, I expressed concern about getting caught by Mr. Fawcett.

"We won't get caught. Gramps relies on his hearing and his sense of touch to know what's going on around him."

This time I didn't wince when he referred to Mr. Fawcett as Gramps. His cozy relationship with the old man no longer instilled envy. It was a minor blip on the scale of problems that Phoenix had dumped on me.

"I'd like to avoid Mr. Fawcett if possible," I insisted.

"Okay, follow me."

Phoenix grabbed his bike, and then pedaled ahead with the corpse wedged between his torso and the handlebars. Leading the way, he rode on a barely visible path that he said would take us directly to the main road without having to bypass Mr. Fawcett's private dwelling.

It was a longer route, but I was relieved to not have to worry about being seen. We made it to the car and Phoenix loaded the body and the bike inside the trunk.

"I know a place we can dump her," he said.

"Where?"

"If you take Route 87 and exit at Alvarado Drive, there's a corn-field nearby."

"How do you know?"

"We ride our bikes in cornfields sometimes."

"We can't put the body in a place where you and your friends hang out."

"None of my friends know about this particular field. I discovered it when I was scouting out new places to chill."

He'd been in Arizona for less than a year and yet he had identified more remote locations than the average person could have imagined. Personally, I would think that being alone in a cornfield was a nightmarish experience, but Phoenix was so depraved, he viewed the massive field as an oasis.

The sky, slate gray with streaks of black, was appropriately grim and foreboding as we embarked on our journey to get rid of Taylor Flanagan's body. White-knuckled, I gripped the steering wheel as my body lurched and bumped along the rugged terrain of Tijera Springs Road.

The treacherous road wasn't my only concern. After tonight I would be considered an accessory to murder after the fact, and my actions could impact Sasha and Zoe for the rest of their lives.

Despite the knowledge that I was jeopardizing my beloved family's peace and well-being, I forged ahead, intent on protecting Phoenix, whom I also loved dearly.

We rode in silence for much of the drive. The rolling and tumbling of the body in the trunk was an obscene reminder of what I'd gotten myself into. For so long I'd yearned for Phoenix and me to participate in an activity that would forge a bond between us. Cycling, fishing, or camping were a few ideas that I'd proposed and that he had shot down.

Never in my wildest dreams could I have imagined us bonding over murder.

I told myself that it was too late to do anything for Taylor, but I could somehow save my son. But I had no concrete plan as to how I would go about saving him. I was in the moment, motivated by unconditional love and an innate desire to protect him at all costs.

We arrived at the cornfield and I instructed Phoenix to stay inside the car. There was no point in both of us being spotted if there were prying eyes anywhere near.

Wearing the flimsy disguise that consisted of only a Western hat and glasses, I popped the trunk before exiting the rental car. As I hauled the plastic-wrapped body out of the trunk and flung it over my shoulder, I was hit with an overwhelming urge to vomit. The body was stiff and heavy like a slab of concrete. Knowing that the lifeless form had once been a lively child who had met her death because she had trustingly taken my son's hand was difficult to deal with.

I stepped inside the labyrinth of growing corn, solidifying my role as an accomplice. Realizing that there was no turning back now, I forged ahead. To keep from panicking, I didn't allow myself to think about the heinousness of the crime I was committing. As I moved deeper and deeper into the darkened rows of corn with their razor-sharp stalks, I focused on the idea of keeping Phoenix safe. I kept walking inside the rows and refused to place the body on the ground until I was satisfied that it was so well-hidden, it would take at least another day or two before anyone detected it.

I needed extra time to prep Phoenix and get him ready for the upcoming whirlwind of activity that would befall our city the moment Taylor's remains were found.

After placing the body carefully on the ground, I removed the plastic to prevent the police from finding Phoenix's or my fingerprints.

Looking down at the mummified form, I whispered, "I'm so sorry."

Then, I fled the scene, batting away insects that buzzed around my face.

Back in the car, I mopped sweat from my brow. The perspiration had not accumulated from physical fatigue but was the result of dread and anxiety regarding the days that lie ahead.

"You may be questioned by the police," I said to Phoenix, trying to keep my voice light.

"Why?" he asked, sounding annoyed by the potential imposition.

"You were seen in the company of the babysitter the night the child went missing, am I right?"

"No! Matt and Dustin were with the girls. I was on the sidelines, keeping an eye on Taylor."

He spoke as if he had been keeping an eye on Taylor to ensure her well-being, when in fact, he was appraising her as a candidate for murder. I wondered if he had sent her a warm smile to make himself appear friendly and harmless?

"If the police question you, don't mention that you saw the little girl standing on her front porch."

"I'm not stupid enough to implicate myself," he said sullenly.

"This isn't my first time at the rodeo; I've had to cover my tracks before."

His admission sent shockwaves through my system, and perspiration began to swiftly trickle from my forehead, pooling around the base of my neck. "But…I thought you said you never killed anyone before."

He gave me a sly grin. "It wasn't a person. It was Bella, my mom's stupid little dog."

"What did you do to the dog?"

"I hung it," he said matter-of-factly.

"Did your mother find out?"

"Uh-huh. That's why she shipped me off to you."

Speechless, I made an indecipherable sound.

It was extremely immoral of Elle to send him to live with me without informing me of his declining mental status. Had I known how deeply troubled he was, I may or may not have accepted the responsibility of being his guardian. Allowing me to have a choice in the matter would have been the decent thing for Elle to do.

"Phoenix, you have to come up with a story about Halloween night. They're going to want to know at approximately what time you separated from your friends."

"Seven-thirty on the dot. I had to get home and begin studying for a chemistry test."

"Is that true? Did you actually have a test coming up?"

"Yeah, and I aced it."

"That's good," I muttered as I drove along the highway.

Before going home, I had one more stop to make.

"Why're we stopping here?" Phoenix asked as I pulled into a Food City parking lot.

"Have to get rid of the plastic that you wrapped around Taylor." I gestured toward the Dumpster at the back of the lot.

"Oh," Phoenix said disinterestedly as he gazed at the screen of his phone.

Clearly, he didn't have a care in the world, and I'd be the only one losing sleep for weeks, months, and maybe years to come.

I watched the news every chance I got. When I wasn't actively watching and waiting for the body to be found, I was on high-alert to hear the dreaded news from another source. Each time someone called my name—an employee, a client, Sasha, or Zoe—I'd brace myself and prepare to arrange my features into a look of surprise.

My nights were plagued with nightmares that featured Taylor. In one dream I was able to save her from Phoenix, but as I pulled away the shirt he used to smother her, she told me in a frantic voice that she was dying. I reassured her that she was fine, but her body began to stiffen and mummify right before my eyes. Experiencing a living and breathing child quickly turning to stone while in my arms was horrific, and in the dream, I could feel nausea rising and burning the back of my throat.

In another dream, she was holding the matching red boot, and when I awakened in a cold sweat, it occurred to me that the body I'd left in the cornfield was barefoot. Panicked, I rushed to Phoenix's room and gruffly woke him up.

"What's wrong?" he asked, aggravated as he sat up and rubbed sleep from his eyes.

"Where's the other red boot?" I hissed.

"I have it. It's safe."

"You have it?" I was incredulous. "Where is it?"

"I'm not giving it up, so don't try to make me."

"Do you *want* to get caught? You can't hold on to a murder trophy, you reckless piece of shit!" I hadn't meant to resort to cursing and name-calling, but I wasn't my normal self. I was sleep-deprived, frightened about the future, and constantly on edge.

He pointed to his closet. "It's on the shelf," he muttered.

I glared at him. It was inconceivable that our family had been unwittingly sharing our home with an item that was connected to the worst crime that had ever been committed in Springfield Hills.

I was a few feet from the closet when I heard Sasha's footsteps approaching. I froze and turned toward the open bedroom door.

"What's going on, honey? Is everything okay?" she asked with suspicion coating every word.

"Everything's fine," I said, guiding her back toward our room. I looked over my shoulder at Phoenix and could have sworn that I saw a smirk on his face.

Back in bed, Sasha cuddled close to me. She placed her palm across my shoulder blades and gently rubbed, allowing her hand to meander down the length of my arm. "You know you can talk to me if there's a problem between you and Phoenix. I want you to know that I'm here for you, and I'll listen without judgment whenever you're ready to talk."

"Nothing's bothering me, Sasha."

"Why were you arguing with Phoenix in the middle of the night?"

"I wasn't arguing with him. I went in his room to remind him that Thursday is trash day. Lately, he's been forgetting to take the cans to the curb."

"You reminded him about trash day on a Tuesday night? That sounds really anal, Malik. You need to relax a little." She kissed my chest as her hand found its way to the crotch of my pajamas. "Do you want me to help you relax?" she whispered in a sultry tone.

It was the last thing that I wanted, but I didn't want to hurt her by telling her that I preferred to sleep. I squeezed my eyes shut and clenched my teeth as she caressed my flaccid appendage, trying to bring it to life.

But it wasn't working. Knowing that the dead girl's red boot was right down the hall killed any desire I might have had to make love to my wife.

"I'm sorry, babe," I said in a voice filled with shame.

"It's okay." She leaned over and kissed me on the lips, and I tried to put all the love I had for her into the kiss, but she suddenly went stiff and pulled away, informing me that she was painfully aware of my lack of passion for her.

"Goodnight, Malik," she said in a hurt tone of voice, and then turned her back to me.

Trying to make up for being unable to perform, I caressed her shoulder and murmured, "I love you, Sasha."

She eased away from my touch and tightened the covers around her slender frame.

"Why do I have to give it to you? It's mine!" Phoenix squawked in a cracking voice, clutching the red boot tightly in his hand.

"That boot is evidence that could come back to haunt you if we don't get rid of it while we have a chance," I said in a hushed voice. I was mindful that Sasha and Zoe, downstairs in the kitchen, could get an earful if either of them chose to suddenly come upstairs.

"But no one is even looking for it."

"Not at this moment, but as soon as the body is discovered without the boots, the authorities are going to start searching for them."

"I'll keep it safe and make sure no one can ever find it." As he spoke, his face was contorted in a way that expressed a mixture of rage and desperation.

For a moment I thought that we might possibly come to blows

over the boot, and I was relieved when he gave up and angrily threw it against his bedroom wall.

Getting the boot from the house to the car was nerve-wracking, and I felt like Sasha was watching my every move as I crept to the front door. After wedging it in with the spare tire in the trunk of my car, I went back inside the house and half expected Sasha to ask me what I'd hidden in the car.

After rushing through breakfast, I told my family that I had to get to work early. But that's not where I went.

Filled with anxiety, I drove to a dense wooded area that was fifty miles outside of Springfield Hills. Along the way, my heart took a dive every time I spotted a police car or a state trooper's vehicle. Super-cautious, I made sure that I didn't exceed the speed limit or switch lanes without signaling. The last thing I needed was to be pulled over and—God forbid—searched.

I finally made it to my destination, which I found on Google Maps, and I hastily pulled a lighter out of my pocket and lit the plastic bag that contained the damning evidence.

Under a blue sky, while birds chirped and the sun glimmered through the top of the trees, I burned the little red boot, adding destruction of evidence to my growing list of crimes.

I went to work afterward and tried my best to avoid getting into a lengthy conversation with the manager of the furniture store that I was servicing. However, the woman who ran the place was extremely chatty and kept finding reasons to come into the server room.

I listened to her bitch about the customers, the state of the country, and the unseasonable heat wave we were experiencing.

I was perceived as a family man and an upstanding citizen. Someone who was perfectly normal. Yet my involvement in covering up such an atrocious murder would render me as guilty as my son—if not more so since I was the adult.

Later that evening, hoping that a change in scenery would help steady my nerves, I attended a recovery meeting. Unfortunately, getting together with a group of ex-addicts didn't help ease my mounting tension.

Ahiga waved at me from across the room. He could always be relied upon to provide a great deal of support and comfort, and I quickly moved in his direction, hoping to draw strength from him.

"Hello there, Malik. Long time no see," Ahiga greeted. "You promised to start attending meetings more regularly. What happened, my friend?"

I mumbled an excuse about family obligations, but when I looked into Ahiga's wise and all-knowing eyes, I could tell that he wasn't buying my excuse. The two dark orbs seemed to peer into my soul, unearthing my darkest secret, causing me to squirm.

"What's troubling you, Malik?" he asked with a light pat on my arm.

"Is it that obvious?" I did my best rendition of a smile, a grudging curve of the lips that was more of a sneer than a smile. I felt tortured inside and it showed on my face, making it pointless to try to conceal my true feelings from Ahiga.

"You can confide in me, Malik," he said.

"It's Phoenix…as usual. We're always at each other's throats, and Sasha is getting tired of the tension in our home," I said with a sad shrug. "I've tried, but I can't seem to make a connection with him."

Ahiga folded his arms. "I'm hosting a pow-wow next week. Why don't you bring Phoenix. I'm sure it would be a great opportunity for you two to socialize without actually being stuck with each other. Native American pow-wows are elaborate events with a lot going on: singing, dancing, and various competitions. And the youth turnout is tremendous. While Phoenix interacts with other kids, you two still get to enjoy a shared experience."

"Sounds good. Thanks for the invite, Ahiga. Text me the information…the time and place and where I can purchase tickets."

Ahiga scowled. "You don't have to purchase tickets; you two will be my guests."

Someone beckoned Ahiga and pointed to the microphone. It was time for him to make the closing remarks and bring the meeting to an end.

"Hang tight for a while. I'd like to tell you more about the pow-wow."

I nodded, but my feet had already begun moving toward the exit sign. There wasn't a chance in hell that I'd bring Phoenix around throngs of young people in such a large setting where there'd be numerous opportunities for him to kill again. Having to deal with another missing child would push me over the edge, and I would never forgive myself for recklessly endangering lives.

My son clearly needed to be institutionalized, but I was putting together a plan that might prevent me from having to take such a drastic measure. Besides, now that I was involved in the crime, I couldn't hand him off to a mental health facility nor could I turn him over to the police without the risk of being implicated. I'd be able to think clearer and make more rational decisions once the body was found and after the uproar of the murder finally died down.

For now, I was in limbo, waiting for the other shoe to drop.

CHAPTER 30

Hardly a moment passed without me thinking about Taylor Flanagan's body being discovered. I had imagined numerous circumstances where I learned of the news, and I practiced my reaction for each one. I had the most practice with the scenario that involved Sasha and me finding out together while watching the evening news. In that situation, I played the role of consoler when Sasha's emotions got the best of her. She would shed tears of anguish for little Taylor and also tears of relief that our children were safe.

Tending to a distraught wife gave me something to do. Grabbing tissues and offering pats on the back to Sasha along with soothing words was busywork that disguised my culpability in the crime and spared me from having to confront my guilt.

In my mind, I had practiced the different situations so often that I didn't leave room for any other scenario, and I was taken completely off guard when I stopped in a 7-Eleven to pick up a Triple Cheese Pizza and a Blue Raspberry Slurpee for Zoe. I wanted to surprise her with her favorite snack—my way of making up for being so distant and preoccupied lately.

As I pulled the door open and heard the store's doorbell chime,

I felt kind of cheerful, a big change from the angst and worry that had been plaguing me for the past week. But the moment I stepped inside the store, my jovial mood vanished.

Standing in line at the register was none other than Heather Flanagan, holding a red basket filled with snacks.

Heather was the last person on Earth that I wanted to run into, and I reflexively stopped in my tracks. My uneasiness quickly built into full-blown panic, and I considered making backward steps out the door. But the thought of surveillance cameras capturing me as I avoided her, gave me a change of heart. Although it was a stretch to think that law enforcement would ever view the footage and question me about my motives for rushing out the door, I watched enough crime shows to know that you could never predict what the police would look at and consider as evidence during a murder investigation.

With my legs feeling like they'd turned to lead, I trudged over to the Slurpee machine. I hoped that no one was paying attention to me and noticing how badly I was sweating, but it seemed that everyone in the store had eyes on me. I was so self-conscious, I had to will my hand not to shake as I grabbed a cup and flipped the lever to dispense the fizzy beverage.

A sudden loud shriek, seemingly from hell, pierced the atmosphere. The sound was so disconcerting, I accidentally knocked over the cup, splashing blue sludge all over the counter, my hand, and the front of my pants. Jerking my head in the direction of the awful cry, I wished I could have instantly disappeared when I witnessed Heather Flanagan collapsed against the counter. The items she'd been holding in the red basket were scattered on the floor, along with her rhinestone-encased cell phone.

"No! No!" she repeated as she thrashed and flailed.

"What's wrong, ma'am?" said the store clerk as he rushed from behind the counter and attempted to assist Heather.

"They found her! Oh, God! They found my baby's body in a freakin' cornfield," she wailed.

"She said they found her daughter's body. You know, the missing little girl," another customer translated to the patrons that stood nearby, gawking.

"They found Taylor Flanagan, and she's dead," blurted a grinning teenager. He promptly held up his phone and began to record the devastated mother in the throes of grief, capturing what should have been a private moment, and no doubt uploading it to the Internet for the world to see.

The store was abuzz with activity and excitement as Heather's wails reached a feverish pitch. Some jackass must have called the police because within minutes, two patrol cars sped into the parking lot.

Never in my wildest dreams did I imagine that this would be the way that I learned that the body had finally been discovered. Sharing the same environment as the grieving mother at the exact moment when she was told that her daughter was dead was quite ironic. Many would say that it was poetic justice for me to have to endure the discomfort of viewing the pain that my son and I had caused.

Customers stepped aside when four uniformed officers rushed inside the store, their faces tense, hands near their weapons, as if a crime were in progress.

"Do you need us to escort you home, ma'am?" asked one of the officers as they approached the grief-stricken mother.

Heather's face contorted in outrage. "No, I don't need an escort. I need you assholes to find the bastard that murdered my child. Why the fuck are you wasting time in here? He's out there some-where, and you guys are bumbling around like Keystone Cops. I want justice! I want you to find him!"

In her hysteria, Heather shoved the cop closest to her, leaving the officers no choice but to arrest her for assaulting an officer.

The same teenaged boy that had filmed her meltdown, now began to film her arrest.

A few moments after she was hauled off in handcuffs, I sheepishly exited the store. Never had I felt more like a worthless piece of shit. My actions in covering up my son's crime had caused additional emotional trauma to the mother of the murdered child.

Somehow I made it home. Miraculously, my car ended up parked in the driveway, yet I had no conscious memory of traveling the familiar route from the convenience store to my home. It was as if the car was on automatic pilot and brought me home without any assistance from me.

As I sat at the wheel wondering if I should mention to Sasha that I'd witnessed Heather Flanagan getting arrested inside the nearby 7-Eleven, the front door opened and Sasha hurried toward my car. She jiggled the handle of the passenger side, indicating that she wanted to get in. I didn't have to ask what was wrong; I could tell by the distressed expression on her face that she'd also heard the news.

I hit the switch that unlocked that door, and she slid inside.

"They found the girl," she said grimly.

"I know." Showing respect for the situation, I spoke in a low voice that was barely above a whisper.

"We should talk to the kids together. We need to be a united front in assuring them that they'll be safe as long as they adhere to the rules we've laid out."

"Sasha, we've pounded those rules into their heads. If we go over them again, it'll be overkill, and they'll probably tune us out."

"I don't care if it's overkill. Until the police catch the madman that's responsible, you and I have to do everything in our power to protect the kids. If that means being repetitive, then so be it."

"All right, Sasha," I said wearily.

"Don't patronize me, Malik," she snapped.

"I'm not patronizing you; I'm agreeing with you." There was so much on my mind, the last thing I wanted to do was get into an argument with Sasha.

"I'm agreeing, babe, that's all," I reassured her, squeezing her hand.

"Maybe I'm overreacting. I've been jumpy ever since I heard that they found the poor child in a cornfield. What kind of monster would discard a child's body like it was trash?"

Wearing a miserable expression, I shook my head.

"The kids are in their rooms, doing homework. Let's go inside and talk to them." In an attempt to make up for snapping at me a few moments ago, I could tell that she was making an effort to speak in a calmer tone.

She caught a glimpse of my blue-stained crotch and wrinkled her forehead. "What happened?"

It was the perfect opportunity to tell her about seeing Heather Flanagan and witnessing her meltdown, but I choked back the words. "I bought that blue Slurpee that Zoe loves so much, but I spilled it on the way to the car."

"Why didn't you go back inside and get another one?"

I shrugged. "I was in a hurry to get home and change out of these wet pants."

"Do you want to change before we speak to the kids?"

"Yes, for the sake of my dignity." I affixed a weak smile to my face.

Inside the house, I raced up the stairs. Phoenix's door was closed, but Zoe's was wide open. She sat on her bed with a notebook and colored pencils spread out.

Holding one of the pencils in her hand, she looked up and smiled. "Hi, Daddy."

"Hi, sweetie. Your mother and I want to have a talk with you downstairs."

"Right now? I'm in the middle of—"

"Yes, right now," I said, cutting her off.

"Okay! God!" she whined.

As I walked to my bedroom, I could hear Zoe stomping down the stairs, making it clear that she didn't appreciate being disturbed while in the middle of a homework project. My sweet Zo-Zo was slowly morphing into a disgruntled adolescent, and I didn't like the transformation one bit.

With Zoe out of earshot, I had the opportunity to speak with Phoenix privately. Instead of changing my pants, I wheeled around and made purposeful strides toward his room. I softly rapped on the door and then entered.

He was sitting at his desk, wearing headphones while reading an ancient history textbook. For the life of me, I couldn't figure out how he could comprehend what he was reading with music blasting in his ears.

He didn't hear me knock, but sensing my presence, he looked up. Pulling the headphones away from his ears, he said, "Hey, Pops." He eyed me curiously and said, "What's that on your pants?"

"It doesn't matter," I said brusquely. "Listen, the police found the body…" I paused, expecting a strong reaction from him, but he kept a straight face. "Sasha wants us sitting down as a family when she and I make the announcement. Afterward, we'll reiterate the safety rules. You need to act surprised and somewhat bothered by what happened to the little girl. No inappropriate jokes and no wisecracks that trivialize the situation. Your lack of empathy will make you seem suspect. Do you understand?"

He gave me a cold stare. "Of course I understand. I get it," he said with a hint of disdain.

With a frustrated sigh, I left his room and returned to mine. I changed out of the stained pants and put on a clean pair, and then went downstairs. I could only hope that Phoenix would be able to act the part of a person hearing shocking news for the first time.

Dreading the discussion with Sasha and the kids, I slowly descended the stairs. They were seated at the dining table drinking sun tea and munching on tamales and burritos. Apparently, Sasha wanted to soften the bad news with some of Arizona's most popular snacks.

I joined my family at the table and slid a small plate in front of me and picked up a burrito from the serving tray. With my nerves badly on edge, I wasn't the least bit hungry but wanted to give the impression that I was fine.

"Your father and I called you downstairs to discuss a new development in the Taylor Flanagan case," Sasha began.

"Is she back home? Is she okay?" Zoe questioned with a glint of hope in her eyes.

I set the burrito on the plate in front of me and cleared my throat. "No, honey, she's not home. Her body was found in a cornfield, not too far from here."

Zoe scrunched up her features. "Her body?"

"That means she's dead," Phoenix offered in a monotone.

Sasha nodded. "She was murdered by her abductor."

"How?" Zoe inquired in a shocked, high-pitched voice.

Nerves getting the best of me, I rubbed my palms circularly on my khakis, creating a rustling sound. "We don't know all the details, yet. But, uh, someone killed her and until he's found…"

"How do you know it's a he?" Phoenix asked, feigning ignorance.

Being that the actual murderer was doing the questioning, I paused for a beat and ran a hand over my forehead before responding. "Uh, it could be a woman, but in most cases of child abduction and murder, the perpetrator is usually male," I replied in a surprisingly steady voice.

"People are saying the mom did it," Phoenix continued. "Do you think that's true?"

Zoe gazed at Phoenix, her head tilted. "Who's saying that Mrs. Flanagan did it? Why would a mother kill her own child?"

"That's only a rumor," Sasha interjected. "The police didn't find any evidence that Mrs. Flanagan had any involvement."

"They say she did it for the money," Phoenix insisted.

"Let's not perpetuate baseless rumors," I said, giving Phoenix a stern look that told him to knock it off and pipe down, but he didn't.

He held up his hands in bafflement. "Why do you guys want to shield Zoe from the facts? So far, Heather Flanagan and her boyfriend, Cory, are the only people the police have taken in for questioning."

"And they were released," I said bitterly while glaring at him.

He was taking the innocent act too far. I'd instructed him to act surprised, but I didn't tell him to reignite the rumor about Heather Flanagan being responsible for her own child's death. After witnessing her meltdown in the 7-Eleven, I felt terrible. She wanted the police to bring in the perpetrator, but I, feeling an innate sense of duty toward my son, was standing in the way of justice.

"We realize you children are tired of having the safety rules drilled into your heads, but we'd rather be safe than sorry during this terrible crisis," Sasha said.

"We understand," Phoenix responded, cueing Zoe with a head nod.

"Yeah, we understand, Mommy," Zoe piped in.

For what seemed like the hundredth time, Sasha and I went over the safety rules we put in place, and both children listened with rapt attention, as if hearing them for the first time.

CHAPTER 31

I had hoped for a day that was as peaceful as possible. No newsflashes about the Taylor Flanagan case. No suspicious behavior out of Phoenix. And most of all, I didn't want to hear that the police had a suspect in custody. My guilt would be unbearable if an innocent person was charged with the crime.

Unfortunately, I wouldn't find anything remotely close to peace.

Midmorning, I was engrossed in work in the server room of a resort and casino that was located on an Indian reservation in Maricopa County, one of Ahiga's old accounts that I was lucky to inherit. I was pulled out of my zone when Dacy Bullard, the casino's IT guy, burst into the room.

Dacy was a millennial in his mid-twenties. His bone-straight, pure white hair, which hung to the middle of his back, was a stark contrast to his brownish, unlined, and youthful face. Like most of his generation, he was somewhat of a know-it-all, and I found it difficult to be in his company without feeling annoyed, and today was no exception.

"The way the police have been dragging their feet, I didn't think it would happen any time soon. But they methodically did their work and caught the guy that killed that little girl," he said.

Heart thumping, I took a deep breath. *Not Phoenix! Please, God—don't let them have my son in custody.* "What guy—who is he?" I asked, dreading his response.

"They caught a known child molester who's on the sex offenders' list. At least that's what they reported on the news. The perv was staying at the Terra Vida apartments, about seven miles from where the little girl lived. It's a shame the way they allow known pedophiles to walk free and work around children. The guy was working as a custodian at the children's hospital and no one did a background check on him. Allowing a sick fuck like that to come into close contact with kids is playing with fire. They say the girl that was found in the cornfield was a patient at the hospital last summer."

I was so relieved that Phoenix wasn't the one who'd been apprehended, I could barely speak.

"How do they know that the custodian guy did it?" I asked when I found my voice.

"The police pulled him over and found some of her possessions in his car," Dacy said.

"Wow!" That single utterance was the only thing that came out of my mouth.

With a slight smile, Dacy nodded. "With that scumbag locked up, parents can start breathing easier."

Dacy chatted for another few moments, but I hardly heard a word he said. I leaned back and clasped my hands at the back of my head and stared into space. Picking up that I was finished with the conversation, Dacy mumbled, "I'll let you get back to work."

Alone with my thoughts, I wondered how many kids the pedophile had hurt. I also wondered what he looked like. I extracted my phone from my pocket to check the local news, and there he was, Glen Mathis, a Caucasian male in his forties, with pockmarked skin and dirty-blond hair that was bald on top. He was the picture of coarseness and indecency. How someone like this had been allowed to circulate around sickly, vulnerable children, I would never know.

Even though he was innocent of harming Taylor, I refused to feel sorry for the man. Who knew how many other children he had hurt in the past and would hurt in the future? The fact that he was a known pedophile made me feel nothing but contempt for him. He deserved to go down for Taylor's murder.

Believing that there was a light at the end of the tunnel, my mood elevated and I called Sasha at her downtown dental practice to tell her the news.

"They got that bastard," I said in a celebratory tone.

"Yes, I heard," Sasha said, sounding preoccupied. "There's a lot going on here today. The new receptionist accidentally double-booked quite a few patients, and it's a zoo right now. Can we talk about it when I get home?"

"Yeah, sure. See you tonight. Love you, babe."

"Love you, too," she said hastily and hung up.

I was surprised that Sasha wasn't as excited as I was. Then again, she didn't realize that I feared that Phoenix might get hit with a murder charge. With a suspect now in custody, I could stop looking over my shoulder and finally relax and get a good night's sleep.

But before I succumbed to badly needed slumber, I needed to show my wife some long overdue affection. I hadn't made love to Sasha for weeks, and I hadn't given her any explanation for rebuffing her advances. It was obvious by the look in her eyes that she was hurt and angry, and tonight I planned to make up for all the confusion and heartache I'd caused her.

As I continued running maintenance tests on the server, I mentally made a list of items that would guarantee a romantic evening with Sasha: champagne, a box of See's assorted chocolates, a bouquet of flowers, and flavored edible oil to give her a sensual massage that would begin with me rubbing her feet and end with me feasting on every part of her luscious body.

Sasha wouldn't be home until around seven, and that gave me plenty of time to shop and transform our bedroom into a sex den. I chuckled, imagining her surprise when she entered the bedroom and found the room decorated, and found me, ready to cater to her every whim.

I texted Phoenix to let him know that I wouldn't be picking him and Zoe up at the bus stop today. I didn't say why, but I was pretty sure that he'd heard the news and concluded that our family was no longer on high alert. I also told him to make sure that Zoe got home okay.

As twisted as my son's mind was, I didn't have to worry about him violating Zoe in any way. He was protective of her and it seemed to me that he loved her as much as Sasha and I did. I had misread the incident in the pool. He'd held her head underwater at Zoe's request and I went into a panic and blew the whole thing out of proportion.

I tried to get back to work, but my heart was no longer in it. I had to run errands at several different shops. Anxious to get started, I packed my tool bag. I left Dacy a text, letting him know that I'd be back in the morning to finish the work. Since it should have been a one-day job, I added that there wouldn't be any extra charges.

It felt as if I had a new lease on life. Being outside, mingling with people felt good. In fact, I discovered an appreciation for things that I'd previously taken for granted, like the Arizona sunshine that warmed my skin. I admired the brilliant blue sky and noticed that the plant life seemed to be more vibrantly green than I'd ever noticed before.

Ever since I'd found out about Phoenix's atrocious crime and after assisting him in the cover-up, my world had crumbled, and getting from point A to point B was like plodding through quicksand. Today, I felt hopeful...optimistic, and it showed in my energetic stride.

Come hell or high water, I was going to get my boy straightened out with a top-rate shrink. Eventually, I'd have to have a discussion about Phoenix with Elle. Without providing her with the damning details, I had to make her aware of how deeply troubled he was. After what he'd done to her dog, she couldn't still be in denial about his mental health. Surely, she'd be on board for placing him in a long-term treatment program for adolescents.

I arrived home with two large bags that contained a variety of items that I was sure would put a smile on Sasha's face. As I pulled into the driveway, I heard splashing water and the sound of laughter coming from the backyard. Phoenix's and Zoe's happy voices echoed as they splashed in the pool. I got out of the car and hastily popped the trunk and gripped the handles of the bags. I felt fortunate to be able to get in the house unseen by Zoe who would undoubtedly want to know what was in the bags.

I filled an ice bucket and took it upstairs. In the bedroom I set the scene by scattering rose petals on the floor and on top of the bedspread. On my side of the bed, I placed the champagne on the nightstand, and set out a box of Sasha's favorite chocolates and two bottles of strawberry-flavored massage oil. From the vase on Sasha's side of the bed, I replaced the silk flowers with two-dozen fresh-cut roses.

Intending to run a hot bath for her when she arrived home, I carried an eighty-dollar scented candle into the master bath and carefully placed it on the ledge of the tub. I didn't typically spend that kind of money on a single candle, but tonight the sky was the limit.

Satisfied that everything was in place, I decided to check on the kids. I bounded down the stairs and strolled happily to the backdoor.

At first I thought I was seeing things, and I squinted at the three figures in the pool. Zoe was lying on an inflatable raft. Phoenix was swimming the length of the pool, underwater, and then shooting out of the water, pretending to be a shark.

If there was only Phoenix and Zoe playing in the pool, I would have considered the shark game to be all in good fun, but the other child in the pool was none other than Paisley, the little girl who'd attended Zoe's slumber party, and whom Phoenix had lured to Baxter's empty house with the intention of snuffing the life out of her.

"Phoenix! I need to talk to you," I yelled from the patio.

He took his time getting out of the water. I could feel heat rising up my neck and settling around my face as I watched him lumbering slowly toward me.

Impatient, I gestured for him to hurry up, but trying to get under my skin, he continued dragging his feet.

"What do you think you're doing?" Aggravated, I gave him a shove toward the backdoor.

"What's your problem, man?" he demanded with a fierce grimace.

"Who're you calling, man? I'm your father and you will respect me as such."

He sucked his teeth and it took all of my self-control not to ram his head into the bricks that made up a single wall of the kitchen.

"Maybe you need to start thinking about returning to Philadelphia." The words popped out of my mouth thoughtlessly, but I was tired of Phoenix's aberrant behavior affecting my peace of mind and happiness.

"I can't go back to Philly."

"Why can't you?" I asked challengingly.

"I can't. My mom and dad don't understand me the way you do."

"It's a little late to start appreciating all that I've done for you." My voice was cold and my face was a hard mask.

"I'm sorry. Okay? I'm really sorry." There was fear in his voice, and I got the distinct impression that he was terrified of returning to Philadelphia.

"Why're you so afraid of going back home to your parents?" I eyed him closely, gauging his reaction, and the mere mention of our hometown caused him to visibly shudder. "Did Everett do something—did he put his hands on you?"

"No, never."

"Then why do you look petrified?"

Wearing a miserable expression, he drew his shoulders up into a shrug.

"There's something you're not telling me."

"No, there isn't." His words came out shaky and his Adam's apple bobbed up and down frantically.

"Talk to me," I said quietly.

He shook his head briskly. His eyes were cloudy, like he was on the verge of tears.

"Talk to me!" I said in a booming voice that expressed my growing impatience.

"Okay!" he yelled. He took a deep breath and then exhaled. "There was this girl at my school—she was there on scholarship, and um, she sort of latched on to me. There were only a few of us black kids, and we went to the eighth-grade spring dance together. Afterward, we came back to my house to watch movies in the basement. Our basement's been renovated. It's a home theater now, with a concession stand, a soda machine…the works.

"She seemed really impressed by everything and it seemed like a good time to bring up the subject of sex. I asked if she wanted to try it, and she said no, but I was able to talk her into manual stimulation…uh, you know, jerking each other off," he divulged with his eyes downcast.

"While I was doing her, I told her that autoerotic asphyxiation would make it feel better—"

I groaned loudly when he mentioned the word, *asphyxiation*. "Why does everything always lead back to your choking and hanging fetish?" I asked with unveiled revulsion.

"I wish I knew. I don't have any idea why I'm this way. Do you know?"

"No clue. You didn't get any of it from me—or your mother—as far as I know."

"So, um, I choked her with the tie I wore to the dance. Gently at first. But I never stuck my fingers inside a girl before, and I sort of got carried away. I pulled the noose so tight, she passed out."

"Oh, God," I groaned.

"But only for a little while," he quickly added.

I pressed a palm against my forehead and closed my eyes.

"When she went home, she told her uncles what I did, and showed them the mark around her neck. Her uncles are bad people… really dangerous. They came after me, and they were serious about killing me, Pops."

"How do you know?"

"They shot at me! I felt real bullets whizzing past my head," he exclaimed with a look of incredulity. "And a day later, they started calling my cell phone, threatening to break my ankles, my knee-caps, and both my legs."

There was a desperate look in Phoenix's eyes that he couldn't have been faking.

"Is that the real reason why you left Philadelphia in a hurry?" I asked in a compassionate tone.

He nodded.

"You told me that you left because of what you did to your mom's dog—was that a lie?"

"No, that's the truth. It all happened within the same time period. My mom was upset that I killed her dumb dog, but her main reason for sending me here was to save my life."

Knowing Elle and how much she coddled Phoenix, it made more sense that she'd send him to me for his own protection rather than for something awful that he did. But I resented the fact that she wasn't straight with me. She could have warned me in advance that our son had a penchant for strangling both humans and animals.

"Did you get into an altercation with the girl's uncles when you went home for Christmas break?"

"No, they didn't know I was in town. But if I spend more than a week or two at home, they're bound to find out. Please, don't send me back there, Pops."

"I won't. But we have to figure out a way for you to work through your issues. You can't go on this way."

"You're right," he agreed.

"But there's something I need to know."

"What?"

"Were you feeling the urge to hurt Paisley while you were playing around with her in the pool?"

The guilty look that crossed his face gave me the answer. He sat down at the breakfast nook. Seemingly distraught, he bent over and started rocking back and forth.

"Tell me! Did you want to hurt Paisley?"

"I didn't *want* to, but when I get that urge, it's hard for me to control myself."

I fell silent, feeling pure compassion for him. I approached him and lay my hand on his shoulder. "It's okay, I understand, Phoenix."

He looked up at me, wearing a puzzled expression. "You do?"

"I didn't *want* to get high when I was in my addiction. And I certainly never wanted to engage in any of the crimes that I committed in order to get a fix. So, yeah, I do understand what it's like to be a victim to your urges. Sometimes I wonder if I passed something on to you when you were conceived."

"Something like what?"

"I don't know, Phoenix. Maybe somehow I passed on my intense yearning. I was craving heroin on that last night that I spent with your mom..." I paused when he made a face, like the thought of his mother and me being intimate was too revolting to imagine.

"It can't be proven by science," I continued. "But I remember that my mind wasn't right that night. I was in emotional turmoil and was feenin' for a hit."

"If that's the case, wouldn't I be born wanting heroin?"

"No, only the mother can physically pass on her addiction to a substance such as heroin. As I said, no scientist would back up my theory, but there's so much we don't know about genetics, and I can't help but feel that my state of mind—the way I was craving drugs—had something to do with this thing that you're dealing with."

"Are you saying that you're to blame for the way I am?"

"I don't know, but I'm willing to take responsibility and help you in any way I can." I glanced out the kitchen window and gazed at Zoe and Paisley as they romped in the pool. "It's time for Paisley to get home, and I'm going to drive her. I can't have the discussion I want to have with you tonight because I planned to spend some quality time with Sasha when she gets home from work."

Again, he screwed up his face like any mention of adult intimacy was reason to vomit. It didn't matter that he had divulged having strangled a little dog and killing Taylor, not to mention, his admission of strangling while digitally penetrating his date to the eighth-grade dance.

"We're going to have a long talk tomorrow. Together, we'll figure out some coping skills that you can use whenever you feel that you can't control yourself. Okay?"

He nodded. "I'm sorry for being so fucked up. I don't want to be this way—but there's something awful inside of me that makes me do the terrible things I do."

"We'll talk about it tomorrow," I said, patting his hands that were interlaced and resting on the tabletop.

CHAPTER 32

Although I had good intentions, my rendezvous with Sasha didn't go well. My mind kept wandering as I gave her a massage, and I frequently caught myself rubbing a listless circle on the same area of her back. The edible oil went completely to waste because my mind was too scattered. Plagued by a zillion troubling thoughts about Phoenix, I couldn't concentrate on giving her oral pleasure. With so much on my mind, I wasn't capable of the level of commitment that it would take to wholeheartedly give of myself.

In my mind, I was engaged in a heated discussion with Elle, asking her why she didn't get Phoenix help sooner—before he was forced to see a shrink after the overdose situation. Certainly there were telltale signs early in his life that warned her that something wasn't right with him. And why did she send such a damaged and dangerous kid to me without any kind of heads-up?

"Malik?" Sasha said my name in a soft but firm voice.

I stopped rubbing her neck. "Hmm?"

"I don't think you're into this. Why don't we try this again some other time?"

"Yeah—okay," I said eagerly, and then scampered to my side of the bed. I turned my back to her, not out of spite or malice, but I needed to disconnect from her in order to mentally sort out what to do about Phoenix.

Clearly, his therapy sessions weren't helping at all. I had no idea what he spoke to the therapist about, but a good therapist should have been able to figure out that the boy had serious problems.

A wave of sleepiness began to overtake me. Realizing that I was exhausted, I allowed my heavy lids to close. While on the edge of a dream, I heard Sasha sniffling. I realized that she was blaming herself for my lack of sexual interest, but it wasn't her—it was me.

Unfortunately, I was too drowsy to turn over and put an arm around her or offer some sort of comforting gesture. I was fortunate to have a woman like Sasha, and I didn't want to lose her.

Darkness engulfed me and I surrendered to the dream state. Throughout the night, I was inundated with bad dreams. The dream that was the most troubling was one where Phoenix marched me to the edge of a cliff at gunpoint. "Jump," he beseeched me. "There's no other way out."

I woke up in a cold sweat at dawn. As Sasha slept beside me, I slipped out of bed and dressed hastily in my work khakis and button-down shirt. Intending to get to the casino early and finish the job I'd started, I scribbled a quick note and left the house.

Arriving at the casino at quarter to seven, it was too early to bump into Dacy. Hopefully, I'd be finished before his work day started. I wasn't in the mood for any more chatter about the man the police had in custody. After listening to how helpless Phoenix felt in regard to his deadly compulsion, I supposed that even child molesters—as vile as they were—deserved a bit of sympathy.

I finished the job at ten o'clock, and was grateful that Dacy hadn't popped in to say good morning. He liked to hear himself talk and I had no doubt that his morning greeting would have escalated to a long-winded rant about whatever was disturbing him today.

Inside the casino's garage, I sat in my car. I pulled out my cell phone to call Elle, but I realized that it was only seven in the morning in Philadelphia, too early to call.

Fuck it! She didn't deserve any considerations, and so I called her anyway.

"We need to talk," I said gruffly when she picked up.

"Why are you calling so early? Did something happen with Phoenix?"

"A lot has happened with Phoenix," I spat. "Why didn't you tell me that our son has a proclivity for asphyxiating people and pets?"

There was a shocked little gasp on her end, followed by silence.

"Are you there, Elle?"

"Yes, hold on for a second."

In the background I heard a groggy male voice that I assumed belonged to Everett ask who was on the phone. She must have mouthed my name because I didn't hear her reply.

"I'm going to put some coffee on," she said to the male voice.

I listened to her footsteps as she took me along with her on her trek downstairs to the kitchen.

"I'm back," she said when she reached her destination.

"Was Everett in on your scheme to blindside me with a troubled kid?"

"No! And Phoenix is not troubled."

"He killed your pup, right? Hung it!"

"That was an accident. He was experimenting. You know how kids are—they're curious."

"About death?" I said dubiously.

There was silence on her end.

"Take your head out of the sand, Elle. Early on, you had to know that Phoenix wasn't like other kids."

"I know that he was smarter than most. More articulate. He easily grasped foreign languages and was more inclined in math and science than most of his classmates."

"Right. But you're not mentioning his dark side. Did you tell Everett what he did to your dog? Did you tell him about the girl he almost strangled to death in your basement?"

"No! Everett doesn't know about any of that."

"Oh. So, in other words, you covered for Phoenix. Made up a story about the dog's death and about the reason for the death threats he was receiving from his classmate's uncles."

"I didn't want Everett to form a bad opinion about Phoenix's experimentations."

I gave a wry laugh. "Experimentations, huh? That's a nice way of describing his destructive activities."

"Malik." She said my name in a world-weary tone. "I hoped that being in a different environment—and living in the same household as his biological father would have a positive effect on Phoenix."

"Well, you were wrong. He was too far gone when you sent him for a mere change of scenery to be the solution to his problems."

"What has he done, exactly?"

It was my turn to go silent as I considered whether or not to tell her about Taylor Flanagan. I decided against it. After all, Phoenix wasn't alone in culpability, and I refused to risk implicating myself.

"He had his eye on one of Zoe's classmates. A few months back, he lured her to an empty house in our neighborhood. I caught up with him before he could harm her. After I questioned him intensely, he admitted that he had an urge to strangle her."

"No, that can't be. He wouldn't hurt a little girl."

"It's true and you know it. What about his date for the eighth-grade dance? How do you think she ended up unconscious in your basement?"

"They were experimenting with breath control play, and things got out of hand. The girl didn't tell her uncles that she had asked Phoenix to choke her."

"Do you hear yourself? How many eighth-grade girls have ever even heard of getting choked for pleasure? And how many do you think would make such an unusual request? Phoenix talked her into it, and she went along, never dreaming she was putting her life at risk."

"That's not true," Elle insisted. "And I resent the way you're portraying him as being out of control and violent."

"He admitted being out of control and violent, and asked for help. That's why I called so early in the morning. I had hoped that we could discuss some kind of treatment for Phoenix."

"Treatment? Certainly you're not suggesting having him put away again."

"We have to do something, Elle. Children aren't safe around him."

"You're exaggerating. Look, if you're tired of looking after your son, then say so. When that girl's thuggish uncles started harassing him, it occurred to me to send him to a boarding school in France, where he wouldn't have to worry about uncivilized people. I should have followed my first mind."

"You're in complete denial, and I was too for a long time, so I understand. Don't worry about it, Elle. I'll handle the problem on my own."

"Don't do anything stu—"

Elle was useless and I hung up before she could finish her sentence.

Phoenix needed a different shrink—a better one. Someone who could read between the lines without him specifically stating that he was a murderer and was bound to kill again. How I'd find such a person was a mystery to me.

I decided to Google "Adolescent Psychiatry for Teens in Crisis," but I hit the local news app on my phone by mistake. My mouth literally fell open when I saw a headline that read: *Violent Child Molester Released from Police Custody.*

Both incredulous and infuriated, I read the entire article with a scowl on my face, while shaking my head in disbelief. According to the report, Glen Mathis was released from the county jail after police surveyed footage of him entering a Sex Addicts Anonymous meeting and leaving around the time that Taylor Flanagan was reported missing. He claimed that he stole her belongings from her hospital room when she was admitted after a tonsillectomy last summer. He said that he'd never had direct contact with the child, and had begun driving with her possessions in the trunk of his vehicle to honor her memory after her body was found.

Now we had two monsters in our neighborhood that were prone to hurting little girls. One monster caused pain in a violent sexual manner, and the other responded to an insatiable urge to kill.

My phone suddenly pinged with a text, and lo and behold, Phoenix was the sender. He said he didn't feel good and wanted to come home. He asked if I would call the school office and pretend that he had a doctor's appointment.

Since we needed to finish yesterday's conversation, I decided to do him one better, and show up at his school in person.

As I drove to his high school, I concluded that the only way to help Phoenix was to convince him to enter a psychiatric facility willingly. I had to get him off the streets, and for his own good, I was willing to risk him inadvertently confessing to a shrink and dragging my name in the mess.

CHAPTER 33

A cheerful receptionist greeted me when I entered the school's office. I told her that I was there to pick Phoenix up for a doctor's appointment and she paged his classroom right away. Five minutes later, Phoenix came into the office, smiling sheepishly. Furtively, he gave me the thumbs-up sign, as if we had conspired together and successfully pulled the wool over the receptionist's eyes.

On our way to the car, Phoenix walked while swiping at the screen of his phone.

"So, you're not feeling well—what's wrong?"

He looked up from his phone. "Nothing. I mean...nothing physical."

"Oh? What's going on? Talk to me."

He stopped walking and I halted my steps as well. "It's those urges, again. They're really strong, and I figured it's best if I'm not around other kids."

The raw pain that I saw in his eyes made me feel scared and helpless. I had promised him last night that we'd find a solution together, and as we commenced walking, my mind was in overdrive.

Suddenly struck by a thrilling idea, I grasped his arm, forcing him to a standstill. "You say that you only target little kids because they're easy to overpower…"

"Yeah, that's true."

"Suppose you were physically able to subdue an adult. Would choking or hanging an adult give you the same satisfaction as asphyxiating a child?"

"Definitely. But I can't take down an adult—unless it's a midget." Phoenix smirked and returned his gaze to his phone.

"But I can." My announcement was so unexpected, he jerked his head upward and stared at me.

"What are you saying?"

"The police set that child molester free. We'd be doing a community service if we got rid of that scumbag."

Phoenix's eyes sparkled with glee. "Really? You'd actually help me kill him?"

"Yes, especially if it'll satiate your craving and prevent you from harming innocent little kids."

"Yeah, I'm sure it will."

"Are you positive?"

"Yes, I'm positive." He smiled so broadly, I wouldn't have been surprised if he'd begun to rub his palms together delightedly.

We got in the car and I started the engine. Before I shifted into drive, I turned and looked at him.

"What? Why're you staring at me? Stop acting creepy, Pops."

The pot was calling the kettle black, but I let the creepy comment slide.

"I have to ask you a question, and I don't want you to lie to me. Remember, you can tell me anything, Phoenix—I'm on your side."

"Okay. Ask the question."

"Is Zoe safe in the house with you?"

"Pops! You didn't have to ask me that. Of course she's safe with me. She's my sister. Well, not by blood, but I love her like a sister. I do have some scruples, you know." Indignant, he became sullen. Pouting, he returned his attention to his phone.

I let him sit there and sulk. I wouldn't have dreamed of apologizing for my concern over Zoe's safety.

We rode in silence for ten minutes. Traffic was heavy and came to a complete stop on the highway. While we were stuck in a gridlock, Phoenix stopped brooding and struck up a conversation.

"How're we gonna get this guy? I'm excited, but I'm also a little scared. I never hunted a grownup before."

Hunted. The word made me pause and look at him askance. How many children had he hunted, I wondered.

"Is hunting part of the thrill?"

"Yeah. After I pick a victim, I find a way to get close to them, so I can figure out their weaknesses."

"Had you gotten close to Taylor Flanagan before you…" I couldn't finish the sentence.

The smile left Phoenix's face and he squinted his eyes as if recalling a bitter memory. "No, that was spontaneous. I saw an opportunity and took it."

"What about whatshername—the girl you took to the school dance?"

He visibly brightened. "Oh, yeah. She seemed out of depth at our school, and I befriended her. Sort of took her under my wing."

"I see. What about Paisley?"

"Definitely. I always talk and joke around with her at the bus stop. For a high school kid to give her the time of day makes her feel important."

"And Baxter?"

A cloud fell over his face and he looked down at his feet. "I don't want to talk about him," he mumbled.

"Why not?"

"Because… I don't want to talk about that gay stuff. I'm not that way, and I don't like thinking about it. Okay?"

"But you're the one who initiated the *gay stuff.*"

"Jeez! Can we drop the subject…please?"

He was able to easily discuss murder and stalking his victims, but any mention of his homosexual activity caused him to react hysterically. It was a shame how screwed up Phoenix was. He was only fourteen years old, yet he was already so damaged that I feared that his actions would destroy him before he reached adulthood. I often wondered what had happened to that seemingly well-adjusted, three-year-old boy whom I'd met in the park so many years ago. That little guy wanted to help feed the pigeons, but today he'd most likely prefer to break their necks for the thrill of watching their reaction.

Traffic started moving again, and I got off at the next exit.

"Why're we getting off here?" Phoenix inquired, his face contorted, as if I were interfering with his busy schedule.

"I want to check out Glen Mathis's place."

"Who?"

"The child molester," I said with disdain.

"Oh!" He sat up straighter.

"I'm off work early, and you're out of school for the day. We might as well do something productive. We'll surveil his apartment building, and maybe we'll get lucky enough to see him outside."

"And then what?"

I shrugged. "We'll follow him, I guess. Figure out his pattern."

"That's it? We're not going to knock him in the head and drag him to the trunk of the car?"

I laughed. "We don't want to be that obvious. There's no reason to rush. If we're patient, we'll find out what time he usually leaves his house, and we'll also know where he's going."

"Sounds boring."

"It is boring, but it's necessary if we want to capture him without being seen by anyone."

"Is he a big guy...or smallish?"

"I don't know. Why do you ask?"

"Just wanted to know how strong the rope I use on him should be."

I pulled up his image on my phone and handed it to Phoenix. He stared at it and then handed me the phone.

"He looks to be medium build. Don't you think?"

"I don't want to burst your bubble, but we may not have time for you to do a traditional hanging, like stringing him up on a tree or something. We may only have time for you to choke him with a rope or maybe a necktie." I gave a little shrug.

"Oh, all right," he said, nodding as grabbed his backpack from the rear seat. He unzipped it and pulled out a length of wire with vertical, metal handles on each end.

"What's that?"

"It's a garrote, a very effective weapon for strangulation."

"Where'd you get that thing?"

"I made it."

Perplexed, I tilted my head.

"I got the instructions from a YouTube video," he explained. "If our dude has a thick neck, this may not be long enough. I made this one especially for Paisley." He snapped the wire a couple of times, smiling devilishly.

"Get Paisley off of your mind," I exploded. "You're not to touch that child. I don't want you talking to her anymore. I don't want you to even look at her. Do you understand me?" I could feel my veins bulging from the sides of my neck as I yelled at him.

"I got it! You don't have to freak out; I was only showing you my skills in crafting weaponry." He smiled, and his smile was sinister. There was so much malice in his eyes, I felt a strong desire to give him a victim as soon as possible. Hopefully, a good kill would hold him for a while. I didn't want to think about what would happen if his urges returned before I had a chance to get him admitted to a mental health facility.

We'd been sitting outside Glen Mathis's apartment building for more than an hour when I dozed off. Surveillance duty was so boring, I couldn't help myself.

"Pops! Wake up. Is that him?"

Groggily, I turned my head in the direction that Phoenix was pointing. I peered through the windshield, and sure enough, there was Glen Mathis, out in broad daylight and looking exactly like his newspaper photo, with his bald spot shining in the sunlight. He could have at least put on a hat to conceal his identity. But he was unapologetic and bold.

I was surprised that throng of angry protesters hadn't gathered outside his apartment building, shouting obscenities. I was sure that the citizens of Springfield Hills most likely wanted the man's head on a spike, but after seeing themselves on TV acting like a lynch mob in front of Heather Flanagan's house, they were probably too embarrassed to act up a second time.

"Let's go, Pops. We have to follow him." Phoenix was more animated and excited than he'd been in a long time.

"Wait. There're probably cameras somewhere. We can't pull out right behind him. We have to keep our distance."

"But he's gonna get away," he said worriedly. Agitated, he craned his neck and watched closely as the sex offender got into his car. "He's getting into a black Hyundai. He's just sitting behind the wheel—not moving. I wonder why he isn't moving? Do you think he spotted us?"

"I don't know," I mumbled.

I watched the man from my rearview mirror. "If he did spot us, he probably thinks we're reporters—not vigilantes."

"But I'm just a kid. How could he mistake me for a reporter?" The possibility of being mistaken for an adult put a note of pride in Phoenix's voice.

"He's on the move," I said, staring at the door mirror on the driver's side.

Phoenix twisted around in his seat, gawking.

"Don't be so obvious. You'll scare him and he'll run back inside," I chastised.

"Sorry," he muttered as he obligingly turned back around, placed his hands on his lap and looked straight ahead. "What's he doing now?" he asked, sitting in his seat with his back ramrod straight.

"He's making a left turn."

"What're we waiting for? Come on; let's go before we lose him." Now he was literally bouncing in his seat, excitably gesturing with his hands.

I gave him a stern look. "If we're going to do this together, I need you to calm down."

"I know, I know. You're right. It feels like I'm having an adrenaline rush or something."

"Just control yourself and trust me. Can you do that?"

He dipped his chin, giving an uncertain head nod.

"Phoenix, if you can't get a grip, we'll have to abort this mission."

He dramatically rolled his eyes at the terminology I used, and I couldn't blame him. Obviously, I'd watched too many secret agent movies.

I shifted the gear into reverse and began backing out.

"It's about time," he muttered under his breath, and I chose to ignore his smart-aleck comment.

I had lots of experience under my belt from tailing Phoenix, and I allowed approximately five vehicles to get between the Hyundai and our car. Phoenix continuously leaned forward, gripping the dashboard as he anxiously peered through the windshield. If he thought his frantic gestures would prompt me to speed up, he was wrong.

"He has his right blinker on," Phoenix announced breathlessly.

"I see him. He's turning on Union Street," I said calmly.

When I drove past Union Street without turning, Phoenix covered his eyes and shook his head in exasperation. "What're you doing? Why didn't you turn?"

"I don't want to be obvious. I can hit Union Street from another direction."

"But suppose he makes another turn…and we lose him?"

"It won't be the end of the world. We know where he lives, right?"

He gazed at me with a look that told me I was the dumbest father in the world.

We hit Union Street and rode past a myriad of small businesses. In the distance, I saw the Hyundai parked in a large lot.

"There he is," I said excitably.

"Where?" Phoenix whipped his head from left to right.

"On your right."

"Oh, shit! That's him."

"Watch your language."

"Sorry."

The overhead sign of the building he was parked in front of read: *Arrowhead Pawn & Jewelry.* I had driven in the area a million times but had never noticed the pawn shop. During my junkie years, my antennae would have been up and I wouldn't have missed the place. Reminiscing about my last venture into a pawn shop, and the way I had met Kaloni, I grew a little melancholic. I had no idea what had become of her after her sad attempt to rob the cashier at Home Depot. I had no knowledge of whether she had survived prison or not. No idea if she was dead or alive.

I felt angry at the system that caged her like an animal instead of helping her. And me too, for that matter. I was sick, and I should have been hospitalized instead of imprisoned. The same screwed-up system had set Glen Mathis free.

Emboldened by a desire to exact justice for Kaloni, I pulled into the lot and parked right next to the child molester.

CHAPTER 34

Glen Mathis got out of his car and was walking toward the trunk.

I rolled down my window. "How're you doing?" I asked in a fake friendly tone.

"I'm all right…as if you care," he spat, revealing tobacco-stained teeth that I noticed were rather small for a grown man.

Stunned that I had struck up a conversation with the person we were stalking, Phoenix gave me a baffled look.

"I just want to ask you a couple questions." I gave him the friendliest smile that I could muster.

"I don't have anything to say to any fucking journalist. You guys are scum!"

"Wow!" Phoenix broke into a grin. "He actually believes that I'm a journalist."

"We're not all bad. So, uh, what are you getting ready to pawn? Hopefully, you're not letting go of a family heirloom."

He laughed, a nicotine-and-phlegm-filled chortle that grated my nerves. "If you consider my bicycle that was passed on to me by a cousin, a family heirloom, then I guess I'm guilty," he responded, and then laughed again.

I hated the bastard. He was proof that the most lowlife types of white men in America could get away with heinous crimes while there was an open season on black men. We were being executed by the police in growing numbers for mere misdemeanors, if for any reason at all. Sadly, many police in America had become the judge, jury, and the executioner of black people.

Many would say that I was living a privileged life and had forgotten my roots, but I hadn't forgotten anything. As a black man who had lived a junkie's life, I had once been reviled and treated like scum, and there were scars on my soul that would never heal.

"How much do you think you'll get for the bike?" I asked after shaking away unpleasant thoughts of my past.

He shrugged. "I don't know, fifty bucks or so."

"I'll give you a hundred and you can keep the bike."

"And what do you want in return?"

"Your story. I think the public would like to know what makes you tick. How you became the way you are."

"Seems like such a psychological piece—a peek into the mind of an immoral degenerate—would be worth a lot more than that."

Phoenix whipped his head in my direction, eagerly awaiting my response.

"Two hundred?"

With a wicked glimmer in his eyes, he lifted both his palms, indicating that I should go higher.

"Okay, five hundred. But that's as high as I'm willing to go."

"That sounds like a deal. So, tell me, what's your name and who're you working for? The local paper or some online rag?"

"*GQ*," Phoenix whispered.

"My name is Malik Copeland and—"

"Malik," he repeated. "Sounds African," he commented with a sneer.

"It's actually Arabic."

"African…Arabic…all the same to me."

"Right, uh, anyway, I'm a freelancer. I queried *GQ* about this piece, and they're interested."

"*GQ*! La de dah-dah. I bet they'll pay you a pretty penny," he said, stroking his chin, his wheels spinning greedily.

"How much they'll pay depends on the content."

"The content?"

"Yeah, how much information you divulge and how well it's written."

"I'll divulge a lot…over a couple of beers."

"That's not a problem. I'll buy you a six-pack."

"Great. So who's the kid?" He nudged his head toward Phoenix.

"He's—"

"I'm his student intern," Phoenix blurted.

"Oh, yeah?" He gave Phoenix the side-eye. "You look kind of innocent. It's a shame for your young mind to be corrupted by a smarmy journalist. I would think that a kid like you would prefer to be somewhere bouncing a basketball rather than hanging out with this guy." He turned his mouth down in distaste and nodded toward me.

The basketball comment was a racial slur that I let slide—for the moment. The motherfucker would pay for it later, though. If Phoenix didn't need this kill so badly, I'd do it myself, giving the racist pedophile a slow and painful death.

"Why don't you follow me to the ATM and then the Wine and Spirits shop?" I suggested. "I'll get your money and pick up some brew, and then we can sit down and talk."

"Sit down, where?"

"At your place?"

"No, that won't work," he said firmly, shaking his head.

"Then, how about a really atmospheric location…"

"I'm listening."

"The cornfield where the girl's body was found."

"You're joking, right?"

"Yeah, I'm joking."

He gave a full-on belly laugh that was intermingled with a hacking cough. "You know I didn't have anything to do with that girl's death, don't you?"

"How would I know. Listen, can we do the interview in my car? I just want to get your story out, and portray your sex addiction in a sympathetic light, if possible. I'm sure there were awful things that happened early in your past that made you the way you are, and the public should know all the sides of your story."

He nodded as he drifted off in thought, frowning with his eyes squinted as if reviewing a harrowing time in his life.

"Let's get out of here." He got back in his car and I reversed out of my parking slot.

He followed me as I drove to a nearby ATM.

"This is awesome, Pops. You're playing that guy like a fiddle." Phoenix mimicked strumming a violin, and I supposed he had no idea how a fiddle was actually played.

"I can't believe you gave him your real name," he said with astonishment.

"Well, he won't live to tell it." I gave him a significant look.

"We're actually going through with it today?"

"Yep, and here's the plan… I want you to get in the back, so that he can sit up front with me. I'll ask him questions while he's guzzling down beer, and then, as a way to subdue him, you need to knock him over the head with something."

Phoenix recoiled and gave me a look like I was crazy. "Knock him over the head with what? I don't have any heavy objects on me. Is there anything in your trunk?" Phoenix's voice trembled.

"Use one of his beer bottles. I'll signal you when it's time to strike."

He looked petrified. "Yikes! Oh, man! Okay."

"Can you do this, son?"

"Yes. Definitely," he said while looking uncertain.

I parked in an out-of-the-way location, near railroad tracks that trains seldom traveled upon. Switching seats, Phoenix climbed into the back. Meanwhile, Glen Mathis took so long to join us, I feared that he'd had a change of heart. After a good five minutes had elapsed, he got out of the Hyundai and ambled over to my car.

Having him seated next to me was surreal, but I kept my composure as I handed him the money I'd promised.

Phoenix, on the other hand, wasn't as calm. He nervously rustled around inside his backpack, putting me on edge. I hoped he didn't plan to suddenly lurch forward with the homemade garrote in his hands. He wasn't strong enough to strangle Glen without subduing him with a harsh blow to his head.

"So, where's the brew?" Glen demanded, eyeing me suspiciously, as if I'd stiffed him for the beer.

"I got it." Phoenix picked up the six-pack that I'd set on the floor in the back of the car. "Here you go," he said, handing it to Glen.

Grinning, Glen ogled the six-pack of Guinness. "Mmm, you got the good stuff. Remind me to call you back for a second date." He guffawed.

Tickled by the date comment, Phoenix joined in with giggly, teenage laughter.

Glen twisted off the bottle cap and downed half the dark brew in one gulp. He wiped his mouth with the back of his hand. "I'm not supposed to drink. That's part of my commitment to the recovery program I'm in. But after the shit that I've been through, I'd say that I deserve to get good and drunk."

"What exactly have you been through?"

"You get right to the point, don't you? There's no fucking foreplay with this guy," he said, glancing over his shoulder at Phoenix.

Once again, Phoenix burst into titters of laughter. Apparently, sex jokes went over big with him.

"Are you recording us, Phoenix?" I asked, attempting to get him in a more serious frame of mind.

"Oh. Right. One second." He tapped on the record app and then held the phone up, near Glen's head.

"Hey, that's annoying. Get that thing away from me."

"Sorry. You can set it in front of you on the dashboard, if you like," Phoenix suggested, handing over his phone.

Glen placed it on the dash and slugged down more beer. Another swipe across his mouth with the back of his hand.

"What have you been through?" I repeated.

"For one thing, I lost my job over this mess they tried to pin on me, which is the reason I'm fucking broke right now."

"Do you think that working around children was the right thing to do, considering your past?"

He shrugged. "It felt all right to me. I put myself in the situation to test my mental strength."

"What do you mean?"

"I had all the eye candy I wanted, but I forced myself to look but not touch."

"Look at what? Those sick kids' naked bodies?" It was hard not to hit him over the head myself. He was a sick individual and the world was better off without him.

"No, I never saw any of them naked. And I didn't work on the cancer ward, and most of the kids I came into contact with weren't all that sick. Like that little girl, Taylor. She had a minor operation, and a couple of days of recovery. I slipped in her room when they took her downstairs to run tests. I stole a few of her possessions, so what? I didn't hurt her."

"What did you steal?"

"A pair of panties, an undershirt, and a cute little pair of pajamas, decorated with stripes and butterflies," he smiled dreamily, and it was a terrible sight.

"Did you masturbate on her clothes?"

"So what if I did," he said defiantly. "It's a coping mechanism. I still didn't hurt her."

From the back, I heard Phoenix gasp. The conversation was getting real, and he stopped giggling.

Glen drained the rest of the beer and then cracked open another bottle. This time he guzzled down the contents of the bottle and crudely belched afterward.

"When did it begin—this obsession with children?"

"I don't know."

"Think," I prodded. "When was the first time you actually found yourself being attracted to a child?"

"I was always attracted to them, even when I was a child. But I became aroused by them somewhere in my teen years. Yeah, my late teens. My best friend at the time had an older sister and he used to help babysit her kids. I would go over her house with him and help him look after the children. He had a niece, Jenny, a real pretty little girl. She used to always crawl up in my lap with a book, asking me to read her a story. I would get a boner out of this world when she'd scoot her little bottom around my groin, searching for a comfortable position. The first time it happened, I made her get off of me and sit down on the couch. But the second time, I just let things take their natural course."

"Their natural course—what exactly is that?"

"I let go of my wad. She asked me if I peed myself." He laughed heartily. "It was the cutest thing." He was well into his third bottle, but showed no signs of drunkenness as he recalled memories of that innocent little child.

The two empties that he'd placed on the floor mat next to his feet were quickly joined by a third bottle.

"Where are my manners? Have some," he asked, offering me a bottle of beer.

"No thanks, I don't drink when I'm working," I said, sounding primmer than I intended.

He turned slightly in his seat. "What about you, son? This'll put some hair on your chest."

Phoenix accepted the beer enthusiastically, and I initially thought he was seizing the opportunity to drink illegally. When I turned to look at him, he smiled and did a double eyebrow raise, letting me know that he planned to use the bottle as a weapon.

CHAPTER 35

I feared that five beers wouldn't be enough to intoxicate the man; his threshold for alcohol seemed unlimited. In hindsight, I realized I should have bought two or three six-packs.

Phoenix would have to swing really hard to sufficiently daze Glen.

I asked more questions about the little girl, Jenny. The way Glen talked about her, it was easy to think that he was referring to a teenaged girlfriend instead of a four-year-old child. Every word that came out of his mouth repulsed me. I struggled not to vomit, yet I had to keep a straight face and act like I was having a normal conversation.

"When the carnival came to town, I walked around with her, holding her soft little hand, and it was heavenly. I bought her every treat she pointed at. I was so in love with her, I couldn't tell her, no."

"Did her uncle know that you were obsessed with her?"

"He knew that I was crazy about her. There wasn't a dad in the house, and he thought I was trying to be a father figure."

"But you were trying to hurt her," I goaded, sick of him trying to turn his twisted fantasies into a sweet story of star-crossed lovers.

"No! I never hurt her…I adored her. I brushed her hair, I bathed her. I gave her piggyback rides, and I bought her lots of toys and nice presents. Everyone wants to vilify me, but I didn't choose to be this way. I can't help being attracted to children; it's just the way I am."

The sick bastard was asking me to empathize with him, but that was impossible. I looked at him, stone-faced, and asked, "Did you molest her? Was she your first victim?"

He didn't respond. He closed his eyes and swilled down the fourth bottle of Guinness, and then the fifth.

He turned and looked at Phoenix. "Are you gonna drink that beer I gave you or are you gonna nurse it all day?"

"Uh, it's kind of bitter. I don't really like it…" Phoenix paused and made an apologetic grimace.

I was about to signal him, but he shocked me when he suddenly pulled his arm back and smacked the side of Glen's head with the beer bottle. The brown liquid sprayed everywhere—the roof of my car, the doors, the dashboard, my neck, the steering wheel, and all over Glen's hair and shirt. I gawked at the mixture of blood and brew that trickled down his face.

Phoenix looked stunned.

"Do it!" I shouted.

Looking punch-drunk, Glen leaned at an awkward angle toward the door. He was muttering incoherently as he lethargically jiggled the handle. Despite his muddled state of mind, he realized that he was in grave danger, and he was trying to get out of the car.

I couldn't let that happen, so I picked up the bottle that had fallen in his lap, and bashed him in the head again. This time he slumped over, unconscious.

I glared at Phoenix. "You picked a hell of a time to choke…no pun intended. Do I have to put this piece of shit out of his misery, or are you going to man-up and handle it?"

"I...I...I can handle it," he stammered and reached inside his backpack.

I noticed Glen stirring a little and I shot a frantic glance at Phoenix. "Hurry up and kill this motherfucker, damn!"

With trembling hands, he held the metal handles of the garrote, but didn't move.

"What the fuck are you waiting for? You don't hesitate to act when your victim is a little girl, you fucking pussy."

"Don't call me that."

"Well, stop acting like one." I had never called my son such a vile name before, but I was infuriated with the world after hearing how Glen had courted a little four-year-old, doing God knows what to her while he had her in his clutches.

I sat Glen up straight so that Phoenix could place the wire around his neck. When he put it in place, I smacked Glen, waking him up, so that he was aware of what was happening to him.

His eyes fluttered open and I yelled, "Go!"

Phoenix tightened the wire and I watched with delight as it cut into Glen's flesh. Glen's eyes widened in shock and he thrashed about, struggling to pull away the wire that would soon cause his demise. He stomped on the floor mat, like he was marching...or trying to run away.

Sweat beads dotted Phoenix's forehead. Straining, he growled like an animal as he yanked as hard as he could on the wire. Finally, Glen stopped moving his feet, and his hand fell away from his neck.

Blood spurted out, running down the front of his shirt.

Amazed, I watched the light go out of his eyes right before he slumped to the side.

"That's it. He's gone, Phoenix. You can stop," I said in a weary voice. I felt drained of energy as if I'd been the one asphyxiating Glen. "Are you okay, son?"

"I'm fine," he said breathlessly and then fell against the back of the seat. "Wow! That was incredible. Really incredible," he said as he smiled blissfully.

I checked his pockets for a cell phone, but didn't find one. He either had left it at home or it was cut off while he was in jail.

We dumped the body on the railroad tracks. I would have preferred dumping him in the cornfield, an eye-for-an-eye sort of symbolism. But the tracks were more convenient.

"We have to get rid of your phone," I told Phoenix.

"Why?"

"The cell towers it pinged off could be a problem. And there's that recording of Glen…" I shook my head. "We can't risk anyone ever hearing that."

"What about your phone? Are you getting rid of yours, too?"

"I turned it off hours ago to avoid any conversations with Sasha. I didn't want her to hear the tone of my voice and worry that something was wrong."

He handed his phone over and I turned it off, then stomped on it with the heel of my shoe. On the way home, I tossed the broken phone into a Dumpster and Phoenix looked forlorn.

"I'll get you the latest iPhone tomorrow," I said, trying to cheer him up.

After we got rid of the phone, I drove toward home. Something caught my eye and I noticed that there were thin streams and tiny dots of blood spatter staining the leather and wood-grain interior of the car. There was even a long streak of blood on the inside roof. I looked around and speckles of blood were everywhere. I hadn't expected to have to deal with cleaning blood from the seats, floor mats, and dashboard. There wasn't a lot of it, but I didn't trust myself to adequately clean away all of the damning evidence.

Two blocks from our house, I turned on my phone and

called Ahiga, asking if he could point me in the direction of a chop shop.

"Why are you asking about chop shops? Are you in some kind of trouble, Malik?"

"No, not at all. I swear. Everything is fine, but I have to get rid of my car."

"Do you want to talk about it?"

"Some other time. I can't get into it right now."

He backed off and gave me an address.

I turned my phone off again and drove to chop shop and dropped off the car. Phoenix and I walked the six miles back home, mostly in silence.

"You're awfully quiet; are you doing all right?" I asked when we entered our neighborhood.

"I feel…I don't know how to put it."

"Try."

"I feel exhilarated. Like I drank five energy drinks. My gym teacher always gets on my case when I have to quit running laps due to my chest burning, and basically, a lack of oxygen. But right now, I could run ten laps and still keep going." He flashed me a grin and I gave him a one-arm embrace as we walked along.

We had finally bonded. It wasn't the sort of male bonding that I had expected. I had dreamed of fishing and camping trips, and father-and-son ping-pong tournaments, but it didn't work out that way.

For the good of our community, I made sure that Phoenix got his fix in a morally acceptable way. Together, we eradicated a scourge, making the world a better place.

Sasha came out of the shower with a towel wrapped around her body and stood in the middle of the floor, looking up at the mounted TV. On the ten o'clock news, there was a report about an unidentified body being found on the railroad tracks.

She shook her head and glanced at me. "What on Earth is happening to our town? There's so much crime lately. Violent crime. It seems like people are being killed right and left. If we wanted to raise our children around this kind of brutality, we would have set up housekeeping in a big city like Phoenix. Should we think about selling the house and moving somewhere safer?" Sasha asked with her brows furrowed.

"It's worth looking into. I think we're going to start seeing 'For Sale' signs popping up all over the neighborhood, and we don't want to be left behind in an undesirable community."

"But we just put in a pool—"

"Right, and we increased the value of our home."

"I hope we can sell it. The Westfields' home is still on the market after all this time."

"They didn't have a pool," I said with laughter.

"By the way, Malik, I didn't see your car in the driveway. Did you park in the garage?"

"No, I meant to tell you that I had transmission problems. I thought that the transmission needed to be flushed or maybe the fluid needed to be changed, but when I took it to the dealership, I found out that the problem was a lot worse than I realized. I had to leave it, and it's going to be a major bill. I might just get a new car. When parts start breaking down, it's one thing after another."

"Yeah, it's five years old, and this is only the beginning of its decline. That's why I lease my car and get a new one every three years."

"Maybe I'll look into leasing my next vehicle," I said, lying with ease and not feeling guilty at all.

I secretly looked Sasha up and down and noticed how sexy she looked wearing a clingy towel.

She walked over to the bed and sat down next to me, her eyes glued to the TV screen. The water beads that had gathered on her shoulders caught my attention and I eased her close.

"I'm thirsty, babe," I said and then licked the droplets of water from her shoulder.

"Malik," she whispered, turning toward me. "I missed you. I missed us together."

"I was going through some shit, but I'm back."

"To stay?"

"Forever, baby."

I lay her down, unfastened the towel that was knotted at her chest. One look at her plump breasts and my lips parted and found their way to her dark cherry nipples. My tongue went from one beaded nipple to the other, drawing slow circles around the hardened flesh.

I patted blindly on top of the comforter, and after locating the remote, I clicked off the TV.

I wanted to give Sasha my undivided attention, and I wanted hers.

CHAPTER 36

A couple of months passed and Sasha let go of the idea of selling the house. Our community was pretty much back to normal after the murder of Glen Mathis. The residents of Springfield Hills accepted that he had murdered Taylor Flanagan and almost got away with it had it not been for the heroism of an anonymous Good Samaritan.

Weirdly, the police didn't work too hard trying to find Glen Mathis's killer, and I took their lack of interest as a green light for us to continue our vigilantism. But it was only when Phoenix really needed to appease his cravings, and at the moment, he was in good spirits and seemed fine.

The feeling of love in our household was palpable. Sasha and I spent quality time with each other by going out for date night once a week. We took turns choosing places to rendezvous, and although I wasn't always crazy about Sasha's selections, making her happy was worth enduring a few hours at Butterfly Wonderland, the indoor home of thousands of butterflies.

With Sasha and I on good terms, the kids seemed to thrive emotionally. Zoe wasn't such a smart-mouth lately, and Phoenix wasn't nearly as withdrawn and anxious as he'd been before our get-together with Glen Mathis. Phoenix's friends came over often and hung out by the pool, and he had a new, extremely expensive therapist that I hoped was helping him learn how to cope with his problem.

I no longer believed that he needed to be locked inside a rubber room for life. He knew that I was here for him whenever his cravings returned. In fact, I was so on top of Phoenix's needs that I began my own research, using the National Sex Offender list to locate child molesters in our area.

There was one that I was tracking on social media, and was able to monitor his movements online. In an attempt to make himself seem like a regular guy, he posted regularly, capturing photos of himself posing next to his SUV, hiking with friends, swimming and mountain climbing. He wanted to be perceived as an earthy outdoorsman, and I had him in my crosshairs for being so deceitful.

The moment I felt that Phoenix needed a fix, Mr. Outdoorsy would be our man.

One Friday evening while Sasha was working late, I decided to try my hand at preparing something a little more wholesome, something that the kids and I both would like. Usually, I ordered Chinese or pizza on Fridays, but I was tired of commercial fast-food. The pizza in Arizona never quite stood up to the slices I used to buy at Philadelphia pizza parlors.

I looked in the freezer and there was an abundance of ground beef. I checked online for a recipe and the first thing that popped up was Cheesy Ground Beef Pasta. The kids loved anything with cheese, and the recipe was simple, so I went for it.

Phoenix and Zoe were out in the pool. After months of lessons, Zoe was no longer afraid of being underwater and was thinking about joining the swim team when she entered middle school in September. She was such a good swimmer that Phoenix routinely snuck up on her and tossed her in the water, and she'd laugh every time.

I sliced cheese and chopped onions on the counter near the window, allowing me to observe the kids. After putting the dish in the oven, I noticed that they had gotten out of the water and were sitting on lounge chairs, talking animatedly. Their closeness warmed my heart, and I was a little ashamed to have thought that it was even remotely possible that Phoenix would ever hurt Zoe.

As I watched them relaxing by the pool, I was struck by the idea to give Phoenix a taste of his own medicine. He didn't have an older sibling to torment him, and it was up to me to assume that role.

Smiling devilishly, I crept out the house and snuck up on them from behind. Engrossed in their conversation, they didn't sense my approach. Only a few feet away, I could clearly hear what Phoenix was saying.

"It won't hurt, I promise," he said.

"But suppose it does," whined Zoe.

"Would I ever hurt you, Zoe?"

"No."

"Then trust me. You might feel a little panicky when I cut off your air supply, but if you trust me and relax, you'll enjoy it. Lots of high school kids experiment with asphyxiation. It's like getting high without using drugs."

"Okay, you can choke me, but only for, like, a few moments. If I stamp my feet, that means I'm not enjoying it and I want you to stop."

"Cool. But believe me, you're gonna love it, and I bet you'll start coming to my room, asking for it."

"I don't think so," Zoe said, giggling nervously.

Outraged, I stepped forward and smacked Phoenix in the back of his head…hard!

"Ow!" With his hand pressed against the back of his head, he swiveled his neck around and stared at me with wide-eyed fear in his eyes.

"Have you lost your mind?"

"I was only kidding with her. I wasn't going to do it. I swear."

I gazed at Zoe. "Go to your room."

"But I didn't do anything."

"Go to your room!" I bellowed.

Frightened, she jumped up and ran to the back door. Once she was inside, I glared at Phoenix.

"After all I've done to help you, this is how you repay me…by violating my trust?"

"But I was only playing with her."

"Stop insulting me with your lies. I told you to come to me when and if your urges returned, but being above board and honest is too much like right, isn't it?"

"No!"

"Sure it is. You prefer to sneak around and dominate defenseless little girls because they're easy prey and because you're nothing but a coward. Too physically weak and emotionally timid to challenge yourself and go up against someone your own size or bigger.

"Don't say that. It's not true," he cried, tears beginning to pool in his eyes.

I looked at him sneeringly. "I'm so disappointed in you, and now I have to figure out how to deal with this. Since I can no longer trust that Zoe is safe with you around, I'm going to have to take drastic measures."

"Like what?"

"I don't know. But I do know that I can't have you lurking around and preying on Zoe, that's for sure."

"Pops, you're scaring me—"

"Good! You should be very afraid."

"I'm serious. I'll kill myself before I let you put me away for thirty days."

Thirty days? Ha! You wish! A lifetime would be more accurate, buddy.

"I was too embarrassed to tell you that the urges had returned so soon. I thought I could handle it myself without bothering you. I wasn't going to kill her…honest. I was only going to choke her enough to knock her out—"

"You don't play around with your sister's life. Repeatedly knocking her out could cause brain damage, you fucking moron! We agreed that Zoe and all little kids were off-limits, but you went back on your word. And now you're going to pay."

Livid, I was absolutely ready to call the men in white coats to come and get him, and I'd give them a heads-up to bring along a straitjacket.

But when he collapsed from his chair and literally curled into a fetal knot, crying and sucking his thumb, I was reminded of the three-year-old preschooler whom I had abandoned in the park.

And once again, my heart broke into a thousand pieces.

I knew that thumb sucking had something to do with the need to feel secure, and the thought of being put away in an institution was so traumatizing that he had resorted to infantilizing himself. And it was a scary thing to see.

I dropped to my knees and vigorously shook him. "Phoenix! Snap out of it."

I tried to straighten his legs out, but he had them balled so tightly, it was impossible for me to unfurl them. I stroked the side of his face and told him that everything would be all right.

"I have a plan," I told him. "There's a guy from Tucson that I've been stalking online. He's a nature guy, always out in the open, hiking and canoeing, and things like that. Next weekend, he's going camping—"

Phoenix unfurled himself and sat up. "How do you know?" he asked with his thumb still in his mouth. It was hard to look at him like that and I quickly dropped my eyes.

"He posted a picture of his admission ticket to the campgrounds," I said, focused on his kneecaps, unable to look directly at him. "How's that sound, buddy?"

"Awesome," he replied and finally removed his thumb from his mouth.

I stood up. "I'm going back in and check on the food. Dinner should be ready in about thirty minutes."

"What're we having, pizza or Chinese?" he asked, sounding like his old self.

"Neither. I cooked. Cheesy Beef Pasta. You'll like it," I said and turned toward the house.

Sasha knew how much I'd wanted to experience a male-bonding activity with Phoenix, and to show some support, she bought me a folding knife with a beautiful mother-of-pearl handle. I felt guilty for lying about the real reason for the trip, but lying to my wife had become routine.

I'd been busy shopping for camping gear the week leading up to the camping trip, and the only thing I hadn't thought of was a camping knife.

I took off early on Friday and dropped Zoe off at the larger of Sasha's two dental practices.

"I want to go," she said for the hundredth time.

"Men only," Phoenix teased.

"You're not a man," she retorted.

"Pops, if only she knew…right?" he said, gazing at me with a cheesy grin.

I ignored him and focused my attention on Zoe. "Listen, princess, the next time we go camping, it'll be a family event. Phoenix and I want to try it out first and work out all the kinks, so that things go smoothly when you ladies join us."

Refusing to be placated, she screwed up her lips, got out of the shiny SUV that I had leased after I'd turned my car over to a chop shop.

Sitting behind the wheel, I watched closely as Zoe opened the door and meandered inside.

During the two-hour-long drive to Tucson, Phoenix and I did very little talking. He mostly listened to music through his headphones while I was in deep thought about the task ahead. Surprisingly, he didn't seem all that excited this time, and hardly asked any questions about the kill. He was carrying the garrote inside his backpack, and was prepared to go into action at my command.

After we arrived, I set up the tent with no assistance from my son. Instead of helping, he chose to sulk. I had warned him that we were leaving technology behind in order to derive the full experience of roughing it in the woods, but he must have thought I was kidding.

"Can't we, like, buy Internet access?" he asked in a complaining tone.

"We're here for two reasons: to perfect our camping skills and to take down Liam Armstrong."

"Who's that?"

I rolled my eyes.

"Oh, that's the guy we're gonna snuff." He laughed. Apparently, taking a man's life had become commonplace for him.

After I pitched the tent, I went out and collected wood and tried my best to get Phoenix interested in building a fire, so that we could roast hotdogs. He frowned and asked why we hadn't brought along some charcoal and a grill like our neighbors to the left of our tent.

Rather than argue with him, I knelt down to do it myself. I'd watched so many episodes of *Survivor* over the past ten years, I thought I had the process down pat, but after an hour elapsed with me still rubbing the same two sticks together, I thought it might be a good idea to take a walk to the camping and rock shop and purchase some flint.

Just when I was about to give up, the friction buildup turned the wood into a hot ember. I quickly transferred the ember onto my bundle of tinder and started blowing. When a tall fire began to grow, I whooped in celebration, as if the Phoenix Suns had just won the championship.

Seeing the flames I'd created, other campers clapped and cheered for me.

We cooked hotdogs and ate them, and having food in his stomach seemed to put Phoenix in a better mood. Feeling good about our venture into camping, I gave him a warm look. "Let's go get some more wood, so we can keep the fire going all night."

It was obvious that he would have preferred playing games on his phone than collecting wood, and he sighed as he dragged his feet toward me.

"Bring your backpack."

"For what?"

"In case we bump into Liam."

"Oh, all right." He brightened visibly and picked up his backpack from the ground and flung it over his shoulders.

The sun was still shining bright as we trekked into the woods, scanning the ground for sizable twigs and fallen branches. The sun began to cast a dim glow as we moved deeper into the forest and we both focused on finding Liam rather than wood.

"There aren't any people around, and I don't think we're gonna find that guy out here," Phoenix stated, looking around and observing the secluded area we had wandered into.

"We'll have to put our heads together and come up with a plan. Let's sit down and talk." I pointed to the ground in front of a tall oak tree with a huge trunk.

"I don't want to sit here. A snake could jump out of those weeds." He gestured toward the tall grass near the gnarled surface roots of the tree.

"This is a camping trip, not a weekend stay at a luxurious hotel. Now, sit down." He reluctantly lowered himself to the ground. "Did you bring water?"

"Only one bottle."

"We can share it," I said, reaching for his backpack. I rummaged through it, but instead of taking out the water, I pulled out the garrote. "You know I love you, son."

"Yeah?" His eyes darted back and forth from the garrote to my face. I knew I looked crazy as I held the murder weapon in my hand, and I started to sweat so profusely, I had to use my shirt-covered shoulder to wipe the moisture away.

"What's going on, Pops? You're starting to scare me."

"I love you and I've tried really hard to be a good father, but nothing I do seems to work. You're sick, son. Very sick—"

"What are you saying?" He tried to rise from the ground, but I yanked him back down.

"Help!" he hollered at the top of his lungs. I briefly covered his mouth with my hand and then released it and swiftly looped the wire around his neck. "Don't do it, Pops. I'm begging you…don't do it."

A deluge of teardrops ran from my eyes. "I'm sorry, Phoenix, but Zoe isn't safe with you around."

"Then send me back to Philly, please!"

"And how many innocent little girls will die when you return to Philly?"

"None. I won't do it anymore. I promise."

I shook my head. "It's too late. I failed you, and I'm so sorry."

He let out a painful little squeal when I pulled on the wire. Instinctually, his hands went to his neck as he attempted to remove the garrote from his neck.

Wanting to end his fear and his suffering, I pulled the metal handles with all of my might. I heard bloody squishing sounds as the wire cut into his neck, causing him to go limp. I let go and he fell forward. When I lifted him up, I saw that I had applied so much pressure, I'd nearly decapitated him.

His complexion was gray and his unseeing eyes were wide open.

I let out a cry of anguish and held him close to me. "I failed you. I failed you. Please forgive me," I murmured as I held his head in place with the palm of my hand, trying to keep it from lolling backward.

To return to my beautiful life with Sasha and Zoe was more than I deserved. But of course that would never happen because there was no way that I could talk my way out of a murder conviction. I was comforted by the fact that Sasha would not have to live in shame. The community would look upon her with pity for being married to a madman that murdered his own son.

Not wanting my wife to be in the dark about the man she was married to, I had written her a letter, confessing everything about Phoenix and me. I mailed it on the way to the campgrounds. She could turn the information over to the police or she could keep it to herself. The choice was hers. I told her to kiss Zoe for me and to tell her that I would always love her.

I'd also written a letter to my parents, expressing my love, and a letter to Ahiga, thanking him for all that he'd done for me and telling him goodbye.

I had expected to live to a ripe old age, to witness all of Zoe's life's milestones, and to one day walk her down the aisle. But it wasn't in the cards for me.

With a sigh of resignation, I kissed Phoenix's cheek and then laid his body down. I reached into my pocket and pulled out Sasha's gift. I opened the glimmering knife, took a deep breath and then sliced open my wrist.

Amazingly, there was no pain, and for good measure, I cut open a vein in my other wrist. Holding my arms on my lap, I closed my eyes and waited to bleed out.

How long is this going to take? Will my life flash before my eyes? And is there actually a place called hell?

As I pondered the mystery of death, I began to feel lightheaded, and I thought I heard Phoenix's voice. I was aware that I was hallucinating because his lifeless body was lying right next to me, still and quiet.

"I didn't cross over yet, Pops?"

"Why not?" I asked, playing along with the auditory illusion.

"I'm waiting for you to finish dying."

"Is that right?" I said, chuckling a little.

"Let's go for a walk."

"All right." I got up with ease, and there was Phoenix, standing right next to me with his throat miraculously closed up. I looked down at my wrists and the skin was smooth and unblemished.

"This hallucination is better than shooting up heroin, son," I said as we walked along.

"You're not hallucinating. Look!" He turned around and pointed. I looked in the direction where he was pointing and saw our two bodies. Mine was slumped against the tree and his was lying on a patch of dirt and weeds.

"We completed our journey on Earth, and now, we can go home," he said.

The sun began to float downward from the sky, and Phoenix took off, running toward its golden glow.

I ran, also, easily catching up with him.

And side-by-side, we stepped into the brilliant light—together.

ABOUT THE AUTHOR

Allison Hobbs is a national bestselling author of more than thirty novels and has been featured in such periodicals as *Romantic Times* and *The Philadelphia Inquirer*. She lives in Philadelphia, Pennsylvania. Visit the author at AllisonHobbs.com and Facebook.com/Allison hobbseroticaauthor.